Praise For

EMBER DRAGON DAUGHTER

It left me desperate for more!

LEILANI LOPEZ, AUTHOR OF *THE DEVIL'S HEIR*

An exciting new novel from fantasy author R. K. Sampson which challenges the love triangle trope through the structure of a magical new world.

TARA QUINN, AUTHOR OF *KINGDOM OF SIRENS AND MONSTERS*

It's impossible to anticipate all the twists and turns, and the ending truly left me hungry for more.

LEA FALLS, AUTHOR OF *GODDESS OF LIMBO*

A beautifully crafted debut with rich worldbuilding and strong writing! Rebecca did a wonderful job making me feel attached to Ember from page 1. I love the representation and diversity in the story as well.

HOLLY DAVIS, *DIVERSITY IS LIT* BOOK CLUB HOST

I loved this book! Sampson's world-building is incredible. It is so easy to understand the context of this vibrant and inclusive world. It was such an enjoyable read!

HEATHER HATALEY, AUTHOR OF *A COLLECTION OF SCARS*

I absolutely loved this book! It gave me serious GoT vibes at first, which I LOVED! All of the characters were so complex and well-developed. The twists and turns of this story kept me guessing, too, and I didn't see any of it coming—which I absolutely loved. Now I'm so excited to see what happens next for Ember & Noor!

E.C. WOODHAM, AUTHOR OF *THE LIGHTS OUT CLUB*

The whole "Fated" system is a really interesting idea, as the novel suggests it's a great thing to be fated, but fate is not always glorious. It was a great concept that was well explained and comes across a but like in *Once Upon A Time* (TV Show) where fairytales are awoken to reality.

R.S. WILLIAMS, AUTHOR OF *KINGDOM OF LIES*

EMBER DRAGON DAUGHTER

THE
FATED TALES

EMBER DRAGON DAUGHTER

FOUR BEASTS.
THREE KINGDOMS.
ONE HIDDEN PRINCESS.

R. K. SAMPSON

*To my fate, Chris, and
to my blessing, Jack.*

CONTENT GUIDE

Content in the Fated Tales series may be triggering for some readers. Reader discretion is advised and potential trigger content is listed per book on the author's website.

Ember Dragon Daughter is book one of the Fated Tales series and should be read first.

This series covers topics such as inclusion, LGBTQ+ characters, adoption, true love, responsibility, and loving and accepting yourself.

Potential Triggers in *Ember Dragon Daughter*:

- A magical system that creates an unavoidable and magically-induced love at first sight
- Depictions and threats of murder
- Family death
- Rejection by a biological parent
- Depictions of a magically-induced mental illness and harm coming to people with this illness

- Kidnapping of a minor and an adult in forced isolation

FATED AND FATELESS

THE PLAYLIST

- 🎧 *Heavy Crown* - Iggy Azalea, Ellie Goulding
- 🎧 *Stars and Moons* - Dizzy
- 🎧 *Jump* - Astrid S
- 🎧 *Leave a Trace* - CHVRCHES
- 🎧 *Sparks* - Hilary Duff
- 🎧 *How Far I'll Go* - Auli'i Cravalho
- 🎧 *Shake it Out* - Florence + The Machine
- 🎧 *Doing the Right Thing* - Daughter
- 🎧 *Feels* - Kiiara

PART 1
EMBER JULIMORE

ONE

FATED TO A DRAGON

"Happy anniversary," Ember said to herself, staring up at the ceiling. She took stock in her mind of the two dates that mattered today: the death of her moms—exactly two years and one week ago on this day—and the second anniversary of her move to Firetop, the longest she had lived anywhere. They'd have hated that she stayed here this long.

Her pupils dilated as she stood up, reaching to light the candle on her bedside table. The room was cold and quiet, as usual. She walked to her dresser and pulled out her long-sleeved high-collar dress. She threw it on over her night shift without a care to how it looked. She had only four clothing items to choose from and one spare outfit in her satchel *just in case*, a habit she didn't know she'd ever break. She glanced in front of the mirror to make sure she was covered up and moved on.

A quick finger combing of her hair was the last step in her morning routine. Ember knew she should try a little harder with her hair. The black color shone rainbow in certain lights, it was the only quality of Ember's appearance she found redeemable. But overall, any extra time spent didn't seem worth the effort.

A wraith chirped at her open window, its small scaly blue body wriggling with impatience. It had been forty years since full-sized dragons were seen in Ashkadance. The demi-breeds, like the wraiths, baomtots, and anchoris, were the sum of their remaining species—at least from within the walls surrounding the kingdom. What was beyond Ashkadance was a mystery. The wraith shook its leg impatiently, balancing for Ember to take the letter attached to it. Ember picked up and unfurled the note.

Meet me at the statue of the First Fating.
-Hasley

Simple enough. Ember straightened her dress, picked up her bag, and locked up the house. Before closing the door, she did her usual sweep for anything of importance. Just like any other day, there was nothing she'd want to keep in the small plain house. It was all in her bag.

She walked the path that led to Mount Pietan, a happy medium between her and Hasley's homes. As a child, Ember would imagine making wings of fabric and jumping off of Mount Pietan. She would soar over the wall into the sea beyond. Ember knew now that was impossible, but the fantasy was enthralling regardless. In another kingdom, her secrets wouldn't matter.

"There is nothing romantic about being fated to a dragon," Ember told her friend, noticing her gaze on the statue.

"I disagree," Hasley replied with a sigh. She was always like this when they were in proximity of anything related to the First Fating.

Hasley loved this spot as much as Ember did, but for entirely different reasons. Rather than focus on the tiny spot of sea visible over the surrounding wall, Hasley paid attention to the statues. They represented the historical beginning of their kingdom. It was also the top of its richest mining resource, but that was a necessity the particularly devout among them tried to ignore. How sacrilegious to cut open the mountain where their first king and queen became fated.

"They were about to kill each other before it happened," Hasley recalled, her tone suggesting that was the most important part of the story. A sword lay discarded at Kariana's stone feet. Her hand extended to the dragon before her. His face was alight with surprise, in opposition to the winged body that posed to kill. How someone's emotions could shift so quickly, Ember didn't understand. The fating was said to be immediate, irreversible, and incomprehensible until experienced.

This was the moment that stopped the Unyielding War. The First Fating over 100 years prior, when all citizens on Mutrien's three continents became encircled with golden light. True hearts met and saw in each other the truth—that they matched. Now, each soul had a mate, waiting to be found. That is, unless you were Fateless.

Kariana's heart twin was a dragon, and it was on this mountain that it was discovered.

Ember looked to Hasley. Hasley's hair was long and curled, like the statues, but that is where the similarities ended. This rendering of Kariana was carved from the same stone that was mined from these mountains. The white gleaming piece did not match the bright blue of Halsey's hair and tan skin. In real life, Kariana's hair had been black.

"You're insufferable," Ember commented, but she still smiled at her friend. Her only friend. Ember wished she had that idealism.

Hasley rolled her eyes, half turning to speak over her shoulder.

"Don't you want to be fated?"

"Not to a dragon," Ember said, incredulous.

"But that's the part that's so romantic. To commune with Aaleia through your dragon love, to fly to other kingdoms..." Hasley trailed off, gazing up into the brightening sky.

Ember shook her head.

"I'd rather not be paired," Ember replied. She didn't need to endanger anyone else. It was already enough of a betrayal to Hasley that she let the girl be her friend. Hasley didn't know the risks of being close to Ember, no one alive did. Keeping this one rebellion, a simple and guarded friendship with a kind girl, wracked Ember with guilt.

"You two should be leaving now," a voice called from the other side of the statue. Hasley and Ember jumped, not expecting to hear anyone else up here at this hour.

"It's almost dawn. Don't you have a purpose to attend to?" the voice added. Ember followed it to see one of the mountain priestesses coming towards them. The elderly woman gave them a stern look, her pink and white hair flying behind her with the uptick of wind.

"Sorry," Hasley called. She snatched Ember's hand and ran in the other direction. When they had started down the slope, Hasley laughed nervously.

"Sorry Hasley," Ember said. She knew how much her friend hated being late.

"It's okay, it's a distracting place," Hasley replied, adjusting a stray blue curl as they rushed down the trail. They only had a few minutes before the miners would begin their work, meaning Ember and Hasley were close to being late to their own purpose apprenticeship.

Ember picked up the pace, her thin soles providing little protection against the ground below. She hiked up the bottom of her long, high-collared dress, giving her legs a little more room to stride.

"Flaming stars," Hasley swore, "I see a sliver of leg!" Her voice filled with laughter as they ran.

"Oh quiet, go faster," Ember yelled over her shoulder as they bounded down the remaining steps. Ember never shared her skin, keeping under wraps in as many ways as she could. While her clothing wasn't shapeless, showing the silhouette of her form, it was still more modest than most others in their province. Ember couldn't afford to stand out. Hasley, however, did not have the same concerns.

Blood pumped quickly through Ember's heart as it beat faster with each step. Skipping over an overgrown root, she tumbled down, the slant of the hill helping her run faster down the slope. They reached the bottom of Mount Pietan just as a wraith chirped past them, a letter gripped in its claws and sun reflecting off of its slim, black body.

Ember put her hand on her chest in an attempt to slow the thumping of her heart.

"Another day and one step closer to purpose," Hasley said, turning to Ember. Off in the distance, the white caps of the miners were visible. A line of men and women on their way to begin work. Soon Ember and Hasley would complete their apprenticeship. Their last names, now representing their birth mothers, would change to their purpose name.

Ember moved into step with Hasley, wiping off the sweat from her brow and body with the handkerchief Hasley handed her. Her breath and heart began to normalize, the rushing in her ears calming with each step. Hasley scrunched her face, accepting the damp cloth and putting it back in her satchel.

They nodded their heads to a woman in a hard top and white clothing as they passed. She was already covered in the white powder from the mines, the sediment of peiradoone stone. It was their richest resource, used in everything around them. Ember was tired of seeing the world in its blinding reflection.

A SHADOW PASSED over her station. Ember tightened her hands over the pearlescent string of beads.

"What did I tell you?" a rough voice asked.

"Never use more than two real pearls in one necklace," Ember replied back automatically.

"Yes," Amlin responded in an exasperated tone, arms thrown in the air. "What? Did you think you were going to jump into the ocean and get some more?" he bellowed, both laughing at his joke and upset at Ember for using more of the resource than he advised.

They had this tug of war every so often. Ember tried to create art that felt right to her. He disagreed. Some materials needed to be used more sparingly. With the wall surrounding their kingdom for almost seventeen years, not every item was replenishable. Often, their materials came from family members selling jewelry from their deceased relatives.

Her boss scowled at her. His already red splotchy face deepened in color. Amlin was messy, and given that Ember herself was a little messy, that didn't bother her too much. But what did upset Ember was his work ethic.

The Fateless were spreading, and no one wanted to be accused of falling victim to it. Lack of interest in a person's chosen purpose was one of the early signs.

"Of course not, Amlin Jeweler," Ember replied. She began moving the materials aside. Her heart clenched at the sight of the pearls being put away in their box. She would release the pearls the second he walked away.

"I don't understand you Ember. So much talent." He swept his arm over her work table as if it were evidence. "But so little understanding of rules and regulations. You'll never get farther than apprenticeship if you don't pay attention to your teacher."

He wiggled his finger in her face, punctuating his last few

words, and Ember felt like setting it aflame. Saying that you won't grant someone a purpose name was not a nice thing to do. Not now, not ever. While Ember Julimore didn't particularly want to give up her mom's name yet, she knew that becoming Ember Jeweler was a necessity to her survival. If Amlin knew the truth about her, he'd turn Ember over to the royal guards. Her body clenched at the thought. Hasley wouldn't want to associate with her either if she knew the truth of her moms' death.

Hasley had forced her way into her heart, and it pained her every day that she let that relationship grow. Her moms paid the price for their relationship with her. Caution was better. Safety was preferable. Life typically trumped death.

"You're right," Ember replied. Amlin's steps scuffled on the floor, echoing in the almost empty room. The wide slate back-room of his shop held two small work tables for herself and Hasley, a storage organizer for the different materials, and his larger desk on the complete opposite end. It was almost as if being next to the work was something he was allergic to. The only work he liked to do was reprimand her.

"When you are done with Crawford Baker's bracelet, I need you to deliver it to her shop," Amlin said as he walked away. With every click of his shoes on the stone floor, her eye twitched.

Ember restrung the necklace to the correct specifications, mourning the real pearls. While Ember created and delivered the jewelry for their customers, Hasley managed the administrative aspects and the storefront. She was the new face of the shop, while Amlin took in all the profits. Convenient arrangement. What would he do when she and Hasley passed their apprenticeship and would move on to create their own shop? Get another pair of apprentices, if there were people available.

The two matching bracelets for Ahnren Farmer and Craw-ford Baker, a celebratory gold fating set, were next on her list to complete. Those were simple enough to make and would be ready with extra time for today's deliveries. This kind of set used to fill the majority of their orders. A thin gold chain with one sparkling crystalline bead in the middle. She set out the supplies, going through the steps in her head, and finished the task quickly. It didn't take long to move down the rest of her list, organizing each package by when she would deliver them. First would be the fating set. Crawford's bakery was close by. If she took too long, she'd have to travel farther to Ahnren's farm home for the delivery.

Ember moved from the workstation. The storefront was much brighter than their stations. Each display case had its own candle to shine on the gems, and the glass was cleaned each night. Hasley knew about presentation, which was why Amlin liked her.

Ember herself was too rough around the edges, not soft or welcoming like Hasley. Her clean and poised look fit in so well with the rest of the shop. Ember had a more angular face with small green eyes and skin tinged grey. It added to her forlorn look. It was impossible to hate Hasley for her natural ease and graceful disposition, for Hasley cared about everyone she met. Ember felt trapped in her secrets.

She absently scratched her chest through the material of her dress and nodded at Hasley as she passed. Ember repeated her mantra in her mind, *there is nothing strange about me*, as she stepped out the door. It was a lie, but it was a thought that surfaced whenever she walked out into the open air. She repeated it again, and it rang even more false the second time. The lie was a comfort, nonetheless.

She walked down the familiar u-shape of shops and stalls, each province fitting a similar pattern. After traveling to all the provinces, she could see that Firetop was more caring about their patriarch God and his Goddess pair. There were more churches and religion-based shops.

When Ember made it to Crawford Baker's shop, she shifted her bag to the other shoulder, unwilling to wear it across her body. The aroma of pie started to waft into Ember's nose as she stared at the long line forming.

"Dragon's piss," she muttered. She did not want to be around so many people at once. But Crawford Baker was now the only baker since her competition had become afflicted. His empty shop lay a few feet away. While little was known about the Fateless plague, it was discovered that it was not contagious. The common thought now, was that it was a curse from the gods. Workers were in there now, salvaging what materials they could from his shop. Now that he was gone, they had to distribute his wares. Nothing would be wasted.

She moved around the line, aiming to enter through the side food delivery entrance. She didn't think Crawford would mind Ember stepping in for this special occasion present.

As Ember approached, voices became clearer behind the shop. She paused beside the loading area, a carriage between her and those speaking.

"Why are we wasting our time here? He isn't going to find her. No one actually expects him to after so many years," a deep voice complained.

"Of course, but he has it in his head that she is out there," a higher pitched voice answered.

She peeked around the carriage to see who was speaking and her heart quickened in her chest. Two men stood there: one tall blond with short hair and a brunette. They wore the uniform of the royal guard.

This was about Jedoriah Knight. Were they waiting for him in the bakery at this exact moment? She should leave. Ember knew logically that this was now an unsafe place and she should mind her own business and walk away...but she couldn't. She had to know who he was looking for. Would they leave soon or stay in town? Should she grab her go-bag and leave Hasley behind?

Ember wished she was like her momma, Echoris. She was good at blending in, spying for needed information. Ember did not have that talent.

"I wouldn't let it go if I were sworn knight to the queen," the deep voice commented. "Failing to find the heir would be inexcusable."

Ember breathed a sigh of relief. If they were looking for the heir, they would have no reason to pay any attention to her. If she snuck away, laid low until they left, she may not have to move towns.

It was a sore spot to mention in society—the continuity of the Drakul line—but with Aaleia denying a second blessing to the queen, many were starting to wonder if it was their intentional downfall. Like the Fateless, the royal family must be cursed by the gods. There had never been a second heir before, but there was no need for one. Ember didn't know what that could mean. If there wasn't a second heir was that proof that the lost princess was alive? She didn't know, but with even the dragons abandoning the kingdom three generations ago, doom seemed more likely.

"No, nothing of importance here." A red-haired guard came out from the back entrance and spotted Ember before she could duck back. She froze like a moth to a dragon flame.

Her mind whispered the lie automatically as her heart catapulted. The guards walked forward. "You shouldn't be here," the redhead said. He left the two guards behind him, his imposing stature advanced towards her.

Recklessly and far too loudly, Ember ran away.

She was aware that this was causing more attention than she needed, but she was unable to stop herself. She pushed her legs as far and as fast as she could. Turning away from the delivery area and out back into the crowd, she ran towards the bookstores. She could not run back to the jewelry store. She did not want these guards to know the general direction she came from and question Hasley. She could not go home; it was too far.

"Stop!" the guard called. He gained ground quickly, his long legs giving him the advantage over Ember's height and impractical dress. If she hadn't have made the fuss, she knew they wouldn't be chasing her. This was making everything worse. But she couldn't stop. She was not as stealthy as her moms had been. She was not as safe. She tried to be, but her instincts failed her there.

The burned and run-down bookstore, yet to be recommitted by the province, came into view before her. Citizens gave her a wide berth, staring agape at the usually demure jewelry attendant running wildly—assuming they even remembered her face.

Part of Ember knew it was already too late. He was too close. He'd see her hide there, or at the very least, knew the direction she went. Feet hit stone but it was barely audible through the rushing blood in her ears. Making a split decision, she bolted in a new unpredicted direction. Could she make it to the mines? That would do, though she could get lost in there. Then again, so could the guards.

Not looking where her feet were landing, Ember's sandal slipped in a hole in the path before her. The material gave way and the strap snapped from her ankle. Ember tumbled down. Her face hit the stone and her vision blurred. She tried to regain purchase, bracing her hands against the floor.

She tried to pull herself up, not noticing that her dress had also snagged on the uneven floor. Her worst nightmare ripped into reality. A simple rip of fabric and it was all over.

"Stop right there," the guard called mere feet away.

Her scales were visible for all to see.

TWO

DRAGONIA

THREE YEARS AGO

"Happy 13th birthday, dragonia," Echoris said to Ember, smoothing her hair and giving her a quick hug. Ember used to hate being called dragonia, a term used for troublesome children. But from Echoris? She knew it was said with mischief. Ember liked thinking that a little bit of herself was mischievous, even if that was far from the truth.

"Thank you, Momma," Ember replied with a smile. They were going out to eat today to celebrate, something she and her moms never did. Outings were not a common occurrence, especially not a celebration.

Echoris smiled at her, adjusting the single pearl on her necklace, a gift from Ember. Her long cream gold hair reflected in the white.

Today was a special occasion. While it wasn't common, it was possible to find your fated pair at thirteen. The next likely celebration would be her apprenticeship start at fifteen. Ember wondered where they would be living at fifteen. They had only moved to Truest two months prior and would move on twice before then.

"Where would you like to go?" Echoris asked as she straightened.

"Anywhere," Ember responded easily. The fact that they were going somewhere, other than school or church, was a welcome overwhelm to her routine. Ember adjusted her black tunic, triple checking it covered the right spots.

"I know just the place then," Echoris encouraged, keeping it a surprise. Julimore didn't speak, instead, she checked her bag for their usual emergency supplies.

Together, the three of them walked down the street towards the market sector, bypassing the shops to walk where restaurants all sat in a row. Ember walked between the two, holding both of their hands as if she were a child again. She had always felt sheltered, separate from the world by necessity, but today she felt welcomed.

Julimore tensed, hearing the sound first. She gripped Ember's hand harder and looked to Echoris with unreadable eyes.

Before Ember could ask what was wrong, she heard it too. Uniform marching steps beat like drums into the pavement. Around the corner of the last restaurant on the street, purple-uniformed guards emerged. At the middle of the group was an anchoris-drawn carriage. Hands waved from windows on either side, one seemingly male and the other female.

Onlookers called out to the queen and her fated pair, Jedoriah Knight, excited to have the royals visiting their province. Julimore and Echoris jumped into action, already working through a plan that was unknown to Ember.

"I love you, dragonia," Echoris said as she dropped Ember's hand. A feeling of dread pooled in Ember's heart.

"Be right back, honey," Julimore said to her pair with strained casualness. They hugged briefly, Ember trapped between them before Julimore pulled away.

Echoris nodded again, her smile not meeting her eyes, and turned to a bystander.

"How lovely to see the queen. What a surprise! Why do you think they are visiting?" Echoris said to the stranger.

Julimore pulled Ember in the opposite direction before she could hear what the stranger replied. She walked with a quick step, but not an outright run. Almost as if she was annoyed to have forgotten something at home, she led Ember down the street. Her palm began to sweat in Julimore's tight grip.

"Don't say a word," Julimore whispered to Ember as they walked. Frantic to be separated, Ember spoke anyway.

"Why is Momma not with us? Where are we going, Mother?" The tears were already starting to break.

"Momma is getting more information. We are hiding, don't ask stupid questions," she answered in a rush. They reached a scribe's bookstore and walked behind it, crouching down between the dumpster and the wall. Julimore knocked on the wall, and a knock rang back a moment later.

Julimore's shoulder-length brunette hair began to fray from her bun, but she sighed in relief at the response. Ember stared at the wall, confused why it would echo back the knock.

"Shouldn't Momma be hiding too?" Ember said with a whimper. She placed her hand on her chest to steady herself and to be closer to her secret.

"Ember," Julimore said seriously. She turned to Ember in the dark of the alley and held her by the shoulders. Her pupils dilated in the low light of the alley, and Ember could feel her shaking.

"There is something you must understand about pairs. Fated pairs complement each other. They have different strengths so that together they are whole. You will see this one day, with your kn —" she paused and corrected with a slight cough, "with your pair.

"I jump into action. I am a quick thinker. Momma gathers

information. She knows how to hide in plain sight and get what we need. She went to do that for our family, to learn more about the royal family's visit, while I protect you."

Ember listened, trying to take in the words, but it didn't seem fair. Why should a fated pair be separated?

"But I've done nothing wrong. Why do we need to hide all the time?" Ember felt the lie like a weight.

"Ember, you know they will kill you," Julimore chided. "You are not a child anymore. If they see the gift Aaeleia and Mutrien have given you, they will kill you."

"It doesn't feel like a gift," Ember whispered. She felt it like a stab to the heart. This supposed gift only led to pain.

"I know. I know. But one day, you'll understand it. Your purpose will be clear to you. Today is not that day."

"Promise me something," Julimore added. "If you ever see the royal family or the royal guard and we are not with you, get away. Run. Don't trust them. Don't. Trust. Anyone."

She punctuated the words with a shake, her emerald green eyes wild. Ember envied those eyes, the beauty she showed in her strength. Ember did not feel as connected to Julimore, not like Echoris. Echoris treated her like a treasure. In a world where Ember wasn't allowed to shine, it was welcome. But Julimore was her protector, and that commanded a certain love too.

"I...I can trust you and Momma..." Ember whispered. They were all each other had. The sad smile that Julimore responded with did not reassure Ember.

They waited behind the dumpster for the sounds to pass. When the marching came closer, Julimore covered Ember's mouth with a firm hand. Their bodies were stiff, keeping as still as possible as the onlookers followed the queen, her knight, and her guards. They stayed like that until the sound had long died away and another knock came from the wall of the building.

Julimore knocked back and stood, speaking no more of the incident.

Julimore and Ember went back home to find Echoris pacing the small hall between their door and kitchen. Echoris covered her mouth to muffle the sound and sobbed when they entered the room. They never had that special dinner.

The next and final family outing was one year later at the annual Aalein festival. Shortly after, Ember never saw her moms again.

THREE

A MONSTROUS SECRET

"Do not resist, Fateless," the red-haired man with the signet ring said. He moved closer, and Ember couldn't help but notice his striking blue eyes. He looked at her with distaste, assuming she was afflicted with the Fateless curse.

There is nothing strange about me. There is nothing strange about me. There is nothing strange about me, Ember repeated over and over again from her crouched position. She wished it with all her might as her hands held the ripped fabric of her collar tighter around her dress.

"I am not Fateless," Ember said through her tears.

The blue-eyed guard crouched beside her and asked, "then why would you run?"

Ember didn't have an excuse they would believe. She was scared and anxious. And to be frank? She panicked. She had been raised to run away and hide in their presence, and she was not as stealthy as Julimore had been.

"It was a misunderstanding," she insisted weakly. She felt like a skittish baomtot, cornered, scaled, and fearful. Feeling her options close in on her, Ember leapt to the right to try and use the element of surprise.

It was an utter failure as the redhead immediately grabbed the back of her dress and pulled her backwards. The dress ripped wider. Ember struggled, attempting to escape his vice grip.

Ember cried out at the ripping sound and cowered to the floor. She wrapped her arms around her chest again, whimpering to herself. The guards took this as submission. The redhead and brunette pulled her arms behind her back to tie them up, releasing the fabric she held. The blond, shorter than the redhead but taller than the brunette, stood in front of her. He looked to be only a few years older than Ember, in his purpose for maybe five years or so.

"We will be taking you to the local security. They'll decide what...?" He halted his sentence, staring at the peek of Ember's chest visible from the ripped collar. Ember shook her head back and forth, a pleading look in her eyes as she stared back at him.

"Don't hurt her," he called and the two guards tying her restraints looked up.

"What? I wasn't tying them too tightly," the redhead said from behind her, indignant at being told what to do.

But the blond didn't answer. He stared at a space above Ember's heart. She couldn't believe this was happening. Two years without her moms and she had already done everything they warned her not to. She settled in one place, made a friend, and became noticeable. And now, her secret was out. Her supposed beastly gift was visible, and she was going to die.

"Please, don't," Ember whispered to him, her knees beginning to ache on the hard floor of the market. She hoped he'd stay quiet about what he had already begun to see. Her arms tied behind her, Ember was powerless to cover what he saw. For what Ember had always hidden was not her body, but what marred her skin. What the guard was staring at now was the death of her, the reason for her moms' passing.

Ember prayed for the first time in years, reciting in her mind *Aaleia, guide me home, heart to Fate, a blessing from Mutrien's wombsake*— a children's rhyme for those desperate to find their pair and begin their family. She had never once asked Aaleia for such a thing, nor prayed to Mutrien for the blessing. But to have those two things, she would need to stay alive.

As if hearing her prayer, the guard began to pull off his jacket. He kneeled down before her, untying her arms and helping her put on the jacket. Ember stayed still, petrified and grateful of the blond soldier.

"I can't believe it," he whispered as his eyes darted back and forth from his hands and Ember's shining eyes.

A tear fell down Ember's cheeks. The surrounding guards moved around her, wanting to see what the commotion was.

"What's wrong?" one of them asked. Ember couldn't see who, her eyes were focused on the grey pools of the man before her. He was searching, unsure what to answer back, his eyes a confusion and exhilaration at once.

"Our mission is complete," he said after a few silent seconds. He lifted Ember up from the ground. Her body shook, in shock and confused. Did they know there was a scaled woman in hiding?

Ember had always thought she was anonymous and alone. Her moms implied that should she be noticed, she would die— not that they were actively looking for the cursed girl. While her moms had never called her cursed, instead saying that she was *gifted* with a sign of the beast, Ember never felt that way. She understood their undertone. If someone was scaled and not in the royal family, she was a threat. With a missing princess and their favor with the gods in question, the royal family would not tolerate any threats.

Not that Ember wanted that. She wanted to be alone.

"Let's go," he directed.

While they did not bind her again, they might as well have. The three guards closed in around Ember, using their bodies to guide her feet. They marched her forward in synchronized steps. It echoed around her despite the open air.

The Fateless, with their mental state broken, were never seen again. She expected the same treatment. As if in flashes, Ember could imagine what would happen next. Amlin would lose his business if he didn't replace her fast enough. Hasley would be promoted to her purpose quicker without Ember to distract her. Ember's home would be ransacked and redistributed. And Ember herself would disappear. Never to be seen or heard from again.

Ember had never expected much for her future. A business partnership with Hasley. A few new unique jewelry designs that she knew Amlin would hate. Quiet mornings on Mount Pietan and sleeping in on the weekends to round out her simple life. It wasn't much, but it had seemed nice. Those small hopes were gone now. All the heartaches her moms went through were for nothing. She had failed them. Their deaths meant nothing now that she was found.

Ember stared at the different guards on each side of her. Their bodies pushed her leftward to the road that forked to housing and traveler inns. Even the guard uniform worked as a propaganda piece, Ember knew. Purple and gold, the color of the blessing and the fating. The royal family was divinely chosen.

Now entering the small cottages that line the row of inns for travelers, Ember paused her steps. Was this where she would die?

"Keep moving," a light voice said from behind her. Ember began to shake her head frantically.

"It's going to be okay. Keep walking," the man spoke

again. She turned slightly to see it was the guard that had helped the redhead tie her arms, the shorter one with the quiet voice. She tried to believe him and keep her body moving, being ushered forward by the sea of bodies that cocooned her.

Ember was not a physical person. She could not overpower the royal guards, and she doubted they would listen to any excuse or reasoning she could come up with to let her go. She'd have to continue with their plan until she had a moment to escape. Ember told herself to look out for weaknesses, to find a window of opportunity. There always was something that could be exploited.

Ember looked up as they passed under a sign and into the stone building. The outside of the inn featured vines across its stones. Ember always liked seeing greenery on buildings. She briefly noted the name of the establishment as they passed the hanging sign, *The Dragon Bevy*.

"We've found her," the redhead said as they entered into the inn. He stood directly in her sight, blocking who he spoke to.

Around the room were portraits of Drakul, other dragons in flight and in battle. There was even a large tooth the size of her head mounted on the fireplace mantle. The room was dark, with red and green decor and dark brown couches. The only item not a dark hue was the fireplace itself, made from the same peiradoone stone that created their walls. The contrast was jarring. Much like her entire day.

Ember tried to look further around the room to see whom the guard was speaking, but the two men holding her arms didn't give her body enough clearance.

"Show me," a commanding voice said. The last syllable held stronger than the rest.

Her line of vision altered as the tall guard stepped aside. A group of men and women in the sitting room became visible before her. One man, in particular, stood out. The redhead gestured to Ember with a swoop of his arm.

Before Ember stood the one person she hoped to never meet in the whole of Ashkadance. Jedoriah Knight, pair to Karwyn Dragon Queen.

FOUR

JEDORIAH KNIGHT

He sat before her in a claw-like leather chair. Not a muscle or hair from his blue mane out of place, the tall spears of the chair curling above him. The calm demeanor of Karwyn Dragon Queen's pair turned to cautious joy quickly.

Jedoriah looked at her inquisitively. As if answering an unspoken signal, the redhead pulled her with him to Jedoriah's chair. With the change in position, she could better see the other guards and staff that surrounded her.

"Do not be afraid," Jedoriah told her. He pushed Ember's jacket away and his hand flew to his mouth in shock. He stared at her and Ember felt her life pulsing into the unknown at too rapid a pace. Ice rolled through her blood, her body stock-still in fear. While her whole chest was not visible, enough of it was. Now over a dozen people knew of her scales.

Jedoriah smiled wildly, the curves of it visible behind his hand. Ember's face reddened in shame. She swore she could almost feel his breath on her skin.

"Thank you, Zhieve Captain," Jedoriah said. Ember glanced behind her, noticing the pin on his lapel that designated his rank. The blond stood behind him and the brunette. Neither had the same pin. There was one captain per guard group. One for the dragon matron, one for the dragon queen (with whom Jedoriah belonged), and one would be chosen for the dragon daughter. If she were found.

Tears prickled Ember's eyes, a hot sting she would always remember from this moment. She was entirely exposed to the room of guards and companions of Jedoriah Knight. The grey, purple, and black patches of raised flesh were as comforting as a burn. These lifts of skin pushed away from her body in strange jagged flakes—the marks of her ruin. The marred skin would be the death of her.

In two silent steps, he was towering in front of her.

"My dragon daughter, at last." His smooth voice slinked onto Ember's skin, and she wished she could wipe it off. He hugged her, and his arms wrapped around her quickly before he backed away, holding her at arm's length.

Ember's eyes bulged and her thoughts sputtered. They had to be Fateless. How could they think she was the princess? She had moms, and they were certainly not members of the royal family. The room grew quieter the longer Jedoriah stared at her skin, so she broke the silence with one whispered sentence. She would not follow along with their misguided notions.

"You are wrong."

It was an act of confrontation that was incredibly foreign to her, but she had no idea what else to do. Ember wondered how deeply her blood would stain the carpet when he struck her down. It was a steadying thought despite the whispers in her head and the racing of her heart.

Jedoriah burst into a laugh that shook the whole room, white teeth exposed. Some inhabitants froze, confused by the outburst, while others exhaled shakily at the breaking of tension. It was unclear if this was usual behavior for the knight of the kingdom.

"I knew you'd have spirit," he said as he wrapped his arm around her and closed the jacket to hide her scales once more.

A strangled sound emitted from her throat, protesting his words. Ember didn't feel like she had spirit. She felt like she was falling down a hole that would never end with a voice hoarse from tears and screams. Ember was sure she would forever dangle in the dark of her mind. Maybe she was Fateless after all.

Jedoriah let her go and the blond guard led her by the arm to the couch next to them. He pushed her down with gentle hands before instructing the other guards about something. She didn't hear him. All she knew was that she was in a den of dragons, a bevy, the name of the inn made flesh, and she had no way out.

When she looked at Jedoriah again, his eyes practically glowed with dark delight at her discomfort.

"I cannot believe it. The lost dragon daughter in my inn," a jubilant woman exclaimed from the corner of the room. She bounced up and down with her hands held in prayer before her. Oblivious as she was to the tension in the air, Ember understood that this woman's reaction would be mimicked all throughout the kingdom. She would never be left alone again.

But she didn't understand. This was not real. It couldn't be real. She was not the princess, and nothing of the past few moments made sense to her.

Ember's memories circled, replaying in her mind. She was not a princess. She was an orphan, a deformed orphan with scales on her chest. Her parents told her it was a gift. A gift that held a death sentence not a crown.

"What can I get you, Embrence Dragon Daughter?"

Ember looked back and forth between the excitable innkeeper and the rest of the occupants in the low-lit room. Fire flickered in the corner, and a stray bit of sun came down from the window. She ignored her question, but the name stuck out to her.

Embrence. Ember. Embrence. Ember. Similar, inspired by the princess. But not the same. She was not that girl. She couldn't be.

"I'm the daughter of Echoris Guider and Julimore Instructor. This is a mistake. I should leave," Ember said. She willed herself to stand up from the couch. She looked pleadingly for the kind guard, trying to steer her body away from Jedoriah.

"No mistake here, my dear. You have scales. You are the princess. Sit back down," Jedoriah answered instead, his suit as dark as obsidian.

Ember, unsure how to get out of this room and the large sum of men and women around her, thought to work with the element of surprise. With nothing to lose and her life already in peril, she pretended not to hear him. What distraction could she cause that was within her control but grand enough that she had the possibility of escape? Her eyes danced around the space. They settled briefly on the fireplace.

"So what do you want me to do with this information?" she asked, asserting more confidence than she felt. She walked toward the mantle of peiradoone. The guards closest to it pushed in around her as if she would bolt. In truth, that is what she planned to do, but she had to distract them first.

She stared up at the portrait of Drakul before he took human form, blowing fire on ships at sea. It was a brutal scene, both men and merfolk floating lifeless on the waters and the banks of the shore. One of Jedoriah's favorite pieces, a small text plate informed her from below the portrait. She could see how that would be something he chose.

She inched closer to it, putting herself within a foot of the fireplace. Beside her was a stand of pokers. She uncrossed her arms, and as if satisfied by her perusal, turned around. She waited for an answer, and Jedoriah was happy to oblige.

"There is nothing else to do but to come with me back to the palace in Azororion. You are the heir."

"So you think I'm the dragon daughter because of these?" Ember asked, gesturing to her scales beneath the jacket. She had never addressed them so bluntly. It felt like a stab to her heart before she put her hands behind her back. Her left hand gripped the poker.

"Yes, you are the dragon daughter," he insisted again. He did not seem like the kind of person that liked a challenge.

"Maybe there are two people with markings on their chest," she countered. No one had ever said before that the dragon daughter had literal scales. If that were true, she would have known about it. Everyone would. They were nothing like the symmetrical sparkling gems of skin that she saw depicted on every dragon portrait and figurine.

"Impossible," came his short and instant reply.

"How do you know?" she asked. Her straight posture wore on her. Her heart hammered, and she wished she could lay down. Just a few more minutes and she could go back to her calm demeanor.

"Answer me this: Why else would someone have scales if they weren't related to a dragon?"

Ember had wondered her whole life why she was born with this deformity. Was she a blight by Aaleia to punish her moms for a reason unbeknownst to her? Did she deserve it somehow? Had Mutrien seen something dark in her soul? Was she actually a beast? A mistake in creation, the wrong child placed in the wrong womb? But she had one reason that she felt was true. One she had thought many times but never said aloud.

The innkeeper walked hesitantly closer, not yet dismissed and testing her boundaries. What would she overhear? What could she share with the rest of the community? Ember disliked her immediately for the invasion into her life.

"I am a curse," Ember answered, "nothing in our kingdom

has gone well since I was born." It hurt her to say her darkest fear, but she needed him distracted long enough. Her hands curled around the iron poker. She felt her life chiseled away chip by chip.

"I'm not the one to give you answers."

Ember recalled her mother's words like a brand. Echoris and Julimore had pushed Aaleia and Mutrien on her as if the Goddess and their God planet were the only beings that had answers to Ember's questions.

It was a theory that Ember felt guilt for every day. Her mother had been on one of the merfolk kidnapped ships 17 years ago. As a tutor in the castle, her mother had been on the trip across the sea with the royals, teaching some of the guard's children. Julimore witnessed what ultimately led Omanox Dragon Queen to build the wall. The repercussions of the kidnapping of Karwyn changed the whole kingdom. Could the gods have cursed her mother's womb for watching it happen and not taking action?

Jedoriah had some questions of his own.

"Don't you think it's cruel that your supposed family would raise you to live in fear, to think you are cursed, a girl with scales in a dragon society? Isn't it more likely that they were keeping your heritage from you?"

Ember blinked repeatedly. This was her life, all she had known. It was who she was. Why would she think any differently?

"They were protecting me," Ember decided to answer, knowing without a doubt that was the truth of it. Her moms loved her, wanted to help and save her. If they were still with her, this never would have happened.

"And where are your captors now?" he questioned, leaning forward from his imposing chair. Ember almost forgot her plan, almost dropped the poker.

"They died in a rebel attack last year." It was something

that broke Ember's heart every day, a sore point of guilt in her heart. They had died while traveling to set up their new home, caught in an attack while Ember had stayed behind to pack up the house. They never came back.

"Convenient," Jedoriah responded. Ember felt like she had been slapped. How could someone say that about someone's parents being dead?

Ember didn't respond.

"What...what is that?" Ember stammered, her eyes going wide. One hand pointed to the opposite corner at the jubilant woman. She looked down at herself, trying to see what Ember was pointing at. All eyes followed Ember's finger to do the same. It was a simple distraction, but she only needed them to look away for a moment.

Ember pushed the gate away from the fireplace with a crash, using the poker to protect her hands. She used it again to push out the logs. Two pieces of flaming grey wood caught the fabric of the carpet and the innkeeper screamed.

Half the occupants in the room jumped up at the same time to try and douse the flames. The rest of the room stood dumbfounded for a minute before comprehension crossed their face. Flames licked across the room. Jedoriah and his captain did not run towards the fire; they bee-lined straight for Ember.

She ran back towards the wide wooden monstrosity of a door at the end of the room. Her arm was already extended, begging the clasp of the door to be closer. A short curvy woman with bright long blonde hair walked right into her path. Ember tried to go around her, but she resisted her with surprising strength and pushed back. The woman grabbed the jacket Ember wore in a spin.

Exhausted by yet another person pulling on her clothing, she screamed in frustration. Feet stomped behind her, both on the fire spreading through the room and with the rush of guards behind her. It was a good effort, but there were too many variables already against her to be able to escape. If Ember was honest with herself, she knew she didn't have much of a chance anyway.

"Don't just stand there! Get a bucket of water," a woman yelled behind them.

"It's spreading! Hurry," another man cried out.

Ember felt a bit satisfied that she at least made it to the door. That initial pride fell into guilt when she surveyed the problem she created for the innkeeper. Hopefully, the crown would cover the damages.

"That was a stupid thing to do," Jedoriah said to her, eyes boring down.

Ember didn't say anything in return. Her bravado leaked from her. She was now a husk, empty and uncertain.

"How about I prepare a room at another inn close by for our company and Embrence Dragon Daughter? I have a feeling the Dragon Bevy will not be operational for our stay tonight," the blonde woman said, still gripping her jacket.

"Go with Cindrea," Jedoriah Knight said to Zhieve, not even looking at the woman as he answered. The two of them stepped away and out the door to prepare the inn. Jedoriah grabbed Ember's arm with a vice grip and called out for assistance.

"Amir Guard!"

The kind guard that gave her his jacket left the commotion and came to their side. He coughed, and Ember let the guilt build in her as she saw his face smudged with ash.

"You are now the princess's captain. Your first duty is to take her outside before the smoke gets too hot. Keep her from escaping, will you?" he asked. His eyes did not leave Ember, and his hand held onto her tighter.

Ember looked away first.

"Of course, Jedoriah Knight. Right away," Amir responded, putting his hands on the back of Ember's shoulders. Jedoriah let go with one final look, then went to delegate the remaining guards as they attempted to stop the fire. The red flames licked blue, gaining steam as they caught on the furniture.

"This is blood fire," Jedoriah stated loudly and opened his arms wide to the room. Immediately the mood changed. The men holding the buckets of water dropped their pails and rushed to the back room. They emerged with shovels and rushed outdoors. Confused by their actions, Ember watched curiously as Amir escorted her from the inn. Outside, she saw the men digging and depositing dirt and rubble into bags.

Amir noticed her confusion.

"Blood fire must be snuffed out. Suffocated not drowned."

Well, she certainly made a mess of things, hadn't she?

FIVE

THREE DOMINANT FAMILIES

Awoken by a chirping wraith, Ember blinked rapidly and stretched out her legs. Soft blankets brushed her skin, unlike the poor excuse for blankets she had in her home. Where was she? Confused and disoriented, she wiggled her body into a seated position. Immediately the reality of the evening came back to her. She was currently in her own personal purgatory, trapped in a royal world she had no business being part of. She sighed, wishing she was still asleep.

Before her stood the blonde woman from last night and Amir, the man Jedoriah claimed was her new captain of the guard. Her body felt like a creaking mess, stiff and tight. It had been a fitful night, bombarded by loud thoughts and dreams of fire and storms.

"I'm sorry, we didn't mean to wake you," the blonde, Cindrea, said.

"It's okay," Ember replied. Though in truth, there was a lot that wasn't okay right now. Cindrea had not left her alone last night, sleeping on a cot beside her bed. She wasn't the only one. Ember also had guards stationed at her window and outside her door all night. She wasn't left alone for a single moment.

"Good morning," Amir Captain said, though he didn't look like he had slept at all. He had seemed nice, much more so than Zhieve, Jedoriah's captain. The jacket Amir had given her still lay in a heap on the bathroom floor from the night before. He seemed to have found a replacement. However, before he'd had the silver dragon pin—two wings joined together to make a circlet. Now, his pin was gold with a shield hanging from the bottom. Ember wondered how he felt about his new purpose name. Did he want this responsibility?

"Dragonia, how about I help you get ready? We have to leave shortly," Cindrea said. Ember winced at the nickname.

"But it already happened. What does it matter now?" Five-year-old Ember whined.

"Dragonia, we must not repeat those same mistakes," she would explain patiently, despite having this conversation with Ember weekly. Echoris was always more level-headed with Ember, while Julimore took everything with a dire seriousness.

"Okay," Ember replied, feeling awkward in the large t-shirt she had been given to sleep in. She would wear anything, as long as it were longer. She pulled the comforters closer around her, a useless barrier between her and the people that were keeping her from fleeing the room.

Now that Ember could see her in brighter lighting, the morning peeking in from the balcony window, Cindrea's age was more apparent. By firelight, she had seemed only a few years older than Ember. But in the daylight, she could see that Cindrea was at least ten years older. Possibly more. Her nose was small and pointed with a small hump to it, and her skin was smooth and a little shiny. Her age shown in her eyes with subtle wrinkles Ember interpreted as wisdom. She wasn't sure how or why, but it seemed to her like Cindrea had been through trials.

But Ember herself had also been through trials, and it didn't look like this period of challenges was going to stop anytime soon. Overwhelm was quickly filling her body, shaking her core. This was real. They were taking her away from her home. Her gut twisted into knots.

"I'll be right outside if you need me," Amir called, stepping into the hall. The door was left ajar and Ember could hear him whispering something to the other guard on duty.

"How about a bath?" Cindrea asked Ember, walking to the connected bathroom. Ember stared back at her from the bed.

"I'd rather not. Just give me some clothes, please," she replied, immediately bringing her hand up to her covered chest. Cindrea's eyes followed the movement.

"We are going to be spending a lot of time together. You might as well get used to it now," she said.

"Why is that?" Ember asked. She curled her toes under the covers, rooting herself and pretending she had more choices than she did.

Seeming to consider the situation again, Cindrea nodded before saying, "Let's start fresh. Everything was a little hectic last night."

Cindrea dropped into a curtsy, and as she came up, she said, "I am now your lady in waiting, Cindrea Waiting. It's a pleasure to meet you, princess." She must have received a purpose change too.

"I'm Ember," Ember replied in a soft voice. "I don't think I need a lady in waiting."

"You are the dragon daughter. Trust me when I say you'll want someone by your side daily. I'll be your confidant," Cindrea replied, taking Ember's hands into her own. Her hands felt soft, as warm as the blanket, but Ember reflexively flinched at the touch. Cindrea noticed, observations being one of her prized skills.

"How is everyone so sure that I'm the dragon daughter?" Ember asked, pulling away her hands and folding them into the covers. More and more of her was curling back into the bed, feeling the quivering fear of the unknown.

"Jedoriah Knight felt it," Cindrea said matter-of-factly.

"What? Felt it how?" Ember asked, confused by what that would mean.

"You were snatched from the queen before you could meet your father, so he never experienced the blessing bond. He had that feeling last night," Cindrea told her with an unblinking expression before she turned away and walked into the bathroom. Cindrea poured water into the tub. When did they bring that into her room?

"What's a blessing bond?" she asked.

Cindrea's head popped out of the room again.

"When you meet your child for the first time, Mutrien shares with you the bonding feeling. It's similar to the fating, so you know your child's true heart."

"I didn't feel anything," Ember responded, hoping that meant something.

"I don't know if children feel it too," Cindrea pondered. "Most of the time children aren't separated from their family, so parents typically feel the bond on the day a child is born. Babies don't remember birth, so I don't know if that's a mutual feeling. Anyway, some of the guards asked Jedoriah last night how he knew for sure, and he explained how he felt."

She fiddled with her hair as the sentence drifted off before grabbing the robe from beside Ember's bed and going back into the bathroom. Pouring water was heard again, and Ember looked down at the hands that twisted and pulled the bedding fabric. All she had felt was fear when she laid eyes on Jedoriah Knight.

Her moms wouldn't have done this to her. They were kind-hearted people who wanted to protect her. She loved them, and she knew that love was real.

But Ember hesitated as she finally stood up from the bed, following Cindrea into the bathroom. She knew her family. She knew who she was. It didn't matter what the knight of the realm said, right?

Cindrea threw in oils and different bubbling agents. The water began to fizzle and turn cloudy before bubbles filled the surface. Her muscles began to relax as she looked at the bath, but she didn't make a move.

At Ember's nervous look, Cindrea sighed and rolled her eyes. She turned around to give Ember privacy.

"So you think it's true, that I'm the dragon daughter?" Ember asked Cindrea as the water splashed around her. The bath was just as wonderful as she imagined. Ember knew that Cindrea already believed she was, so she wasn't sure why she bothered asking her outright. She closed her eyes and leaned her head against the tub and realized why she asked. She hoped for a different answer. Ember wanted that validation from someone living.

The water held Ember loosely, the darkness behind her lids a comfort. Ember submerged her own head beneath the water of the tub, wetting her hair. She heard the response from above it, her ears clogging as she became enveloped. The response jarred her, despite the hollowing sound that came from hearing it below water.

"Without a doubt."

***

"TRAVELING to the castle will take a day and a half if we leave now," Cindrea provided as she handed a toweled Ember a pile of clothes to wear. Ember clutched the clothing to her chest as the towel did not reach high enough. They were items from Cindrea's own closet, thankfully high collared. She didn't think she could handle anyone else staring at her chest.

When she put the clothes on, Ember was happily surprised to find she actually liked the outfit. It featured long black suede boots over grey trousers and a high collar beige blouse. She felt comfortable, and the clothes were finer than she was used to. Her dress from the day before was not worth saving.

Ember wondered what Amlin thought when she didn't come back. More so, what Hasley thought. She'd have to send them a note at her next stop.

"Can I send a letter to someone, so they know I'm leaving?" She didn't want Hasley to worry, especially when she was leaving with no warning. Julimore and Echoris could have been wrong. Having scales wouldn't be a problem to the royal family, Ember hoped, and she could lead a normal life. She'd move to another province, and maybe Hasley would come with her. Ember would pretend this was a dream, her scales representing nothing but a deformity. No beastly gift. No curse. No scales. A dream life by comparison.

Ember didn't know how to feel about the blessing bond Jedoriah had felt, but it must have been a mistake. Once she got to the castle, the queen would sort things out. While they hadn't known each other personally, Julimore and Echoris had worked close to the palace tutoring children of the royal guard. The queen could remember them and want to help her.

"Of course, once we get to the palace. Right now it's a little too chaotic to send mail. We don't want it tampered with," Cindrea responded. Cindrea tugged out more stubborn knots from Ember's hair. When she braided it back into a face-framing style, Ember almost smiled into the mirror. She never imagined her hair could look so pretty. She immediately turned red. She had never paid attention to her looks before. It felt uncomfortable, almost shameful, to care about it now.

"Why chaotic?" Ember asked, circling her thoughts back to the statement.

"Everyone knows we've found you. The streets have been celebrating," Cindrea said.

Ember's body froze. If the people believed she was the

dragon daughter already, how would that affect the queen's opinion? Would they find out she wasn't the princess and then kill her for not being the answer to their prayers?

"How?" she whispered, looking at Cindrea from the mirror.

"The innkeeper knew, so her pair must know. The staff also saw you, so their pairs would know, their children as well. These things spread," Cindrea replied with a nonchalant shrug, used to the way that news travels with the royal family.

"Alright, let's go." Cindrea gestured to the guards.

The five guards positioned around her room grabbed the bags Cindrea had prepared for Ember. They held a mismatch of other people's clothing and items, a temporary solution to clothing while they traveled. The guards corralled Ember into the middle of their group and she noticed Amir drop her satchel in with the other bags. She hadn't noticed him pick it up when she ran from them yesterday. Ember's steps stalled. Her movements were clunky as the implications laid in on her.

The queen wouldn't want to let the people down, but she would hopefully want to find out the truth about her daughter more than that. That is, assuming she didn't already know what happened to her daughter. For all Ember knew, the truth was too horrible to share.

Filing outside the inn, Ember watched as Jedoriah bid farewell to the innkeeper from the substitute rooms they used, as well as saying goodbye to the one whose inn now had a few char marks. Ember didn't meet either pair of eyes, feeling guilty about the fire. People were lined up at the ends of the row of inns, trying to come closer. Occupants even peeked from the other inn windows. The number of royal guards seemed to grow overnight. They blanketed the street, keeping citizens clear.

Cindrea pulled her away from her observations. "Our carriage, dragonia."

"Ember," she corrected with a snap. She did not welcome

this familiarity. As nice as she was this morning, Cindrea was still a stranger.

Drawing their rather large carriage was a bull-like beast with stunted wings and a rough hide as tough as armor. Ember paused in front of the creature, reaching her arm hesitantly toward it.

"Be cautious," Amir called as he drew up their rear. The warm honey eyes of the creature seem to beckon to her. Ember slowly pet the creature behind the ears, guiding her hand lower to stroke over the wings. She could tell from the way they clamped that they could not open. An animal with the instinct to fly that could not.

"Embrence, in the carriage," Jedoriah commanded as he passed. He climbed into his own carriage ahead of theirs. The anchoris flanking that carriage seemed to look at her, observing her petting his brother.

"I'll see you soon," Ember whispered to the anchoris, running her hand behind his ears. Its eye twinkled at her, and he made a squeaking happy sound, tilting his head to move into the scratching. His happiness shattered a chamber in Ember's chest. It didn't seem like he got that attention often.

Ember sat down in the carriage and turned away from the window to address Cindrea. They were the only two on the red cushioned seats.

"Jedoriah Knight seems..." She was unsure what word to use. Cindrea caught her meaning quickly.

"Intimidating, impatient, a little cruel?"

"Yes," Ember said.

Cindrea smiled, pushing a strand of platinum hair behind her ear and adjusting her grey dress. Purple thread accented her curves with each nip and tuck of the fabric. It looked expensive.

"He is all those things, but he is also a proud man. He

wants what's best, and he mostly knows what's best," Cindrea said.

"Mostly?" Ember questioned, her right eyebrow quirking as the carriage began to rumble forward.

"No one is infallible. Least of all Jedoriah Knight." She rolled her eyes and Ember wanted to laugh. Could she say that about her monarch? Cindrea seemed oddly comfortable with challenging him.

"It's great to get to know you, Embrence Dragon Daughter," Cindrea said with a smile.

"My name is Ember," she replied again. She did not like having to repeat herself on something as important as her name.

"How do you know?" Cindrea patiently asked.

"It is the name I have always had." Ember didn't understand the question.

"Have there been people in your life other than your mothers that were there? People that saw your blessed mom pregnant? Do they have any other family?" Cindrea gestured around them as if the empty jostling carriage were proof that there was no one else involved in Ember's life.

"My moms were orphans," Ember replied, offended by Cindrea's judgment of her family.

"Convenient," Cindrea pronounced slowly.

That word again. Ember wanted to slap her. Ember didn't see how her not having an extended family proved she was a missing princess. Her mothers had no family, that was that. She ignored the woman and turned to the warmth of the window, laying her head down.

The carriage stopped, and Ember jolted forward. How long had it been?

"Why'd we stop?" Ember asked as she stretched her legs out in front her, pushing out kinks in her neck and back with a little twist. She felt grateful her scales were covered, as it would have been hard to sleep so soundly otherwise.

"It's dinnertime, Dragon Daughter," Cindrea said, standing up in the tall carriage.

"Already?" Ember rubbed the sleep from my eyes. Outside her window was a still forest.

"Yes, you seemed to need more rest, so we didn't disturb you for lunch." She picked up something from a basket on the floor.

"Here." She handed Ember a thermos. "Have some hot chocolate, the night is growing colder."

Ember accepted the thermos and took a sip. The heat from the treat warmed her hands. Thoughts nudged her. Acceptance that it wasn't at all what she had been lead to believe crept into her subconscious. It was as if her sleep betrayed her, putting clues together. Ember pledged then and there that no matter what happened and what she uncovered on this crazy journey, that she would still think of the happy moments with her moms.

"Dragon Daughter."

She turned, finding Amir waiting at the opening of the carriage.

"Captain," she replied back, not moving from her seat.

Amir gestured for her to join them outside of the cabin. She picked up the velvet cloak and joined them under the night sky. A happy sigh escaped Ember's lips as she took in the darkness and the shadowed trees surrounding their camp. The twilight of stars was her favorite thing about their world, with the exception of the ocean she and many others had not touched.

"Are we stopping for the night?" Ember asked as she followed Amir to the fire pit.

"Yes, we passed the local inns in this province so we could gain more time. If we camp here, we'll be at the palace by midmorning."

Reaching the fire, she stopped to find only two free spots available, both in close proximity to the knight. Ember was beginning to dislike Jedoriah more than she did before she knew him. As the right hand and fated pair the dragon queen, he helped influence everything that happened in this city.

So much had gone against her and the citizens of Ashkadance, that many were feeling the sting of resentment. Each year, the people grew poorer, the Fateless grew in number, and the rebels became more of a threat. It didn't help that most of the mistreatment of the Fateless came from royal decree.

"Hello, my Embrence." He turned his brown eyes to her, ashen blue hair twinkling in the amber glow. Ember did not like his use of the term *my*.

"Please call me Ember." Ember did her best attempt at civility, even though she'd rather crawl away from the slither of his voice.

"Of course. My apologies." He nodded, not taking his eyes away from hers. "Sit. Please." He gestured towards the seat beside him, scooting farther down the log.

Ember obliged him, wrapping herself in the warmth of the flame and attempting to ignore the stares from the men around her. It was a losing effort.

"Every night, my men and I tell a story around the fire. Tonight it's my turn, so I thought I'd share the story of the dragon king in celebration of finding you."

Ember gritted her teeth but did not reply. It's an overplayed story, one every child hears from the moment they are born to the night they fall into the endless slumber. To some, it's a favorite. To Ember, the child of two teachers that frequently visited the priestesses, it was shared too often for her to feel its intended impact. But maybe, she reasoned, there would be more detail if it came from the royal family.

He started the story the same as all of the history lessons do, with a callback to the Unyielding War.

"The world of Mutrien was in chaos," Jedoriah began, taking a deep inhale.

"Three dominant families fought to control the planet's only continent. The people were divided, and the beasts of the world intervened with an unfair advantage of power. After years of conflict, later known as the Unyielding War, Mutrien decided he needed to use his power to take action against the people and beasts that inhabited him. Magma erupted from beneath the sea, and our one continent became three. Mutrien cried for his broken body and for his hurting people. To his greatest fear, the separations between them all did not help the conflict. Fighting continued, using the sea as a battleground of ships and fire.

"Aaleia, a goddess floating through the universe looking for a home, heard Mutrien's call of sorrow and pain. She found our planet and fell in love with what it could be. The First Fating began—starting with Mutrien and Aaleia themselves."

Jedoriah looked at Ember as she turned to listen more intently. This was the part she wanted to hear, how he interpreted the fating of beasts to mankind.

"And so one morning, after a week of storms and chaos, the citizens and beasts of Mutrien all awoke to find the world changed. Sparks lit up each city as the people found their pair in their neighbors, in their enemies, and even in their best friend's partner. There was confusion, but there was also peace. Every citizen across the three continents found the person that held their heart, waiting to help them reach their true purpose. Someone chosen for them, delivered when they needed them most.

"Love changed and so did family, as Aaleia granted fated pairs and Mutrien granted blessings to each couple when it was right for them and their purpose.

"Aaleia's gift went one step further. She set to honor us and bestow the chosen families on each continent the power of beasts into our hearts and lineage. Aaleia chose a beast for two women and one male, granting the humans a pair strong enough to protect their borders and giving the chosen beast a human form.

"Meira of Grydagia was fated to a griffin peacekeeper. For Quiro of Faeinto, a unicorn diplomat. And for the most powerful kingdom, Ashkadance, our Kariana was chosen for a dragon known as Drakul, a general in the dragon army. He became our first and only dragon king, as Kariana became the first of our line of dragon queens."

As he continued, Ember felt more eyes pierce her, studying each movement of her face and looking to where they knew her supposed scales to be.

"And so the world grew stronger, balanced, and more powerful with the legendary beasts introduced to the bloodline of the high houses. Aaleia was pleased, and Mutrien has blessed us ever since."

A story for children, and only the parts that made Ashkadance look victorious. She finished the plate of shredded meat and grains that Cindrea had deposited onto her lap in silence. For what was left unsaid was the most important part of the story. Beasts were now hard to come by. The years of war before the fating and then the commotion that came afterward hurting their many species irreparably. Not just being killed in the Unyielding War, but now the birth rates were lower as well.

There were barely any dragons, griffins, or unicorns anymore, and what was left of the dragons was unknown. They abandoned Ashkadance in the rule of Sheran Dragon Queen, the current dragon queen's grandmother. There was barely anyone alive that had seen a dragon. And relations with the other kingdoms? Nonexistent. Not after the merfolk conflict. Not after the wall.

Standing, Ember ignored the conversation that followed

after Jedoriah's story. She instead chose to put away her plate where Cindrea designated and laid down in the damp grass to stare up at the stars. This road was her favorite, the main highway to Ashkadance's castle. While she had never journeyed as far as the castle, she'd used this route before. To their left lay the white expansive wall that bordered their continent. In the darkness, it appeared like a subtly glowing and impenetrable sky, the stars popping up at its end. If you knew the wall was there, it wasn't that scary. But without that knowledge, it looked like an empty hole in the universe. Ember once hugged the wall, pressing her body against its cool surface.

"Are you alright, Dragon Daughter?" Ember saw one of the younger guards standing in her peripherals, peering down at her. It was the brunette that had been with Zhieve and Amir. They had yet to be introduced.

"Just enjoying the sky. What's your name?"

"Waldorph Guard, but call me Wally. Can I sit with you?"

Ember smiled at him, but then grew weary as he tumbled into the grass beside her. She had talked more in the past two days than she had in weeks to Hasley. It felt strange having so many people around her that wanted to be a part of her life.

"What's the palace like?" she asked him as he settled down next to her. She might as well know more about what she is getting herself into.

"Well," he began, not sure how to describe it, "there is a lot of space."

"I mean, how does it feel to be there?" She felt him fidget next to her, a silence extending longer than it should.

"It's quieter," he finally decided to say, "than most people would expect."

"I like the quiet," Ember replied, but she felt there was more left unsaid in his words. Either way, she would find out sooner rather than later.

Before he could say anything else, a struggle was heard

from behind them. Ember jumped up and Wally pushed her behind him. Cindrea ran towards the pair, coming to cover Ember's other side. She was surprised to see Cindrea pull a dagger from a pocket; it held a blue jewel at the end of its hilt. Even in the darkness, the firelight reflected back on the gem. Ember began to shake as voices grew louder around them.

A person rushed out from the trees, running towards the camp. He was a tall man with black hair like hers. It sat shaggy and unruly across his face. His eyes were wild, almost bulging in the light. Cindrea and Wally came in tighter around her, waiting to see what direction the man would run. He was barefoot, mud splattering his appearance. His shirt and pants were ripped, holes across them showed peeks of his golden skin. He screamed a shrieking wail that echoed around them in something more animalistic than a roar.

"He's Fateless," Cindrea said, eyes not moving from his figure. As if he heard her, the man's face whipped in their direction, and he flipped his feet, running almost sideways at them in an ungodly angle. Ember stumbled back into Cindrea, her heart jumping into her throat.

Guards rushed for the man, but not before he came to slide in the dirt, propelling him faster towards the trio. Wally pushed Cindrea and Ember back, but the man crashed into them before anyone else could get close.

"Princess! Dragon!" he cried, voice hoarse and desperate as his arms encircled Ember in a crushing hug. He pulled back to look at her, but his eyes couldn't focus. They darted back and forth around her face as if unanchored to any part of him.

"Stay back," Cindrea called, pointing her dagger at him but not getting any closer.

Wally pulled out his own sword from the hilt of his purple uniform and tripped, stumbling in the dirt. The guards charged forward, her captain and Jedoriah's leading at breakneck speed. They'd be there in seconds.

"Save me. Save us, princess," he whimpered. He let go of her and fell into the grass at her feet. Wally held him down, a knee on his back. He looked scared, his arms shaking as he sheathed his sword and pulled the man's hands behind his back. Ember looked down at the man, unsure of what to do. She couldn't save him. She didn't even think she would be able to save herself right now.

"I have him," Wally said as Zhieve reached them, Amir only steps behind.

Without warning, Zhieve pulled his own sword from its sleeve and held it high over the Fateless man's head, striking down. Cindrea screamed at the abruptness, Wally throwing himself back. But Ember wasn't looking at him. She was looking at the Fateless man staring back at her. She didn't see the blade coming until it struck the man's neck and his gaunt face fell down into the grass and dirt. Blood splattered on her pants, and she fell backward too, almost kicking the head of the man that pleaded for her help.

His eyes stayed open, staring back at her. The tears that had gathered now unleashed as blood leaked into the spaces around his eyes. Ember lost all breath, lost all meaning. She looked up from his wide eyes, this nameless person, to Zhieve. He stood tall, blood dripping from his sword, but his eyes didn't even dare look at the man he just killed. Instead, he stared at Wally. Zhieve's eyes seemed to judge—almost as if he believed Wally should have killed the nameless man, that he shouldn't have had to do it. Wally's eyes judged back. No, they seemed to say.

"Why?" Ember croaked. "He just wanted to talk to me." Though she knew it was a lot more complicated than that.

"The Fateless cannot be trusted to survive," Zhieve responded. He wiped his sword on the body, cleaning his blade before he turned away from them. Ember caught Amir's eyes as Zhieve walked back to Jedoriah Knight. Amir looked upset, and

Ember knew instantly that she could trust him and Wally. They had compassion. They never would have killed this man, at least, not in such a brutal manner.

Jedoriah didn't even seem to blink, uncaring as they went back to setting up the camp for the night. Some of the guards had the decency to look uncomfortable. Cindrea helped Ember stand, and together they walked to their shared tent. Amir and Wally disposed of the Fateless man's body.

Ember wished she knew his name. She wished she could tell his family a beautiful lie.

SIX

A WORLD UNDERWATER

"If I could be queen, I would not turn it down."

Ember opened a bleary eye to see Cindrea sitting on top of the cot opposite hers, a blanket around her shoulders. She looked younger and more vulnerable bundled up in that way. The movement and subtle streams of light coming in from the corners of the tent flap suggested the day had started again without Ember noticing. It had been a long night; sleep didn't hold a prominent place in it.

Ember squeezed her eyes tightly shut before she opened them again and took a deep breath. She wanted to be honest with this woman and set their boundaries before they entered the castle. Ember feared they would never let her leave once she set foot on the palace steps, and if Cindrea would be her lady in waiting, it was important they understood each other.

"If I accept that Jedoriah Knight is right and I am the dragon daughter, that would mean my whole life was a lie. That would mean that my parents didn't love me. I don't know how to accept that and survive. Until I see irrefutable proof, I am not going to believe it." Ember sat up herself, throwing off her dew-dripped blanket. She wished Hasley was here, and she couldn't wait to write that letter and tell her she was okay.

"Ember, just because your moms weren't your Blessed parents, that doesn't mean they didn't love you. They raised you as a newborn. They could have killed you. In fact, it's more strange that they kept you alive. What is the point of taking you and keeping you ignorant of your heritage?" Cindrea questioned, pulling on her shoes as she stood up from the cot. She handed Ember a change of clothing and turned around.

That was something Ember desperately wanted to know. If they weren't her moms, then why? They didn't ransom her. They didn't torture her. None of this made sense.

"Let's just forget it for now, okay? We have to go." Pulling on a new pair of pants that were not stained with blood, Ember put on her boots and stood up. The road ahead of them was about to diverge into two paths, one that went straight to the gates of the castle and the other continuing its circle around Ashkadance.

Amir, Wally, and the other guards Ember had yet to get to know were all packed up and ready to go. Her tent was the last to be packed. Jedoriah already stood near his carriage speaking with his captain. They both turned to look at her and Ember was struck by the cruel beauty of the captain. His red hair and an undertone of yellow kept his skin bright in the burgeoning morning. Dark eyes stared back at her. Ember passed the two talking men.

"Good day," Jedoriah said behind her, but she didn't acknowledge the greeting. Ember couldn't understand how either of them could have been paired. Whoever was fated to them must be just as wicked. Ember wondered, not for the first time, what the queen must be like. Ember helped dismantle the tent with Cindrea. Her thoughts drifted to the queen and her predicament, no matter how hard she tried to focus on the task at hand.

They were asking her to give up her life, to be part of a family and a legacy she didn't want. But it didn't matter, she pledged to herself that she was going to be herself no matter what happened. She may not be a princess or a warrior, but she was a thinker. Her isolated life taught her to listen and observe. She would find her way out of this, she just needed the right moment. She couldn't rush it, or she would be in the same situation as yesterday. But being trapped in an inn with the knight of the realm after setting someone's world on fire? She didn't want to repeat that.

Ember pet the anchoris behind the ears as she passed, slipping a snack to him before their journey.

WRAITHS FLEW AHEAD OF THEM, notifying the castle of their approach. Ember began to focus on her breathing, doing her best to stay calm despite her racing heart.

She absentmindedly scratched the scales on her chest, still covered by her cloak. Ember had tried not to think about her supposed birth mom. Blinking suddenly, Ember realized that if her moms were not her moms, then Julimore and Echoris were probably not their real names. Who was she if not Ember Julimore?

The palace was much larger and more foreboding then she expected it to be. It was a large monument of hedged stone that peaked up from the ground. There were many spiraling towers to it, with two exceptionally tall ones that protruded up into the sky on opposite sides. But the most interesting piece of architecture was the long flat landing space. Her memory reminded her it was originally designed for Drakul to land and turn into a human without entering from the front gates. Later in his life it became a regular outdoor room, no longer needed as a landing strip when he gave up his dragon form for a human life.

The grounds around the main entrance were pristine, a perfectly manicured lawn. Along the drive were two single-file lines of people, one on either side of the walk. Their uniforms pressed, faces a mask of calm. It was a smaller group of people than Ember expected for such a large space, but still, more than she was used to. The line at Crawford Baker was nothing compared to this. More than fifty people waited to greet them.

She and Cindrea walked behind Jedoriah Knight, guards preceding them and pulling up behind them. The men and women greeted Jedoriah with bobbed nods of the head, but as soon as he left their sight they settled on Ember with an unmistakable excitement. It was a jolting contrast that happened with each staff member. Calm and collected for their knight—something he must demand of them—with a wild shift to curious jubilance when he passed.

They reached their hands out to her, touching her cloak and shoulder. Ember shrank away, feeling more claustrophobic by the moment. Should they be able to touch her? Was that allowed? Ember began to shake and Cindrea gripped her arm, pulling her into her side. Cindrea nodded at the staff and gave stern looks to those that tried to get any closer.

"Captain!" Cindrea called when it became clear she couldn't guard Ember against both sides effectively. Amir caught the look of panic in Ember's wide eyes and moved to her other side.

Ember didn't know how to feel, to have so many people pulling for her, happy to see her and unable to control themselves. A life of invisibility was all she had ever known. They stopped trying to touch her, but the whispers followed as she walked up the pathway. Again and again, she saw the faces morph, and she wondered how Jedidiah could not see what was happening right behind him. Or did he know and not care?

"Welcome home, princess."

"Welcome back, Embrence Dragon Daughter."

"Dragon Daughter returns!"

"She's here. She's really here!"

"It's the princess. She's real."

"You're alive!"

Ember tried to absorb their faces, never having seen so many people happy to be in her presence. It was a moment she didn't want to forget, even if she felt she didn't deserve it. Who was she? A woman born with a deformity she always thought would kill her, not give her a crown.

When they reached the end of the drive and approached the palace doors, Ember stopped dead. A new feeling burned into her soul. The queen.

Karwyn Dragon Queen stood at the entrance of the palace, staring stoically at Ember. Jedoriah Knight walked up to his pair, his smile demure as he kissed her cheek and turned to stand on her right. Karwyn did not move a muscle, did not greet the heart that was said to match her own. Her eyes stared straight into Ember, and she couldn't look away.

After such a strange three days and after speaking with the men and women in Jedoriah's employ, Ember had already naturally begun to question the life she had been living, thinking on all the weird behavior from her mothers. They weren't perfect, she reasoned, but they had been her family and she loved them. Ember had told herself that she would find out for herself what the truth was when she got here. She had no doubt now. She was not born to the family that raised her. It gave her peace and immediate pain.

Was this the blessing bond?

"My queen," Cindrea began, "I am pleased to that announce your daughter, Embrence Dragon Daughter, has returned." Cindrea's hand gestured to Ember as she fell into a curtsy.

Looking at the queen, Ember felt a warmth in her chest expand outward. She felt comfort, home, the elixir of life itself.

She lifted a hand to the woman and then paused. Her hand, her skin, her entire body had a soft purple glow. Different from the blessing, the purple spark-like fireworks surrounded a woman at the moment Mutrien blessed them with a child and different from Aaleia's fating of golden sparks. This was subtler, but still, an awareness that could not be denied. And Karwyn was feeling it too. Her own skin glowed the same hue, and her stoic face grew a slow smile. A blessing of a different kind, a mother and daughter coming together after sixteen years apart.

Ember felt tears roll down her face. Her mother. This was her mother. It was an earth-shattering certainty that both broke her heart and finally sealed it into one piece.

The guards and servants around them began to cheer at their reunion. Ember couldn't hear them.

"It's you," Ember said.

"It's me," the queen answered. She stepped toward Ember, her black and silver dress sashaying with her. Ember walked forward as well and their bodies meet in the middle for the best hug Ember had ever received. She dropped her cheek onto Karwyn's shoulder, inhaling her cinnamon scent. Karwyn dropped her head on top of Embers and whispered, "You don't belong here."

As if jolting awake from a dream, Ember tensed.

"What?" she whispered back.

"You should leave," the queen responded. Ember pulled back, watching as her mother did the same. Her sleek black hair was pulled into a tight lifeless chignon. She shared with her the same quiet smile before stepping back to Jedoriah's side. They stood still next to each other, the main palace doors behind them.

Ember's heart stumbled in her chest, a wild beating of horse hooves. Her palms began to sweat, and the breath caught in her throat.

Karwyn blinked, and her mouth transformed into a bright pearly smile, her emotions changing in a blink. She turned around and walked briskly through the entryway. The queen called back, "Let's come inside."

Ember couldn't move. She felt trapped. *You should leave. You should leave. You should leave.* Cindrea brought an arm around Ember's shoulders and guided her into the castle behind Jedoriah and their gaggle of guards. Ember barely noticed the movement. She didn't hear the bustle of the servants overjoyed at the viewing of this reunion. Ember couldn't see through the tears welling and spilling rampantly from her eyes. A world underwater, it almost seemed preferable.

At the destruction of her life, she found no hope to stay calm. Her sobs became desperate gulps of air, her blood tingling her insides and numb pricks of skin all across her body. *You don't belong here.*

SEVEN

THE VIEW BEYOND

"Jedoriah!" Cindrea called, forgetting formality in her attempt to get help. The knight turned, seeing Ember panicking in the hall. The queen walked on, her shoes clicking across the grey stone floor. Either unaware or uncaring, she did not turn to see the commotion.

The servants, however, cluttered the space behind Ember. Their whispers caused her more heartache.

"Poor dear, what a shock."

"Reunited after so long, no wonder she is crying."

"Did you see that glow? What a moment."

Ember tried to drown them out, to keep their prying thoughts from escalating into her subconscious and latching there. It must have looked like a pretty picture. An over-whelmed princess and her mother reunited after sixteen years. Ember felt more abandonment now than she ever had before.

Jedoriah called for the guards to go down the hall. Amir came up from behind Ember and Cindrea, sweeping Ember into his arms. He rushed her to the room mentioned. Her breathing escalated, and she felt a tingling in her bones.

"Can't breathe," she wheezed, her chest pulsing at the

effort. Amir ran faster down the hall.

Reaching his intended destination, Ember was swept into the small infirmary. Five beds lined the room, impractical small beds that would barely fit a child. There was a couch and several cabinets that an old man was rifling through, seeming to organize papers. Amir carried her passed the sofa, depositing her on the closest bed.

"What is going on?" the new man asked, addressing Jedoriah and Amir. His eyes turned to the bed, finding Ember curled tightly into herself, body shaking. His long purple coat looked new, a shimmer in it that spoke of his status as the physician for the royal family.

"Hello, my name is Jair Doctor, and I can help you. Sit up. It'll help open your breath," he said as he approached her.

Ember did her best to do so, slowly stretching out her scrunched body and trying to slow the heaving of her chest. Jair reached into the cabinet behind her. He pulled out a thick blanket lined with silver on one side and black velvet on the other. He wrapped Ember in the blanket and tucked it around her like a cocoon. It was warm and heavy. Her shaking began to ebb.

"Now, everyone back up," the grey-haired doctor instructed. He gestured for Jedoriah, her captain, Wally, and Cindrea to move back. They give her five feet of room.

"Do you get panic attacks often?" Jair asked.

"First," Ember gasped out, "time." Was that what had happened to her? She shivered, a little more restricted in the weighted blanket. It hugged her and she could feel the ache in her chest calm more, the tingling of her arms and legs subsiding.

"What did she say to you?" Jedoriah asked, his voice seeming both annoyed and upset over this introduction to the castle.

"That I don't belong here," Ember responded, feeling the

sentence like a gaping wound.

"She should know," Cindrea answered back, looking to Jedoriah.

"Clear the room," the doctor responded immediately.

Amir and Wally begrudgingly left, indicating they would wait for Ember in the hall. Why didn't Amir and Wally get to stay? Wally she could understand, he was a regular guard, but why her captain?

Ember felt lightheaded, unable to question or ask what was happening. She wished she were still in Firetop, laying on her hard bed with her mom's hand knitted quilt on top. She'd tell Hasley she was sick today, have her relay the message to Amlin, and she'd lay there thinking on what a horrible dream she'd had.

Jedoriah sighed and looked at Ember, his posture stiffening while his arms swung loose for a moment at his sides.

"Your mother is Fateless," Jedoriah said and adjusted his jacket, flicking off a non-existent piece of fluff. He spoke as if it was only a minor inconvenience to him, as bothersome as a smudge on his shoe.

"I don't understand," Ember responded. How could her sovereign and blessed mother have the Fateless plague? Wouldn't everyone know that the queen was slowly going insane? How could she have been fated and blessed if she were one of the Fateless?

"I assure you, she is. Don't listen to anything she says," Jedoriah snapped, impatient in his task to share this. He turned and walked back to the door. "Cindrea will help you to your rooms," he added before the door shut behind him.

Ember adjusted herself in the small bed, the blanket falling slightly from her chest. This was too much for one day.

"I assure you, we are providing her with the best care," Jair said and nodded at her kindly, sympathy shining in his brown eyes.

"How did this happen?" she whispered, worried for the queen's safety. The moment she saw her, she felt a kinship that was unmistakable. Would the fating, when her time came, feel similar? It made her feel guilty, such an instant love for her when she had two moms who cared for her for all her life. Is this why they never seemed to be connected the way Hasley was with her parents?

The Fateless were killed, like the man in the forest. They were a threat. With little insight into it other than the fact that it wasn't spread through contact, there wasn't much else they could do. How could they stop it? If the queen had it, was anyone safe? How long had she been sick?

"Are you familiar with the merfolk conflict?" Cindrea asked.

Ember nodded. Everyone knew to various degrees a little about the conflict. Although, "conflict" was putting it lightly. The merfolk had kidnapped Karwyn when she was the dragon daughter, it had led to the closing of their borders. The citizens rallied to protect the monarchy, but when people had to start changing their purpose and the Fateless began to grow, unrest festered. It still did. No one expected the wall to have no way out.

Quickly doing the math in her head, Ember realized that was almost seventeen years ago.

"When Karwyn Dragon Daughter returned, she was fated to Jedoriah and they were blessed. For a time, everything was fine, but those close to her could see that Karwyn was different. It wasn't until some time had passed and the first cases of the Fateless were made public that we realized what we had done," Jair answered patiently.

"And what was that?" Ember was afraid of the answer.

"We trapped ourselves inside an infested kingdom. The merfolk infected the future queen, knowing there was nothing we could do," Jair explained with an exhaled breath.

For the second time in less than a week, her whole world tumbled down.

"The queen was the first case? It was given to her on purpose?" Ember whispered. Could this horror be real?

"That's the confusing part," Cindrea answered. "We minimized the staff, minimized her public appearances, and still the Fateless spread. That's how we learned it was not spread by contact. While it spread, it was not to those that have been in immediate contact with her. She was the first, but she is not the carrier. Something else is spreading it."

The god's curse, Ember thought. This was a punishment. She felt it in her bones.

"And you used to serve my mother?" Ember asked Cindrea. She nodded.

"Then why are you serving me now?"

"To help you prepare for what is needed of you," Cindrea said.

"And the queen?"

"She is well taken care of. Guards are with her at all times, and she still has one other lady in waiting," Cindrea responded. Ember pulled the weighted blanket back up to her shoulders.

Coming back to her earlier questions, Ember turned back to the doctor.

"But I thought the Fateless didn't have pairs?"

"Your mother is a unique case. We believe that since she was the first to contract it and has dragon blood in her veins, then she could have different symptoms," Jair finished. He pulled out a pad of paper and writing utensil from his desk.

"Shouldn't the kingdom know about this?" Ember asked, her eyes following the stethoscope on his shirt.

"That would send everything into disarray. No, that would not do. Only the people in this room and a handful of her guards, of course. With you gone, the continuity of the crown was in question. We couldn't jeopardize that."

"I'm back now," Ember muttered to herself, still in shock that it was true. She was the princess. Would that mean this key to the history of the Fateless would soon be public knowledge? Going from no family to having her family be a lie, to then having a royal family, to feeling rejected by them? It was dramatic enough to handle within the span of years, but days and minutes? Ember's heart ached.

"Cindrea," Jair Doctor started, "why don't you show Embrence Dragon Daughter her rooms?" He then addressed Ember, "And my princess, once you are settled we'll need to do a diagnostic of your health. It can wait a few days. I'm sure you are tired. For now, we'll begin you on an herb cycle to make sure you are getting the proper nutrients. Alright?"

Ember nodded weakly and unwrapped herself from the blanket, and Cindrea took her hand to help her off the small bed and lead her to the door. Jair walked behind Ember, a hand on her shoulder.

"It's great to see you again," he said with a small smile.

"We've met?" she asked, her hand on the door latch.

"I helped deliver you to this world," he said, "I'm happy you are in my care again."

Ember smiled, a real, albeit a hesitant one, and opened the door to her new life.

———

AS CINDREA LED her down the hall, Ember couldn't help but feel the coldness of the decor. It didn't feel like a home, it looked more like an empty war museum. She knew logically it was a castle and that amount of space was difficult to make personable, but did there need to be portraits of death and destruction across the walls? The homes she shared with her moms always felt lived in, despite the little time they spent in each location.

When they made it into the wing that led to her tower bedroom, Ember had the sense that the area had been closed for some time. It smelled like musk and stagnation, old air trapped within these doors without the circulation of many lungs. Dusty chandeliers hung from the ceiling with spider-webbed corners as thick as she'd ever seen them. Each painting on the wall was covered with a sheet. Ember itched to see what was beneath them. More death like the outer chambers?

"We'll be cleaning up this space, of course," Cindrea commented as Ember stood in the middle of the large room. It was an entryway, one door in and out. No windows, yet there were torches lit. Did they come to this space before her to light the way? She hadn't seen any servants on their way to this wing. Around the flames there were no cobwebs. The fire glowed with a blue center. She walked a step closer, compelled.

As if sensing her thoughts, Cindrea said, "These torches have been lit since the death of Drakul Dragon King."

Blood fire then, like at the inn. Lit with diluted dragon's blood. It was difficult to contain once it spread, but on small torches like these, it could stay lit for centuries—if it went untouched. Ember felt pulled to the flame. Where did they get the blood? Was this the blood of Drakul Dragon King? Given it was lit on his death, she assumed so, but it could be another dragon as well. Blood fire was uncommon, she had no clue where the innkeeper got it, but it's appearance in the castle wasn't a surprise. If anyone had access to dragon blood, it would be the home of the first, and only, dragon king.

Outside the entrance to the stairwell, there were two suits of armor from the Unyielding War. They appeared both clunky and nimble, a metal that was strong yet still somehow breathable. Across the breastplate of one appeared to be the imprint of a large star, its bottom sparkling angle transformed into a sword. It was the emblem of the ruling family of Ashkadance, before the end of the war.

"There will always be two guards at this door. They'll be joining us shortly," Cindrea explained. "There is only one public entrance into this tower. It's a security measure."

Ember also thought it made for a good trap.

They walked single file up the cramped and musky stairwell. It felt cold, solitary. She wondered briefly how they got any furniture up these stairs. They probably had to bring it up in pieces and then build everything in the quarters. That must make renovations frustrating.

"Every dragon daughter has stayed in this tower before they were crowned," Cindrea explained as they trekked up. She was a good pick for a lady in waiting, understanding the intricacies.

Knowing that Ember's biological mother had spent her first twenty years in this room made Ember even more interested to see it. She hoped there would be some clues to who the queen was before she became Fateless. Was she always mean? Unwelcoming? Or was that only to Ember?

When they finally reached the top of the stairs, Ember was greeted by a long hallway. On each side was six tall doors, with one wide door on the end. The walls a grey brick, the floors a dark wood. There were more paintings, though they too were covered with sheets. She moved forward, glancing back at Cindrea.

"Why the extra rooms?"

"For any personal staff you want close by. I'll be here, of course, but you can add anyone else once you determine who you'd like to serve you," Cindrea responded.

Ember didn't see herself utilizing twelve rooms; that seemed excessive to her. She had been alone too long to imagine ever having twelve people she felt safe near. The contrast her life had taken the past few days was startling. Why would she need more people? Or maybe Amir and Wally would also sleep up here? She felt safe near them, especially after seeing their contempt for Zhieve.

Ember braced herself as she stood in front of the door to her presumed bedroom, a large door at the end of the hall. Her hand hovered above the handle. She took a deep breath, her fingers curling around the latch. When the heavy door, no doubt made thick for her protection, creaked open, her exhale pushed out of her in a rush.

It wasn't just one room, but rather a complete home in this one space. The only thing that was missing was a kitchen. The grey stone walls were painted a cream peach, the red of the floor matching nicely. A soft glow emitted from the room, amplified by the firelight. There was a table to her right, spacious enough to seat six people. A long couch and fireplace were to her left. Past both living spaces was a slide-away door that was left open showing a large bed.

She walked through that door to see what else lay behind it and found a second fireplace, a large walk-in closet, and another bathroom. Across from the bed was a balcony, Ember couldn't wait to sleep with a view of the stars.

There were three large rugs beneath the three different main pieces. One beneath the bed, one under the table, and one more under the couch. All three rugs were the same, a shaggy black that matched her hair. In certain angles, it shimmered rainbow hues. The bed itself was also covered in a similar aesthetic to the carpet. There was a large throw fur piece for warmth, but the rest of the bed items were a breezy black silk with silver woven every few strands. Her room was a forest at starlight. Ember didn't think she had ever seen a place that felt immediately like her own.

"It's called soul-thread," Cindrea commented, noticing Ember looking at the sheets. "Not an easy material to come by; it's very delicate. Few people are able to weave it without ruining the thread, but we have several for the castle." Cindrea looked at it wistfully.

The walls held romanticized portraits of Drakul Dragon

King with the first Queen of Ashkadance. The paintings in this room were not covered. In fact, it was cleaner than every other part of this wing. No dust on the mantle, no cobwebs in the corner. One showed Queen Kariana riding Drakul in dragon form as it soared over the city. Another with her in an embrace of a man with black as night hair. It was hard to know whether it was the truth or artist rendition, but Drakul's hair shown with a subtle purple undertone. His hair kissed his jaw, a full and curling beard grazing it.

What a striking pair they were, two beautiful people of dark hair. Other than the statue on Mount Pietan, she hadn't paid much attention to their renderings. Looking back, she felt it was more in retaliation to her parents. It was the only rebellion she could afford without endangering her life. Now here they were in her room.

"This is..."

"Enchanting," Cindrea finished for her, looking at the portraits as well.

"Would you like to clean up from the journey, Dragon Daughter?" Cindrea added, already walking towards where Ember assumed the bathroom was to draw a bath.

"No," Ember started quickly, "I'd rather be alone for a little while." She sat on the edge of the beautiful bed with a heavy plop. She hadn't had a second alone, which was something she needed right now. There was too much to absorb, a lot to take in about the past few days.

"Of course," Cindrea answered with a bow. "I'll come back later to bring up dinner."

Ember nodded and asked, "Can you bring some paper for letters?"

Cindrea agreed and left the room, leaving instructions for the guards as their heavy boots echoed closer. They stopped in front of her door and settled. So, not completely alone, but at least she didn't have to interact with them.

Ember opened the glass door of the balcony and the breeze fluttered the white curtains in a dance. She walked past them, one curtain curling around her fingers before letting her through. Immediately her senses became overdrawn with salty air. When Ember saw the view, she automatically felt moisture gather in her eyes. It was the sea. The sea was closer than she had ever seen. She could actually make out where the sun kissed it.

Her room lay high in the castle, its tallest tower giving a view not of the wall, but of the world beyond it. A glittering sea reached her vision and the sun crested over the water. Where the sky met the sea, that strong line across the world, that's where Ember wanted to lay her soul to rest.

Her body rocked with the waves, and she pushed forward, gripping her fingers on the balcony edge. The sea, this sky, this room—it felt like home.

Later that night, when her heart had calmed, her belly had been full, and her thoughts were transcribed onto paper for Hasley, Ember decided to leave her room. She walked out into the hallway amused to find Wally asleep on the floor. Ember stepped over him to one of the covered paintings.

She lifted her hand and pulled off the white fabric. Illuminated by the torches in the hall, she could see Kariana Dragon Queen and Drakul Dragon King holding a small child. They gazed down at the baby smiling. On the child, Ember could see flecks of scales.

She wasn't the only one, Ember realized, but rather the first after many generations without.

Ember re-covered the painting and walked back into her room. The cold of the open balcony brushed her cheeks, saying hello and simultaneously goodbye to her last night as Ember Julimore.

EIGHT

ONE HEIR

Covered up to her neck in furs, Ember's eyes rested on the night peeking through her balcony. In the lightless tower, the only glow in her room came from her soul-threads and the actual stars out in the sky.

Without understanding why, Ember had always felt a pull to the sky and to the world beyond the wall. When she mentioned it to her moms as a child, they had called that feeling a nudge from Aaleia, a hint of her future pushing into her consciousness. She replayed that conversation over and over again now. Why would they tell her that? Why hint at all that there was more to her than met the eye? She couldn't make sense of her moms' motivations no matter how she puzzled it. For in Ember's heart, they were her parents, her moms, whether she was kidnapped or not.

Yet here she was without her moms and scared of the new relationship she could have with the queen. Impossible thoughts in an impossible week. How did they do it? She didn't think their tutoring of the royal guard's children would get either of them anywhere close to the queen. More questions that she would need to find answers too. Was there anyone she could talk to about them? People in the castle that had been their friends?

Overwhelmed by the possibilities of her new environment, Ember fell into a dreamless sleep without trouble.

When Cindrea knocked and entered the room the next morning, Ember felt the sun had come too soon.

"Can I have a little more time?" Ember groaned, turning onto her back and looking up the canopy.

"I'm sorry, Ember. We have a long day ahead. Breakfast will be served shortly."

Ember pulled the blanket up over her face. *You don't belong here*, a voice echoed in her mind.

After some convincing, Ember got out of bed and pulled on the robe Cindrea handed her.

"Thank you," Ember said.

"It is my purpose," Cindrea said in a sing-song voice. Ember nodded her thanks, unsure if Cindrea has meant it as a slight to herself or a compliment.

The clothing that Ember was forced into minutes later felt foreign on her body. The dress was form-fitting along the waist, billowing outward to stop right at her ankles. The dark purple looked almost black, and it reminded her of the night. The dress's main flaw, however, were the exposed scales above her neckline. Ember protested left and right, and demanded to wear a covering. Cindrea eventually relented.

"Remember this," Cindrea said, "the quicker you embrace your scales and show them to others, the more power you will gain here."

The thought made Ember want to both cover up and strip naked at the same time. Conflict stirred and she pushed it down. Today she needed to get more of a layout of the castle and what her days would be like. That was her only prerogative. Get a grip. Know the lay of the land. It's what she did in every new house she lived in prior, and she tried to make this new life fall into that pattern.

Cindrea selected a few different shawls for Ember to look through, eventually choosing a simple black one. Feeling calmer now that she was covered, Cindrea braided Ember's long hair back and they walked from her chambers to her living room.

After getting a crash course in the subtleties of having her own court, Cindrea pointed out which door was hers should Ember ever need to find her. She was told she could have more women and men at her beck and call if she wished, but Ember immediately told Cindrea that was not necessary.

Amir entered her vision from the open door.

"Good morning, Dragon Daughter," Amir Captain called as he deposited a box in the room across the hall.

"Hello, Amir Captain." She felt excited to see him again. His grey eyes sparkled with kindness and from their small amount of interactions the past two days, he genuinely seemed on her side. She was glad he was chosen to be her captain.

"I'll be right back," Cindrea said as she opened the door to her personal chambers.

"Do you have a minute, princess?" Amir asked, leaning his body against the open door.

"Of course, if you call me Ember," Ember replied.

He smiled at her but didn't say he would. Instead, Amir gestured to the empty table and they both took a seat.

"We have a few things to settle today, mainly who will be my second and live in the room beside me."

"What would a second do?" Ember asked.

"They will be available to you if ever I am sick, help with shift changes, and would be my replacement if I were to die," he explained. He spoke of his death as if it were a normal thing to discuss. Perhaps for a captain, that was a normal thought process, as easy to accept as getting the occasional burn as a baker.

"What about Wally? I don't know the other guards, but he jumped into action quickly on the journey here." Ember shuddered at the memory of the Fateless man. She brushed the fabric of her dress as if that would push away the memory.

"Wally was my thought as well, but whoever would be chosen would need to move into the tower and that would mean separating him and his pair." Amir crossed his arms.

"Wally's pair could move in as well," Ember answered. It's not like there wasn't enough room for his pair. She had all this space, and if this person was with Wally, they must be trustworthy.

"That wouldn't be possible. Zhieve has to stay in the queen's wing." Amir's arms uncrossed and re-crossed. His gaze moved away from Ember and to the table.

It took a moment for Ember to understand the implications of his response. What would Zhieve have to do with...

"Oh," Ember answered, not sure how to put her thoughts into reality. Her mind jumped back to just two nights ago. Had it only been two days ago? She saw again the glint in Zhieve's eye when he looked at Wally's, judging his decision not to murder a confused man. That look meant so much more now that she knew. That judgment held a stronger weight.

"I see how that wouldn't work," Ember said. "Right, so what do you recommend instead?" She asked, unsure of where to take the conversation from there.

"Honestly, he was the only one I was thinking for the position. It's possible he could sleep here every other day? Or stay part of each night," Amir thought aloud. "If he and Zhieve felt comfortable with that."

"Okay," Ember answered hesitantly. "Whatever you think is best." What if there was more to this than met the eye? Was

Wally more wicked than he seemed, or Zhieve more good than he seemed?

Before Amir could say more, Cindrea popped back into the room.

"Ready to go?" she asked.

Ember followed her out of the room, affirming first to Amir that he'd make the right decision. They both stood up and followed Cindrea into the hall. Without thinking, Ember picked up a box from the hall to help Amir. Her hands needed to do something, to do anything at all. She wanted to string beads.

"Thank you, Dragon Daughter," Amir responded sincerely, taking the box away from her hands. Cindrea pushed them along. Ember realized what had changed when Cindrea left the room. Her complementary styled dresses now also had coverups that matched hers. Together the two of them looked like a team. She smiled for the second time in one morning, it was a personal record.

They walked down the steps single file, Ember glanced back just as the portrait of Kariana holding her scaled child blinked from her view.

AMIR CAPTAIN PULLED open doors that led to the courtyard breakfast room.

"Here we go," Ember breathed before stepping forward. Amir and Wally waited around the perimeter with guards from her company, Jedoriah's, and the Queen's. So many men and women lined up in jewel-toned purple suits made for a dark comparison to the greenery. Ember herself stood out in her darker dress with iridescent beads, soon realizing that Cindrea overdressed her for her first breakfast in the palace on purpose.

Cindrea bowed to the occupants of the table and left, leaving Ember with her family and the gaggle of guards.

"Hello Embrence," Jedoriah Knight crooned from his seat at the head of the table. His face barely moved when he spoke and the hair on Ember's arms raised from her skin. Karwyn sat on the opposite end, her eyes looked straight through Ember. Ember wished she could stop and hug herself, but instead she broke into a bow. She lowered her head first at the queen and then at Jedoriah. She was thankful for a reason to look away from their faces.

"That's not necessary," Karwyn said after Ember finished, a crease forming in her brows. Her dark hair contrasted the pale yellow of her dress.

"I agree." Jedoriah followed, glancing at the queen briefly.

"Come, sit," he said, gesturing Ember towards the seat on his right. Not wanting to sit next to her mother after her rejection was so fresh, Ember nodded and moved to the empty seat that Jedoriah motioned to. Fear immediately made Ember regret her choice, and her skin became clammy beneath her cover-up. There was an imposing presence around Jedoriah that she had trouble quantifying. She pushed her knees together, trying to keep them from shaking as a bead of sweat developed on her chest. He was the one her moms would emphasize as more dangerous over the queen. She did not yet know why. If Jedoriah saw her discomfort, he didn't say anything.

Noticing for the first time the extra guest seated at the rectangular glass table, Ember tried to smile. Seated near her mother was a tall woman with caramel hair and a wide nose. Like everyone else in the garden, she had taken a liking to stare straight at her.

"Hello. I'm Ember."

"I'm Ahnika, your tutor. We'll be meeting right after breakfast so we can access any educational lapses and get you into top shape." The woman nodded curtly to Jedoriah and then Ember as if her thoughts were the beginning and end of the conversation. Her blue eyes were slitted, taking in everything about Ember. She didn't seem unwelcoming, but she did appear cautious. Her eyes hovered over where Ember's scales would have been visible if she weren't wearing the cover-up.

"They'll be no lapses there," Karwyn responded. "They'll have made sure of that!" Her eyes glazed over as she looked up to the sky.

"Who?" Ember asked, but she knew the answer. The queen referred to Ember's moms as if she knew them.

The queen smiled at Ember without answering, her expression turning softer before she closed her eyes. She appeared serene, sitting at the head of the table with her eyes closed and not a care in the world. The wind blew and the leaves of the surrounding trees swayed behind her.

Jedoriah dropped his water goblet down with a loud clang on the thick glass table. What did guests and regular visitors like Ahnika think of the queen's behavior? The thought of having a tutor immediately made her think of her moms.

Ember was scared to be in this place of power, scared of the spotlight in her new place of residence. But after the feelings that coursed through her when she met her biological mother, she knew she could not go, not yet. And after what was just said, it was clear Karwyn knew something about her moms. Maybe they had actually been friends? Her moms had taught her about the kingdom, sharing more information than Ember thought she would need. All of her memories seemed different now. There were multiple meanings in this new day.

"A pleasure to meet you," Ember said to Ahnika.

"Of course, Ember has a lot to learn in the next two weeks," Jedoriah said, continuing the conversation. He cut up the piece of sausage on his plate and ignored the queen's words. Ember's attention drew back to him.

"Why two weeks?" Ember asked.

Her mouth watered as the sugary delights passed before her, each pastry a sight for sore eyes.

"No, Embrence. Jair Doctor had something special prepared for you." He dismissed the server and someone else came forward with a tray. Ember grimaced at the brown mush. At least she could put a little cinnamon on top.

"We'll be holding your debut ball in two weeks' time," he explained as he bit into the puff pastry Ember was not allowed to have. Red goo crushed out from one side, sliding onto his fingers like oozing blood.

"My debut ball?"

Ember found it quite funny that they labeled the ball as if it belonged to her since she had no idea that there was one being planned after her arrival less than twenty-four hours ago.

"Yes, for morale," Jedoriah answered as if those three words addressed every concern Ember would logically have. But they did not. She needed to know more about what the queen meant.

"It will be combined with the annual Aaleian festival, a wonderful affair," Ahnika added.

She had no say in her world when she lived with her moms, but when they were taken from her she had a small taste of control over her life. It was stripped from her just as quickly as it was gained.

Now she was here, in a decorated box of foliage and flame.

"I'll make sure we go over the different traditions you'll have to take part in at your debut, Embrence Dragon Daughter," Ahnika said.

Zhieve came through the garden doors and handed a note to Jedoriah. "Those rats," he spat, crumbling the note after a quick read-through.

"Is everything alright, Jedoriah Knight?" Ahnika asked formally.

"Another rebel brawl," he muttered, stabbing a bit of food.

"Where?" Ember asked, daring to speak again. Her body felt cold at the thought of them.

"Near Borderain. Two groups raided a farm and then a factory." He quickly stabbed and cut more pieces, chewing loudly. "Nothing to be done now, the guards in the province are in high alert."

Was that how they treated the death of the moms that raised her? A quick bit of anger, then an *oh well*? Ember didn't know what she was getting into here, she wasn't looking forward to finding out.

"ARE YOU ALRIGHT?" Amir asked after breakfast. His eyes trailed Zhieve and the retreating company that followed the queen and Jedoriah's departure from the table.

Ember nodded, gripping her hands together in front of her dress. Ahnika had left early to prepare the classroom for Ember's first lesson. She and Amir were alone in the breakfast garden.

She flicked a crumb off its surface and watched it fly off into the grass. The circle of trees around the rectangular table was a lovely sight, but she did wonder the purpose. The castle held many of these pocket gardens it seemed. Rooms placed outside when there were many empty within.

"Can you show me the way to Ahnika's classroom?" Ember asked, hoping to get done with her tasks for the day quickly.

Amir smiled at her, offering his arm to her.

"Follow me, Dragon Daughter, to the library."

Walking through the library made Ember want to do anything but go to class. Not being able to socialize had given her an affinity for learning. Her moms had always loved that byproduct of her upbringing, especially given that they both taught different subjects across the realm. Ember paused in her trek, her eyes looking up at the long stacks of meticulously numbered books. Reading and jewelry-making were her only hobbies.

Every bit of furniture in the library was a light wood, almost more grey than it was brown. Ember itched to trail her fingers along the shelves and study tables. The books were stacked to the ceiling, and giving a cursory glance around the room, there was next to nobody here enjoying the tomes except someone she assumed was the librarian. The shorter woman sported her green hair in a tight top knot, skin a deeper brown than the shelving. Ember watched her move one book from her cart back into the stacks.

They would have loved this. Actually, they must have. With the small doors along the wall, those must be the tutor rooms for the guards and servants' children. Clues sparked through her. Which books had they read? Who would they talk to on the staff?

"There you are, come, hurry up," Ahnika said, poking her head out from a door to the left of the tall entryway. Amir nodded in her direction, patting Ember on the arm.

"I'll be right there," Amir said to Ember, pointing at a table a few paces from the door.

"Thanks," Ember said as she moved her way to the ajar door. Inside, she saw Ahnika, shuffling through some papers on her desk. Her high waisted trousers accentuated her figure. Ember liked her style.

Ahnika's desk was cluttered with books, piles segmented in what she assumed were purposeful stacks. Ahnika took a sip from her stone mug. There were over a dozen torches in this small room, more than she had seen in other comparable spaces. There were three small desks across from Ahnika's busy table.

Ember took the closest desk to her teacher and Ember was

reminded how uncomfortable she felt in her overly formal dress.

"Since we only have two weeks until your debut into society, we'll have to start with the most pertinent information and work to fill in the gaps after that."

Picking up some paper and writing tools, Ahnika handed them to Ember before straightening her own pile of papers on her desk. Ember thanked her, realizing she'd probably need to write many more notes than what these pages could hold. The instructor glanced down at her own personal notes before speaking.

"So tell me, Ember Dragon Daughter, what do you know about how your kingdom is run?"

"When the dragon daughter finds her fated pair through Aaleia, that person becomes their knight. When they have their own dragon daughter then Mutrien has given her the right to be dragon queen."

"Yes, all very good, that is part of the process. We pass on our royal crown based on the birth of the next generation, symbolizing the acceptance of your rule as a mother to your child and to the kingdom. The other kingdoms have different rules across the sea, some systems basing the passing of the crown on the death of the monarch," Ahnika lectured, leaning against her desk.

"Praise Aaleia, that is not our way. If the queen, long may she reign, were to become incapacitated or die by illness or an assassination, then the dragon matron will take over as monarch until the next dragon daughter produces an heir.

"The dragon matron, as you know, is the former queen, living in the palace opposite this one in Cruelindime. She is available for guidance and support."

Cruelindime was another province her family had avoided along with Azororion.

"What happens if the dragon matron has also passed?"

Ember couldn't help but ask. She made a chart on her piece of paper, the succession drawn out with little effort. It didn't seem like enough people. Too unstable. What would they have done if they hadn't found her?

"Then the dragon daughter will ascend before she has her child." Ahnika sat on the edge of her table, settling in to talk with Ember. She had a feeling the royal family was Ahnika's favorite topic. Her blue eyes were practically sparkling at each word.

"What if there was no one left?"

"You mean if the whole royal family were dead?"

Ember nodded. That could have been their reality; they must have had some sort of plan. What if the dragon matron passed and the dragon queen was completely taken over mentally by the Fateless? It was a miracle that her birth mom was not farther gone, Ember realized.

Ahnika appeared almost stricken by even saying the thought out loud. She questioned, "why would you ask such a thing?"

"Shouldn't I be asking those questions?" Ember asked her. All thoughts beyond survival would take a while to form in Ember's mind.

"Aaleia and Mutrien would never let that happen to Ashkadance," her new instructor responded, oblivious to the fact that it was something that the people were actually worried about. She had heard those conversations whispered in the streets, that kind of dissent and lack of confidence grew quickly. Ember hadn't been found, and the crown didn't have another heir. It was no wonder the rebel attacks were more frequent and the public sympathy for them rising.

"I just wanted to know all the variables," Ember followed, feeling suddenly like this wasn't the person she should be discussing this with. Ahnika either ignored or didn't care to see that her answers made Ember uncomfortable. Instead, Ahnika continued, bringing up another topic that Ember didn't particularly want to be involved in.

"And the fating," Ahnika began. "Do you understand the reason for it?"

"To find your other half," Ember responded automatically, spouting the line she had been told since birth. As a child, she didn't like thinking that she was only half of herself, but the thought made more sense the older she got. Though how anyone could find their other half in a dragon was a startling thought. What kind of person were they, Kariana and Drakul, when they were together?

"Yes and no. It is considered by the crown and our scribes that the fating is Aaleia's way to help you meet your full potential, whether that be good or bad." Ahnika held her arms out as if good and bad were displayed easily, one side versus the other.

"It's your companion that will help drive the stakes and get you to where you need to be. Whether everyone takes that opportunity or goes in the opposite direction is up to them. Aaelia does not judge whether your balance in the world is good or bad. She helps every person strive to their best."

"How do the scribes know that?" Ember asked, shifting in her seat. This wasn't what was taught in her schooling. She scribbled a few quick notes. That explained some of the subtle changes in the campfire story Jedoriah had shared.

"Well, as you know the scribes help monitor the world, inscribing its history and their observations. They've noted that since the First Fating, more of Ashkadance's citizens hold one to three purposes in their lifetime rather than jumping around between purposes until they die. People are more defined with their intentions and meeting those goals with the support of their fated pair."

Ember was going to be a jewelry maker. She had decided on that purpose for herself. Now she was here, a future queen.

But if her purpose was to be queen, how would a knight

help with that? As her confidant so she could take on the challenge more eagerly, or as a means to help her co-rule? Take on duties she could not? How would she help this person? She wondered what their goals would be.

"To sum it together," Ahnika furthered, "your pair helps you reach your full potential."

But then another thought came to Ember's mind. "Why does Mutrien only bless the royal family with one child at a time?" Ember asked.

Aaleia found each person's pair. Mutrien created their children. Together, they balanced love, purpose, and life. There were celebrations each year to cover those balances. The Mutrien ball was a few months away, and Aaleia's in only two weeks. Ember felt incompetent for not realizing that connection. Pairing the ball with the reminder of the goddess definitely did help morale.

"All rulers in Ashkadance have one child to discourage conflict."

"How so?"

"If there is only one heir, there is no competition. No rivalry. No jealousy. This keeps our kingdom safe."

Having one heir didn't seem like a safe bet in Ember's eyes.

"Then, of course, there is your dragon history," Ahnika continued. She moved around her desk to pull a book from one of its drawers.

Ember perked up, curious on this topic. She scratched at her scales from beneath her shawl, a habit that would be hard to break.

"Here," Ahnika said, handing Ember a worn leather book.

"What's this?"

"Your family tree, going back to Drakul and the dragons he named as his family before he became fated to Kariana."

Ember accepted the book, excited to read that history and learn more about these mysterious figures that she had only ever dreamed of. She couldn't wait to tell Hasley about it in her letter that night. She knew her best friend would want to hear any insight she gained on the dragons, including the scaled portrait of Kariana's baby—the first Dragon Daughter of Ashkadance.

"Other things we will be covering is how each province governs itself through the keyholders. Our history, the disappearance of the dragons, the merfolk conflict, of course. A short history of Grydagia and Faeinto from before the wall—"

Ember listened on, but her thoughts lingered on her moms. She wished they were here instead, explaining the missing pieces of her past.

NINE

LET ME GO

"Embrence," Jedoriah called, opening the door to her room without notice. It had been one week since she had been in the palace, and the ball was quickly approaching. With friendships slowly forming among her new companions, she didn't feel as cut off as she expected to be at the palace. That could not be said for her relationship with Jedoriah.

Her body immediately reacted in discomfort to his call, her pulse skipping erratically. He hadn't visited her since she was forced into this castle last week. Ember closed the box of beads she was sorting through and stood from her small table. Cindrea glanced up from her spot on the couch but did not seem concerned. Would she one day feel that indifference to the knight of the kingdom visiting her room?

"I have a surprise for you," he said as he opened the door wider. An elderly woman shuffled forward, her smile wider than her face. It was a cheshire look, pulling her teeth out from her mouth but much warmer than Jedoriah's serpentine grin. Her eyes sparkled, green depths with gold specks.

"Hello, I'm Ember," she said, meeting the older woman

half-way. She glanced back and forth between her and the rod straight form of Jedoriah.

"I know who you are. I'd recognize you anywhere, even without the scales," the old woman spoke with a laugh, gesturing in a hobbled fashion to Ember's exposed marks. While it hasn't gotten easier to show her scales this past week, she was trying to get used to keeping them uncovered while she was more isolated in her tower. She knew that her ball gown would feature them, so she was trying to open herself up to how that would feel while she wasn't surrounded by hundreds of eyes. She shuddered at the thought.

"Though you probably don't know me," she continued, "I'm Omanox Dragon Matron. I'd be honored if you would call me Oma though."

Ember's eyes widened. "You are my grandmother?"

Reaching her, Oma opened her arms for a hug and said, "yes, Fireheart, I am."

Her voice warmed Ember's fears. Her moms had been orphans, or at least, that is what she had told her. Ember had never had the figure of an older matriarch in her life. She didn't know it was something she needed until now.

Ember stared at the woman's long thick white braid. It fell down past her back like a dragon tail, but it barely moved as she shuffled forward.

Ember accepted the hug, the only physical touch she had welcomed since that first day. Being in Oma's arms felt like a warm day in the sun, despite it actually being a cold bitter night. Oma herself was not warm, however. The cold air from Ember's balcony window chilled her skin. Ember ushered her forward into the warmth of her bedroom. She stopped by the balcony to close it.

"Leave us, Jed," Oma commanded, her voice not offering any room for negotiation. Ember was startled to see he didn't fight the order. Instead, Jedoriah bowed before backing out the door. While his face showcased his displeasure, he didn't speak his thoughts aloud. Her heart unclamped and she could now focus on her full attention on Oma. Cindrea took the opportunity to follow him out from her seat in the corner and grant them privacy. She left her sewing basket beside the couch.

"Come, get warm," Ember said, helping Oma to sit on her bed. She pulled out her fur throw blanket and wrapped it around her grandmother. It was freeing to be in the presence of someone maternal again. The way that Oma looked at her, with a hope that was almost palpable, it helped Ember feel that hope again as well. Ever since she came to this dreary palace, it had been small isolated smiles across hours of cold, moments she felt welcome with her guards and ladies mixed in with a complete lack of control.

"I can't believe you're here," Oma whispered, reaching out to pet a strand of Ember's hair. "You have no idea how hard it was for us when you disappeared. We were prepared for a happy time, a coronation and a christening, but all that was left was the Fateless curse." She shook her head, referring to both the chaos and the sickness that had infected her only daughter. Oma's tanned skin appeared brighter in the firelight of Ember's bedroom. Ember made note that Oma too, considered it a curse. Those that said curse, plague, or used them interchangeably seemed to have an intent. A plague could be an accident. A curse was on purpose.

"It took her that quickly?" Ember asked. No one else had been willing to go into the details. As far as Ember could see, her mother did have random spells where she said the uncomfortable and unconscionable truth. While other moments, she said the fantastical things you would never believe. Regardless, her Fateless symptoms looked different than that of the man in the forest. A side-effect of her dragon heritage, most-likely. She was almost lucid in some moments and that must make going mad even more difficult.

"No, it was slow," she recalled. "We didn't see it happening until it was already gripping her. She went on a diplomatic mission to Grydagia. There was a shipwreck and that retched merman didn't return her until days later." Oma named the beasts as if it were a burning brand. "She met Jedoriah the day she returned and Mutrien blessed their union with you. It was beautiful how it all came together, despite the wreck in the sea."

Oma tightened the fur around her, small thin fingers curling in what looked like pain. Ember almost looked away, not wanting to disturb Oma when the memories plagued her.

"I was not with her when the ship took on water. I was here, mourning the loss of my pair. I believe this trip is when the Fatelessness took hold of her. As the pregnancy progressed, she changed. By the time you were born, she was gone to us."

Oma's eyes glistened, remembering how her daughter used to be.

"Why did the merfolk take her? Not much is shared in school about the reasoning," Ember asked, hoping she wasn't stepping over a boundary she shouldn't cross. If Oma and Jair Doctor believed it was the merfolk that infected her, possibly even purposefully, shouldn't Ember be made aware of that threat too?

"They were prideful because they were half beast. They claimed to talk to Aaleia and Mutrien, commune with them as the old kingdom heirs could. They said a message needed to pass on through them to our kingdom. They cursed her," Oma confessed.

Ember was shocked by that detail. That ability had been said to be possible to the royals in the First Fating but not any other generations. If the merfolk could still commune with the gods, what were they saying? How could they have cursed them?

"What did they say was the message they had to pass on?"

"That a new heir was coming, that the ways of our people had to change," she emphasized the words with an ungraceful curl of her mouth. "It was a threat," Oma concluded, her eyes grave.

"So we brought up the wall. Initially because of their treatment of Karwyn, saying we had to listen or they would keep her. The other kingdoms did not help, leaving our calls for aid unanswered. When the Fateless started spreading and the rebels grew, I had to keep our people away from the water and the dangers they posed. These outside influences, we can't have that." Oma shut her eyes, circling in memory.

"We rallied. We knew we had to protect our people from further infection and influence from the outside world. We closed up our lines. No more trade, travel, or merfolk. With no foreign aid received, cutting ties with Grydagia and Faeinto seemed like a necessary sacrifice to keep the merfolk away from my kingdom."

Before Ember could interrupt to ask more questions, Oma grabbed her hand, rubbing her thumb across the tops of them.

"I wish you would have known her before. She was bright, curious, rebellious like her father, but still, she was something special. They damaged her, and it spread to our people. She wasn't the same after that."

Ember felt that description like a weight on her chest.

"I wish you had been here my first day," Ember said honestly.

"Me too, Fireheart. At least you had Jedoriah here with you," Oma responded, patting Ember's hand.

"I don't feel safe around him," Ember admitted. She re-adjusted the comforter. Feeling like she could speak freely with this woman, even though they have only met moments ago.

"How does he make you feel unsafe?" Oma's eyes narrowed.

"My moms always told me to stay away from him, that he

wasn't who he seemed. When the royals visited the provinces, we'd run away, hide in alleys. I know now it was because they were hiding me, but I don't think all of that fear was for one reason. And honestly, he is cold around me. Intimidating. It's like he wants me to be even more afraid."

Oma's eyes moved from squinted to speculative.

"It makes sense that they would instill that fear in you."

"Why do you say that?" Ember asked, startled.

"Jedoriah saw your kidnappers daily in the castle, probably for hours a day. Even a glimpse of them would be enough for him to know you were close."

"Was one of his guards getting his child tutored? Why would they interact so closely?"

Oma seemed puzzled by the question, her head pulled back as her spine straightened.

"Because they were your mother's ladies in waiting. Didn't you know?"

The world spiraled.

"They told me they were tutors for the children of the guards," Ember answered, not comprehending how this part of her life could also be a lie.

"No, my dear, they met the first day of Karwyn's debut ball. They were assigned to help Karwyn and met in this hallway."

Ember stared at her closed bedroom door as if she could see through it. Her moms had been in this room, had fated in the hall next to her. Their life had begun here with her birth mother.

"I... didn't know."

A tear rolled down Ember's face. The queen had known them. They had likely been friends. And yet, they stole her.

"Oh Fireheart, it's okay," Oma said as she scooted closer to Ember on the bed. She laid her head down and took Ember into her arms. It was a slow and endearing move, a movement filled with so much love that Ember immediately began to tear up.

"Tell me about them," Oma said, stroking Ember's hair. Jedoriah made her feel welcomed in an uncomfortable way, acting as if she had always been there and should accept all tasks without question. Duty, loyalty, it all blended together for them. Cindrea, Amir, Wally, they were all more understanding of the war raging inside of Ember. And now Oma, a breath in the fire.

"My moms—It felt real. It still is real. I thought they were my family," Ember whispered the last word. It stung her. She held it in her heart. *Family*.

Ember told her everything, about how she was raised to hide her scales, that she was told they were a gift. She told her that her moms had always talked about their love for teaching and that they told her they were tutors here.

Ember shared her fears, that Aaleia and Mutrien had cursed her too. Oma's eyes told her that no, it was not her fault, but she did not say a word then as Ember spoke from her heart.

She shared the day her moms died too. It was not an easy conversation, but one Ember was finally able to have. She believed Oma wanted to know what her granddaughter had been up to without her. And she wanted to tell her, to tell anyone, that her parents weren't bad people. She didn't understand why they took her, but she knew they couldn't be bad. And she loved them.

"I think you are right," Oma had said then, "they were the first to report to me her changes. They could have had a twisted sense of duty."

It was the story she wanted to believe, but she needed more concrete answers than that. But still, she was more at peace with her current situation. She felt lighter after their hours of talking. Oma paused occasionally, asking questions and sympathizing with how strange this situation must be for her. She hoped she could share these same comments with Hasley when they met again. Then she could bond with the only person that thought to be kind to Ember, despite how often Ember pushed her away or acted strangely. Finally, she could share all of herself with Hasley. She looked forward to that happening soon.

Ember was tired after their long conversation. Her head lolled back on the pillow, and her eyelids drifted downward in heavy blinks.

"Tell me about dragons. Where are they?" Ember requested in delirium, only half awake but wanting her last thoughts to drift away from loss.

"The dragons are far away, where the sea can't catch them and the stars listen to their story," Oma answered in the dark, stroking Ember's hair. Ember smiled softly. She didn't understand, but it seemed peaceful. Like a bedtime story.

"Do you have a pair yet?"

Ember barely registered it. A pair? She didn't need to be fated. She had her Oma now, a real companion. First, she needed to survive her debut ball, then she'll think about the future.

Cuddling closer to the body next to her, Ember's eyes fluttered closed as the dawn peaked over the sea.

"CINDREA, DON'T BE LAZY," a stern voice said.

Confused at why anyone would call Cindrea lazy, Ember's thoughts muddled and reformed.

"There are spots on that plate," the same deep voice said with disapproval.

Ember squinted one eye open and spotted her bedroom door ajar. Through it, she could see Cindrea setting her meeting table. She carried a stack of plates with one arm and a handful of cutlery in the other. Cindrea faced away from Oma as she attempted to put down a plate at each seat. Oma, clad in the same clothes from last night, crossed her arms and followed Cindrea's movements with a stiff back and squinting eyes. Ember had never seen anyone be rude to Cindrea before and her reaction to it was not what she expected. Cindrea seemed willing to take the verbal lashing and judge of her work without complaint, though her movements were more rushed. Having never seen her flustered before, Ember decided to intervene.

Ember groaned loudly and stretched, letting them know she was waking up.

"Good morning, Fireheart," Oma said brightly, the mood immediately shifting. She glanced at Cindrea struggling with the plates before walking to Ember's bedside. Sitting up, Ember smiled warmly at her grandmother.

"Good morning, what's this?" Ember asked, her head tilted around Oma to see back into the living room.

"We're having breakfast together as a family," Oma said with a smile, brushing a hair from Ember's face.

"Don't we usually do this in the gardens?" Ember said, pulling back her soul-thread sheets and reaching for her robe.

"Yes, dear, but we overslept. Breakfast was two hours ago."

Cindrea deposited a bouquet of flowers to the center of the room and bowed at the both of them before leaving them alone. Ember was about to call out and say she could stay but then Jedoriah strode in without knocking, a servant behind him carrying a tray.

A full family breakfast then. Ember sat down on her hands to prevent from fidgeting, waiting for her mother to walk through the door.

"Good day, Embrence Dragon Daughter," the servant squeaked. His voice more high-pitched than expected for his filled-out figure. She smiled at him, and he tripped, strawberry pasties spilling on the table. His skin turned practically purple in the mortification of his blunder.

"We'll take it from here," Oma said, taking the tray from his hands before he could apologize.

"Thank you, dragon matron," he sputtered again in that high voice as he rushed through the door.

"So much incompetence," Oma muttered. Jedoriah agreed, taking a pastry for himself before shutting the open door. Was Karwyn not joining them? Ember had never been in a room with Jedoriah in such an intimate setting before. Ember glanced at the closed door.

"Here we are," Jedoriah commented as he buttered a piece of toast. Oma rolled her eyes. Seeing her grandmother being both strong and caring, while also commanding, she wondered if that was how Karwyn would have been. What would her and Jedoriah's relationship be like? Those thoughts fleeted through her mind before stumbling back to the weird scene unfolding before her.

"Ember," Oma started and Ember smiled at the use of her preferred name.

"What we wanted to talk to you about today is your mother," she continued.

"Is she okay?" Ember asked.

"As okay as she always is, but Jedoriah..." She gestured to him. "Mentioned to me the situation in the forest and how you reacted to the death. Given what I've been coming to think these past few years, Jedoriah's experiences, and the public's thoughts on the topics as well," Oma trailed off. She took a bite of toast and Jedoriah picked up the thought.

"We want you to lead a new project, have a cause to share with our people. We think the Fateless is a good opportunity for you to bring goodwill and change to the kingdom."

How in the world would the pain and suffering of others

benefit her? Ember blinked, trying to push the thought away and understand his meaning.

"Especially as a voice of the people," Oma added.

"What kind of project?" Ember asked cautiously.

"We believe that you would be perfect to head a community home project. Some place for those that become Fateless to move into so that they can be comfortable, cared for, and part of a research project for us to learn more about how to resolve their illness," Oma finished, sharing her wide smile with Ember.

Unsure of how to react, Ember grabbed a pastry and took a bite. Thankfully there was no predetermined nutritional food for Ember here from Jair Doctor. The few chews didn't give her much time at all to think but at least it schooled her features. No more disappearance and death? Actually pursuing the cause? It seemed to Ember like something that should have happened a long time ago. Maybe it would have if the queen hadn't been inflicted.

Whether it be a curse or plague or some other concern entirely, this would give her cause to find out.

"What would I do in this project?" Ember asked, dusting the powder from her fingers and staring excitedly at Oma.

"It would start with awareness, bringing the people in on our commitment and dispelling some of the ideas we've let grow over the years."

"Yes, we should present your participation at the ball," Jedoriah added.

"That's only a week away," Ember stated deftly. This seemed like a large project, not something to rush into and share at the first opportunity.

"It will help morale," he replied and Oma agreed, citing this needed to be shared at the peak of interest. She hated how often that reason defined actions. Was it best to talk about something before the details were ironed out? Would the kingdom be happy or upset this was her first campaign to bring to them?

Ember regretted the thought immediately as Oma and Jed then began to plan the new initiative right then and there. Apparently, they had already decided a lot of the initial needs of the project before bringing it to her.

Ember felt as if her brain was melting after hours of conversation and planning. There were even two locations already chosen to be repurposed for these community homes, one on each side of Ashkadance. They scheduled a day for her to visit the closest location so that Ember could add her input into the changes they were doing to the internal structure of the homes.

Servants came in at the ring of a bell to provide paper, maps, and writing utensils and at one point, Cindrea as well to leave a letter on the couch. Ember noticed the handwriting immediately to be Hasley's and stood from the table.

She heard the conversation between Oma and Jedoriah move towards the topic of the ceremonies for the ball as she opened the seal to the letter.

Her smile fell as she read. Why would Hasley leave it like this? Her first letter back to Ember had been long, excited, a little messier than her usual penmanship but it was a surprising topic. And here? Hasley had only one line to share.

Amlin won't let me go to the ball. I'm sorry.
-Hasley

PART 2

EMBER DRAGON DAUGHTER

BE KIND

Her debut ball was in an hour. One hour. Tied in with the annual Aaleian celebrations, it had been a full house this week. Every waking moment the past few days were spent with Ahnika in various lessons and dress fittings. There was even a last minute dancing lesson with Wally. But what prepared her the most was the guidance from Oma. Ember loved having her grandmother available to answer her questions and help aid her speeding thoughts.

Ember felt like only moments had passed since she met Oma. While she hadn't been involved in the castle's preparation for the ball, she had seen how everyone else around her was preparing. More staff were cleaning, her measurements had been taken, sample fabrics were shown, and Ahnika had spent two whole lessons going over the traditions of this day with her.

The combining of the Aaleian ball with her debut set a new precedence. For prior dragon daughters, the two celebrations had been separate so that each occasion could shine on its own. Ember wished she wasn't the one breaking the trend.

"No one is ever ready until they are forced to be," Cindrea

said softly as she dusted gold powder over Ember's exposed shoulders. Ember supposed that was true, but it didn't make her feel any less vulnerable with her newly short hair. She fiddled with the length, a full inch above her collarbone. No hiding now, in more ways than one. Her relationship with Cindrea had grown too. While a little more maternal than a regular friendship, Cindrea had that tough love that Ember needed to hear every now and again.

"It's a strong look for tonight, Ember, embrace it," Oma said in an attempt at reassurance.

After getting into her dress, Ember turned back around to face the floor length mirror. Her breath caught in her throat.

The deep blue dress was tight at the center, coming up to a sweetheart cut. It billowed out at the waist in a storm of fluffy material that Ember didn't have a name for. It had little shining green gems inlaid into the big bell of a dress. Oma moved the material in the light, and it reflected twinkling fractures of color around the room. This blue was so dark it was almost black, a color that seemed to become a regular in her wardrobe.

Ember's chest fluttered looking at the dress. She rarely felt such a want for physical items. After a life on the move, literally, she didn't feel an attachment to anything she owned prior to this new life. But this? Ember felt pride in how she looked for the first time.

When her eyes traveled up, however, Ember began to feel a cold sweat leak from her pores. Her scales looked lovely too, the gold powder heavily concentrated on her shoulders were dusted onto her scales in a gradient. They would be adorned and celebrated today in a way that Ember had never had before. She didn't know how to feel about this fact, this new reality she was thrust into. But she did know one thing: she still felt like she didn't belong here.

Ember wiped away the sweat from her brow as Cindrea began to braid the crown of her hair. They had decided on minimal jewelry for the evening, only two dark blue stones dotted her ears. If only Hasley could see her now.

Ember had sent an additional note to her friend in the form of a formal royal request, addressing that Amlin had to permit her to go. She was either already lining up to join her at the ball or she wouldn't show up at all. A response wouldn't come in time for Ember to know.

"Stay still," Cindrea said as she tugged a strand of Ember's hair. Ember stared at her reflection as Cindrea completed the small braid at her temple. Her head moved again despite Cindrea's request as she tilted her head to the side, confused briefly when she saw her face duplicate in the mirror. This face, however, retained the long hair that she now missed.

Karwyn stood by the ajar door, her eyes meeting Ember's in the mirror.

"Hello," she greeted, hands folded in front of her. Her hair contrasted with the glimmering gold of her gown. Their outfits stood in opposition to each other. Ember in a deep blue of the early night, Karwyn the hue of the morning sun. While Ember's skin tone had become slightly less ashen with proper nutrition and ample rest, she still leaned closer to grey in an undertone. That was the main difference in Karwyn and Ember's appearances. The pink undertone beneath Karwyn's pale skin complemented the yellow of her dress. Not a touch of grey reached the queen. Her outfit was complete with a slim golden tiara, the only crown Ember had seen her wear in the two weeks she had lived in the Azororion palace.

Oma spoke before Ember could think what to say.

"Come in, Daughter. We are almost done," Oma said. She gestured towards an empty chair next to the racks of dresses that did not make the cut.

Karwyn Dragon Queen obliged, sitting down and delicately crossing her ankles. Ember wondered if some of her own princess training would be so ingrained in her that she would do them no matter the circumstance.

"A fitting choice for your station," Oma said as she surveyed the final hairstyle, her hands on Ember's shoulders as she looked into the reflection of her eyes.

A knock sounded at the door.

"Finally," Oma exclaimed. Wally came into the room, holding a tray of treats and a pitcher of water from the kitchen per Oma's request.

He stopped dead at the sight of Ember's hair and dress. He nodded, pondering the change before replying: "That's a good look."

Ember smiled wide at him, giving herself a moment to not doubt the situation.

"I love the sparkles," he commented as he placed the tray down on the table.

"Me too," Ember replied automatically. It reminded her of her different boxes of beads and jewelry at her apprenticeship.

Wally jumped when he saw the queen before skittering into a bow and turning to do the same for the dragon matron.

"Your staff has no penchant for procedure," Oma complained. Ember was starting to see clearly what things set off the dragon matron.

Amir Captain knocked as he strode in. He paused and exclaimed aloud when he got into the living area. "Wow!" He turned his head and saw the dragon matron. "Pardon, Omanox Dragon Matron. I did not see you there."

Oma's face showed less displeasure towards Amir than Wally. The bow that he transitioned into was a lot more graceful than any of the other occupants of the room. He understood.

And as the moment came, it faded. Cindrea hid a smile with an angle of her head, picking up the comb again to adjust part of Ember's hair.

"Stop. There is nothing to be done to improve her."

The room grew silent briefly at Karwyn's words. She stood from the chair and began pulling her own hair as her face washed with a myriad of emotions. Ember wasn't sure what to do or how to react.

"Be kind, Kar," Oma said quietly as she too stood from her seat.

The fight left Ember, as did all color from her face.

Cindrea whispered loudly to Wally, "I told you she was cruel." He looked back at her with a squinting eye, not recalling that conversation.

Oma shifted gears, turning her tone to Ember's lady in waiting. Unable to save her daughter, she seemed to take a lot out on the fierce Cindrea.

"Cindrea, why don't you leave to get ready. We no longer need your services."

Not seeming to mind; Cindrea left without complaint.

"I'm here to walk you down," Karwyn said, as she walked to the door, staring down the hall at Cindrea as she walked into her neighboring room to get ready. It was as if the past few minutes hadn't happened at all, as if she had just arrived and didn't insult her daughter seconds prior.

Amir and Wally stood awkwardly by the fireplace, awaiting their departure and pretending not to notice the strange behavior. A cough came from the hallway and Ember realized the queen's guards, whom she had yet to get to know outside of Zhieve's behavior, must have been waiting in the hallway this whole time.

With a hug from her Oma and a nod to her guards, Ember squared her shoulders and walked towards her mother. This was not the time for fear or upset. This was her first day addressing the people she would have to one day rule.

Maybe one day she would get used to it, but Ember knew that day wasn't today. This ball was non-negotiable, so she reminded herself that this would be the most hectic her life would be for a while. After tonight, she could ease into it. Oma could guide her. Maybe Jedidiah would even ease up with Oma here to support her.

There were many traditions for this night, her debut into society, and the first one was about to begin. The current queen would always present her successor to her subjects, as an acceptance of their monarchy and a passing of the torch when Mutrien willed it.

"You'll do great," Amir said as she passed. She smiled back at him. Karwyn's eyes were unfocused as she took in the hall and stairs before them. Her hand reached for and now gripped Ember's tightly as they moved down the stairs. As the former dragon daughter, she must have walked down these stairs many times. In fact, so did Ember's moms.

She glanced at the queen, recalling all that her moms had said about the woman. Knowing now how close they must have been to each other, she didn't know how to act. She knew she'd have to get her alone to speak, but she has never seen her mother without her guards. And now, Zhieve was here, leading them down the stairs.

"We need to take care of the people that take care of us," Oma told her when they first began ball discussions. One tradition that had alarmed her were the parties outside the palace gates and how long the party would last. At sunrise, Ember would greet them from the balcony and discuss their new plans for the Fateless.

Anyone and everyone could come to catch a glimpse of the future queen during her debut, but only those formally invited could be in the main ballroom and its private gardens. Even as an invite-only event, those in attendance were large since every keyholder could bring their family and prominent guests from their province. Many people had a day away from their purpose to attend and celebrate, which made Amlin's refusal to let Hasley attend the ball even more infuriating.

Ember glanced at her mother behind her as they walked single-file down the stairs with their guards. The faraway look she saw there startled Ember. Karwyn was haunted, memories swarming in her eyes.

"You look like him," Karwyn said.

Ember turned around, not seeing the connection at all, and forced herself to focus on putting one foot after another. Ember began to shake in nervousness, her knees almost turning inwards as they paused at the end of the stairs.

"It's just one night," Ember said softly to herself, not realizing that she had until the queen answered.

"No," Karwyn replied, taking Ember's hand again on the bottom step. She forced Ember's face to look straight into her own again as she pulled her daughter forward. In a moment of lucidness, she seemed to think and speak clearly. "This is a day you will always remember."

Ember knew there was truth in that. This ball was a demarcation in her life. An unstoppable moment that was bound to come and would likely come again for every ruler afterward. The last moment she was free.

There is nothing strange about me.

ELEVEN

"IT'S YOU."

"Good luck, Dragon Daughter," Wally said, taking one of the large doors as Amir opened the other. Zhieve walked through first with two other guards, followed by Ember, Karwyn, and then the rest of Ember's guards.

The second they came into sight, a hush spread as if on a wave. The elegantly dressed men and women in a myriad of colors stilled. The further along they walked, the more the quiet became an ache in Ember.

She noted some of the traditional decorations Ahnika had described to her during their lesson. Along the entrance of the main ballroom was a garland created from tree branches and fallen leaves. They combined branches from previous celebrations with ones from the current year. It symbolized Ember entering into a relationship with the past and future generations. Many of the decorations were created with that symbolism in mind. Both old and new, present everywhere. The life Mutrien provided and the pair Aaleia brought to you. While this was supposed to feature more Aaleian influences than Mutrien, some aspects snuck into her debut.

As she stepped past the threshold and into the space designated for the ball, she felt crushed by the sudden weight of silence. Dozens of bodies looked expectantly at her. They judged her movements, her outfit, and her entire life in the split second first impression. The dragon daughters before her had several years to build up to this. Three weeks was not enough time.

She took one step forward and felt their expectations curl around her. Karwyn pumped her hand twice before leading her into the center of the room. The guards fell back. Karwyn took a deep steadying breath before addressing the crowd. A collective breath was held as the queen opened her mouth to speak.

"I give you, Embrence Dragon Daughter."

Karwyn stepped away from her daughter, and Ember was left alone in the center of a sea of guests. She turned 360 degrees around the space, not seeing Hasley in the crowd, she stopped when she saw someone she recognized. Her eyes trailed to the thrones at the end of the room. Jedoriah stood there by the thrones in his completely black attire. He walked purposefully towards her. His slow pace left her feeling vulnerable, but she didn't look away. The familiar, albeit intimidating, man she knew was a better focal point than the hundreds of hopeful faces in her periphery.

Ember pinched the inside of her wrist to keep herself standing tall. She would not slouch or cower. She would not scratch her scales. There were many things that Ember told herself that she would not do at this moment, but the main request she asked of her soul was that she not cry. The attention surrounding her was a suffocation she was not used to. The instinct to hide was too ingrained in her life up until these past three weeks for the habit to have died down.

Finally before her, Jedoriah's boot hit the floor with a click. His hand extended for her left and he placed his right onto her waist. Without any commentary, he pulled Ember into a dance, and she followed on instinct as he led her around the room. While spinning, she couldn't ignore the world around her. At each step, a new group of faces emerged. The whispers began to climb, a crescendo of voices and soon she was spinning and spinning into them. They moved with her, taking her through their hopes. Faces of excitement, trepidation, reverence, and more swam in circles around them.

Whispers left behind, the crowd started to cheer and clap. All around her, Ember heard her birth name shouted. In honor and in horror, she took their praises. She looked to Jedoriah, still spinning her gracefully around the room. His face played an act she hadn't seen before, displaying affection and care for her as he smiled and twirled her with force around the room. The lit lanterns blurred around him, and spots formed in her vision as he danced faster, taking her through unfamiliar steps as the music changed. He looked almost handsome, the blue of his hair bright in contrast to his black clothing.

They stopped their dance back at the center of the ballroom as the music gracefully fell away. Jedoriah put his hand into the air with an unspoken command. The voices joined the instruments back into the quiet. Once they obeyed, he projected loudly for all in the palace to hear. Ember held her arms behind her back, restraining herself and trying to open her body up for more air. Her breath disagreed with her own personal orders to remain calm as her heart also began to dance.

"We hoped this day would come, but dreaded that it never would," he began, calling to their fear of being without an heir. To her knowledge, it was the first public acknowledgment that it was a possibility they considered.

"We are so grateful to our royal guards, men charged under my duty with the task of finding our only daughter unharmed. And she was found, only a few days travel from where we now stand." He gestured to the men bordering the room and Ember smiled back at them, their faces beaming with pride.

"She was taken," he proclaimed, "from my pair's birthing chambers by two of her ladies in waiting. They did not harm her; they were just misguided in the ways of the gods. They misinterpreted the will of our world and wanted to protect our dragon daughter themselves."

When Jedoriah told Ember that he would need to address her kidnapping during the ball, Ember had insisted that the family that raised her not be tarnished during her debut. Thankfully, Jedoriah had agreed that more unrest was not necessary.

"And now, we are all gathered here today to bring honor to her life, her return to us, and to the people of Ashkadance. So, we invite you to get to know our Embrence Dragon Daughter. Dance with her, speak to her..." His voice trailed, looking back from the crowd to Ember. He moved forward and Ember saw the show he was projecting. The difference in how he looked at her when they were among those that knew about her mother, and how he then looked to their people.

His hands came down on top of her shoulders, and he projected again to the crowd, looking Ember straight in the face as he did so. While his voice seemed proud and kind, Ember saw in his eyes something much more sinister.

"As she will one day be our queen."

"Hello." Her first dance partner was next to her in moments. A tall and imposing man that stood stoic in front of her. She complimented the buttons on his coat, naming the gem that adorned them as a distraction from her nerves. The man barely noticed as he stared at her scales the whole dance, not saying a word. She let him go the second it was appropriate, and before she knew it, another person was in front of her. This time a female anchoris trainer. Ember immediately disliked her for the way she talked about the beasts. It reminded Ember to go and visit them in the stables the next day.

Queasiness overtook her stomach after her seventh spin

and as many partners. Her feet ached, and she wished she could cover her scales again. Wouldn't there be another break for speeches soon? What about a break for food? Or even prayer? Ember would take any excuse to stop as her chest began heaving, and she completely ignored what her next partner said. The world began to close its ugly mouth, and she felt its teeth prickling her neck.

"Are you well, Dragon Daughter?" her latest partner asked. She nodded, unable to form more than a sobbing gasp. Ember told herself it was only another minute longer.

But she was not okay. In fact, she could barely keep standing as the crowd seemed to push closer to them. Many people primed to jump away from their current dance partners as soon as she was available. Ember looked desperately for any familiar faces, having yet to see Cindrea in the crowd and needing someone to take her away from the close heat of these bodies. Her eyes searched wildly until she spotted Amir standing before one of the glass doors that lead to the garden entrances

Ember detached her arms from her dance partner and squeezed between bodies, the touch of so many people surrounding her felt slick and balmy. Her body began to heat.

Finally breaking from the crowd, Amir recognized the panic in her features. He met her halfway, pulling Ember with him to the garden door. He gestured for Wally to guard the entrance and they escaped. The garden was blissfully quiet.

She fell almost limp as Amir helped right her stance, her breaths coming in shallow puffs. She tried to force her breathing to slow, taking in whiffs of the white Gardemonian flower bushes that surrounded this outdoor sanctuary. Ember shut her eyes tight, wrapping her arms around her upper body in a choking hug. Amir Captain put his arms around her shoulders.

"It's going to be alright," he said. Ember heard the concern in his voice and looked up. Her eyes slid into the background of twinkling lights and suspended candles. She froze as a figure from behind Amir came into focus.

"Are you okay?" the new voice asked from behind them.

Ember lowered her arms, and Amir turned to see who had spoken. When he was out of her vision and only the stranger stood in her sights, the world became alight with a gold and glittering glow. Sparks shot from her chest, bouncing off of her heart and scales. A light erupted from his chest, electricity pulsing between them. She felt an unexplainable current drawing her closer to this man and tingling up from her toes to her ears. He felt the same, approaching as if pulled towards her on an invisible thread. Their eyes locked on each other.

"It's you," Ember whispered.

"It's you," he said back, eyes widening as his hand outstretched towards her.

TWELVE

"YOU'RE A GUARD?"

Ember met him in the middle, staring into chocolate eyes rimmed with blue. Their hands entwined and gold sparks shot between them. A shower of heat surrounded them as they pulled closer.

She knew now what the fating was. That feeling that every other dragon daughter and what most of Ashkadance had felt before her. And Ember did understand. She believed a woman could find her home in a dragon's arms because she had never felt as safe as she did now with this stranger. Barely a second had passed between them, yet she knew. Her pair. The one person Aaleia had chosen for her. He was here before her eyes, and she couldn't look away.

His arms enveloped her, and Ember inhaled the sweet scent of his skin. She heard sounds around them: Amir speaking, the opening of doors, and a fluttering of the ball's music. It muffled around her like a bubble popping in the sea. Her head landed on this man's chest, and it was the single most comforting experience Ember had ever had. She felt the sparks between them break and grow stronger as their bodies held each other. She noticed the uniform he wore as her eyes fluttered open after a moment in his arms. She asked her first question.

"You're a guard?"

He laughed at a joke she didn't know.

"Yes, from Cruelindime. My first week."

His first week as a guard, and it happened to be to provide assistance at the ball. Aaleia worked in mysterious ways.

He looked down at her, lifting his cheek from the top of her head so that he could stare into her eyes again. Ember lifted her head instinctually to do the same.

"And you are the long lost dragon daughter." His voice held a wonder to it.

Ember blushed. "It was a surprise to me too."

"I bet." His pearly teeth shone with laughter, and his eyes twinkled at her.

Ember felt mesmerized. She couldn't look away as gold reflected from his dark skin and square-shaped face. He laughed again, finding it as easy to feel joy as it was for him to breathe. Ember laughed back as she felt tears slip down her face. She put one palm up to his face, catching a spare tear from his own eyes.

"Why are you crying?" she asked.

"I don't know, why are you?" he asked. She brushed his tears away, his face leaning into her hand. She felt serene and exhilarated, a heart that beat an extra thump when in love rather than pain. She hoped the feeling never ended, that this moment stayed frozen with her.

A shuffle came from behind her, and Ember half-turned to see her Karwyn coming out of the ballroom. She glanced frantically in both directions before settling on their golden forms. Amir sat on the bench to the left, waiting. He jumped to his feet at the sight of the queen.

Ember wanted to know more about the person that had

become her forever. She ignored her mother momentarily, turning back to her pair. She needed to introduce him.

"What's your n—" Ember began. His mouth opened to answer, but they were pulled away from each by the queen's surprisingly strong arms.

Amir walked towards Ember, pulling her back from the queen, eyes wide in shock.

"What are you doing?" Amir yelled at the queen, disregarding the fact that she was his monarch. Ember protested from behind Amir, blocking her path from Karwyn and Ember's new pair.

"Inside! Now! They! Must! See!" the queen screeched each word, her hair wild around her slim face, crown missing. Ember's fated pair reached towards the queen rather than recoiling back, his kindness coming to the surface instantly.

"Are you alright, Karwyn Dragon Queen?" His arms braced in front of him to stop the queen, but with surprising strength, she grabbed his arms and began tugging him to the door. Shocked and not willing to fight back, he followed her. Gold sparks trailed behind him, and Ember felt them fray away from her heart.

Feeling sick at the thought of being away from him, Ember pushed Amir to follow the queen. Karwyn did not wait or explain; she opened the door back into the ballroom.

The soft glow of the night sky left their skin and the sounds of their guests filtered through. Karwyn pushed Ember's pair through the door. He turned back towards Ember, and she grabbed his hand. Their skin exploded in sparkling lights as they touched again. The crowd gasped and the queen composed herself, smiling and standing tall. Amir awkwardly followed, not sure what to do now that they were in public. More composed now, Karwyn pushed back her hair behind her ears and spoke.

"My daughter has found her pair," Karwyn announced.

She gestured to the man that Ember could not tear her eyes from. She inched closer to him.

"Introduce yourself, so all may know the knight of my dragon daughter," the queen commanded. She circled around them to Jedoriah's side, folding her hands in front of her and wearing the smile of a cat that caught a mouse.

Ember needed to know his name too. She held her breath, squeezing herself closer. In their surrounding glow, she could almost forget the sea of faces. Ember was sure he must feel the same, as his hand clenched hers and he pulled her to his side. Her pair took this intrusion in stride, startled but charismatic, the opposite of Ember's anxious mind.

"I am Noorworth Guard from Cruelindime," he said. He took a bow to the crowd in a grandiose fashion and twirled Ember at his side with a flourish. She loved him already, care-free in a way that Ember felt she never could be.

He circled his body around hers. They stared into each other's eyes as the crowd began to cheer, their united voices becoming louder at the next statement from the queen.

"And Noorworth Guard now becomes Noorworth Knight!" Karwyn yelled.

The crowd rallied, and the dragon matron clapped in excitement. She walked forward and embraced her daughter in probably the most tender exchange anyone has ever seen them in. Ember's eyes didn't even graze their exchange or the stoic look that was Jedoriah Knight. She couldn't help it. All she wanted to do was stare into Noorworth's brown eyes.

Noorworth seemed to have more awareness of their surroundings then she did, for Ember didn't even notice when the crowd called for a dance and music answered that call. She did notice, however, when his arm moved from her waist to hold up her hand. The other hand following up to her back. Rather than beginning another swirling dance of their capital, he took her into the slow waltz that Cruelindime was known for. For once, Ember felt grateful for her dance lessons and the guides that Ahnika had shared with her. She was able to follow enough of his steps as to not trip him. A natural rhythm she knew she could keep up with for the rest of her life if Noorworth was her partner.

Their eyes bore into each other, weights falling away each second. A trail of gold followed their movements until the whole room sparkled in their radiance, reflecting from the windows and the recently waxed floor. Their eyes shown and Ember's eyes shed pearlescent tears again.

"I'm Noor," he whispered, introducing himself again.

"I'm Ember," she replied.

"It's nice to meet you Ember."

"And you."

"I didn't expect this," he told her honestly, looking around the large circular room in surprise.

"Me neither." And Ember hadn't. She had not anticipated what it would be like to have a partner in all of this, either. All she had wanted was to survive the attention. Instead, this was the few minutes of her life that made her feel like she didn't have scales.

"So you're the princess." His eyes spoke of a hesitance that the slow turning of his words echoed.

"Yes, is that okay?" she asked, knowing there was nothing she could do about it.

"I don't know," he answered honestly. His bushy eyebrows knitted together, and Ember felt a strong urge to kiss the spot where the two met.

"I don't know either," Ember said.

Noor smiled brightly again, seeming almost relieved that it was strange for her too.

"I can't wait to know everything about you," his soft voice said.

Ember smiled back at him, knowing completely what he meant.

"You aren't much of a talker, are you?" Noor asked.

Ember shook her head. "I'm more of a listener and a thinker."

"Great! I have a lot to say," he joked and added, "a perfect match."

The song came to a close. Noor kept her in his arms a few seconds longer. He kissed her hands and rubbed his thumb across them.

"Is this okay?" he questioned, his lips still hovering over the knuckles.

"Yes," she said. Every second since their eyes locked was the most stellar sensation she had ever experienced in her life. Everything was new. She had never been near someone this intimately before. And it was in a room with hundreds of people.

There was a lot they did not yet know. While his body was almost stone still, Ember felt like she couldn't stop shaking. She vibrated at the intense emotions coursing through her. Her wide shimmering skirt kept their bodies about a foot apart, and it felt way too far for their newly magnetized souls.

A cough sounded behind them, and Ember turned to see Jedoriah with a crew of other men and women. Behind him stood the keyholders of the seven provinces, designated with their small key pins on their outfits.

"Congratulations," Jedoriah said dryly. "Our keyholders wanted to say the same."

He stepped aside and eyed their closeness as they spoke and hugged the people gathered. Soon it became more than the people sanctioned by Jedoriah, but a long procession line of most of the ballroom guests. Omanox greeted them, pulling Ember and Noor aside for a hug and congratulations.

"Already pulled away from me," Oma commented sadly to

which Ember and Noor protested. Ember could understand her Oma's feelings, however, they'd only know each other for a week and all new relationships needed time to grow.

The keyholders spoke to Ember and Noor of their excitement and love for them, of their hopes and dreams for their family and what they'd like to see in their hometowns. Ember was touched by it, calling Cindrea over to her to take note of everything. She happily did so, in between asking Noor questions. They began to speak to the last of the keyholders, Amic from Borderain, and Ember and Noor found themselves laughing together at his easy jokes and smooth manner of speaking. There wasn't enough time to continue their conversations, however, as Jedoriah came back to them to begin the meal celebrations.

"We brought in an extra seat for Noorworth Knight," Karwyn said as she walked past them.

"We welcome you to come to visit Borderain. The performance we are working on will blow you into the sea," Amic commented with a charming smile and a twinkle in his eye.

"Lovely," Oma commented dryly before dismissing them.

They sat down to eat. Ember glanced at Noor from beneath her lashes every few bites. She found that more often than not, he was staring straight back. No wonder there were songs about the fating, stories and rhymes, poems and prayers passed along to children to explain the phenomenon. Ember did not pray often, but each look felt like a prayer answered.

The night proceeded as planned: a series of dances, a course for dessert and drinks, and a group prayer to Aaleia right before the sun rose in the sky. The guests reveled in the night, dancing and thriving conversations surrounding Noor and Ember wherever they went. Trailing sparks never left their side, and Ember embraced her new life in the glow of love.

A hand grazed her back, a brushed back piece of her hair, and even a tickle on the inside of her elbow as more people shared their hopes and congratulations. Every second was scrumptious and memorable.

"I can't wait to be alone with you," Noor whispered in her ear, and she found she leaned into his hot breath. She couldn't wait either.

A booming clap was heard in the center of the room and all constituents paused, looking towards Jedoriah. He gestured for Ember and Noor. She hesitantly led her love to the head knight. It must be time to make the announcement.

"Dawn approaches. It is almost time to greet a new day with not only our dragon daughter but her knight." Jedoriah gestured to Noor, who waved at the crowd. They ate up the informality with smiles and cooing sounds.

A new lineage would now begin, a dragon daughter raised away from the court and a knight that had no idea of the formality the court required. In truth, they were a new royal family, raised among the people. Ember wondered if that was what bothered Jedoriah about her too, that she was not prepared from birth. She thought differently than him and their people knew that.

Oma led the way, looping her arm around Karwyn as her face lost focus. Jedoriah walked closely behind. Ember and Noor followed them up the stairs and through the wide doors that lead to the public viewing balcony.

Ember kept her hand in Noor's as the balcony doors opened and the light from their fating became apparent to the crowd below. At once, the sea of shadowed faces surged closer. "Get back!" The guards called from below, pushing the groaning gates back into position. The crowd cheered loudly, all amazed to get a glimpse at the future dragon queen and her knight. The sun peeked from behind the wall and began to soften the darkness of the sky around them.

It was a wide balcony meant for the whole family to be visible in one swoop. Ember looked at the queen, who leaned the most over the edge of the balcony. She cackled, her arms reaching for the sparks that flew over the edge. Oma stepped forward, pulling her daughter back by the waist with startling strength. Jedoriah peered forward as well, his face aglow as he stared into the crowd that grew louder at the second.

"They are here for you," Noor whispered in her ear. He seemed almost dumbstruck, overwhelmed by the sheer volume of people that came to the capital. All to stand outside and see a glimpse of their future rulers. His breath lingered behind her ear, arms encircled around her, and she shivered, not used to having someone so close and actually appreciating the proximity.

"And now for you," she answered back, gripping his arm with her own. She feared to let go, his love floating away with the receding star-clustered sky. Could he truly be hers, forever?

As the subtle pink and blue hue climbed up their world, Ember found a moment of peace despite the chaos below. As she looked back and forth between Noor and her people, a crowd of citizens that a few short weeks ago knew nothing about her, she became energized.

At Oma's nudge, Ember raised her hands up as she had seen Jedoriah do to request silence. The effect was immediate, even in the low light. The crowd hushed in a wave, reverberations coursing through them as neighbors and friends nudge each other into silence.

"Hello," Ember said to the crowd, waving dumbly to them. They echoed the sentiment back in a crash of joy that she felt in her bones.

"I have some news for you," Ember called out to them. She had agonized the past week over what to say, what details to impart and what would mean the most to them. She hoped her intentions came to the surface.

"We all have been touched by the plague of the Fateless. We have all lost people to the incurable sickness."

The tone immediately moved to somber. She took a deep breath and continued.

"From today onward, we are going to house those that have been infected. We will work with our doctors and scribes to understand what is happening to our people. We will keep them safe. And hopefully, one day, we will heal them."

Ember exhaled, relieved to have spoken her memorized speech. She leaned back into Noor, relieved and grateful to have started down this path. Now she waited. What would people think? Did they want this as much as she was surprised to find that her heart wanted it too?

For a few seconds, silence and shock was the only response. But then one person clapped. And another. A hesitant murmur ate through the crowd. Ember felt twisted in a knot. They wanted this too, right?

A few more claps echoed and soon, the response was overwhelming. The rushing of applause mirrored Ember's own galloping heart, pulling her out of her body. She felt numb, tingling across her skin as thoughts swarmed her. What if she failed? What if there actually was nothing she could do to help these people? Noor gripped her hand, and Ember felt grounded again, pulled back to the here and now. Ember mentally reaffirmed her commitment to this new path, a responsibility to people she avoided most of her life. Life trumped death, and this project would keep more of her people live.

Ember glanced at the queen. It was not apparent to the crowd, but from her vantage point, Ember could see how the dragon matron was holding her daughter back from the balcony. The look on Oma's face was unforgettable. A mother, protecting her daughter, in the only way she knew how. Jedoriah's face did not mimic that same concern. Instead, his eyes glinted with wide pupils. The louder the crowd got, the harder his stare burned.

Ember turned away as the sounds from the crowd

expanded outward, as each person told and retold what those close enough to hear had witnessed, applause and shouts became renewed.

For the first time, Ember felt like she was part of something bigger than herself. Swept into this life, she had pledged to survive. There was more to it now. So much more.

THIRTEEN

A KISS

There was a man in Ember Dragon Daughter's bed.

"You're actually here," Ember whispered to herself, staring down at the lock of curls that spilled across her pillow case. Even in sleep, Noorworth Guard—No, Noorworth Knight—looked like someone too perfect to exist. There wasn't any snoring, nor any funny sleeping faces. He was still, near silent sighs escaping from a small opening in his mouth. And a little bit of drool.

"Should I not be?" he said with a muffled voice as he rubbed his face. He stretched wide, his arms and legs momentarily taking up all the space in their bed. She smiled at his ease and as if on instinct, he opened his eyes and smiled back at her.

"Hi," he said to her, a sing-song quality to his morning voice.

"Hi," she replied back, horrified at her hoarse morning voice.

When reading about the fating in school, all the books said it would be difficult to conceptualize until the connection snapped into place. Ember was now part of that group of people who understood, but also did not at the same time. It was as if their feelings jumped to the end, to their height of growth that would have happened over time in any mature relationship. But it was instant. It was breath.

While things with her moms were muddled and confusing, this certainty was welcome in her life. The feeling she had when she met her birth mother, Karwyn, was beautiful and similar, but not the same. Although at the time, she had envisioned fating would be similar. It was not. The world was sharper. The light in the room was brighter as she stared into his eyes.

"You have the rest of my life to stare at me. Don't do it while I have bed head and drool on my face," Noor said as he turned onto his back. He rubbed his eyes and despite what he said, stared straight back at her.

"You know, that's a security risk," Noor commented as he stood up, leaning his back against the headboard and gesturing to the balcony.

A cold breeze drifted into the room tickling Ember's shoulder blades, and she looked down. She wasn't in her dress from the night before, that would have been impossible to sleep in. She vaguely remembered stumbling into her room gripping Noor's hand, refusing to let him get too far. With little fanfare, Cindrea pulled her into the bathroom. As the door closed, his head tilted with it to watch her until the last possible moment.

"This is the only way in and out of the room with the exception of a hatch for bringing up food and water in the hall." Ember heard Amir Captain say from behind the door.

"But over here," a sound came to her right, *"there is a hideaway."*

Cindrea wasted no time disrobing Ember, and the sharp cold brushing her skin made her jump.

"You'll wear this tonight," Cindrea said as smooth silk passed over her shoulder. Ember barely paid attention to it, despite her usual unwillingness to Cindrea helping her dress.

Instead, she stared into the wall, waiting to hear her knight's voice.

"Good morning," Ember said, still wondering if she was asleep.

"Is that how you greet your knight?" he asked, his new title a joke on his lips. While Ember wouldn't be the dragon queen until she gave birth, the dragon daughter's pair immediately became a knight. While not the head knight, for Jedoriah held that position, Noor would be once she was crowned.

"How should I greet my knight?" Ember asked, feeling a flutter in her heart.

Noor wiggled back down onto the bed, finding the head-board uncomfortable. His shirt was wrinkled from sleep.

Nothing had happened, physically, from the night before. While Ember thought about it, she knew she needed more time before jumping into that level of intimacy. They hadn't yet kissed— that Ember didn't want to wait for. The thought made her stomach flipflop.

Instead, they had talked and held each other. They would do so much more of that, for which Ember couldn't wait.

"You know, I don't know." He smiled at her, new to this experience as well.

His gaze turned more guarded as he said, "I am a big believer in honesty. Honesty and bread are probably my two favorite things."

"I agree on both counts," Ember tried to joke, but she could tell the conversation would grow more serious.

He pushed some of his floppy curls away from his face, smiling at her, but his voice was hesitant.

"Everyone wants to get paired. Well, maybe not everyone. But you expect it. I knew it'd happen for me, but I never factored helping rule Ashkadance as part of the deal," he admitted.

"Neither did I. I didn't consider anything grand for my life at all," Ember said. "My two favorite things are beads and sleep. Combined with honesty and bread, we'd have had some great nights at home if it weren't for..." Ember gestured to her scales.

"Sleeping, eating, talking, and making bracelets in bed sounds like a great way to live. Especially with someone as beautiful as you next to me. But I think we'll have more to do most days of the week."

Knowing that they both had some trepidation about their upcoming responsibilities opened up a tunnel between them and words came out in a rush.

They talked about life before the palace and their prospective life after. The fear of being alone and the loss of both Ember's moms through death and then through a tainted memory, how hard it'd been to accept that she wasn't born to them. That Ember Julimore was a lie. Noor shared his own parental concerns, how their relationship was strained and not as loving. He teared up when he spoke about his sister, who died after becoming Fateless. Killed for being Fateless, he tried to say but couldn't mouth the words. She wondered what he thought of the community homes.

They spoke about how the wall impacted his father as he had been a fisherman and his mother a trader as Ember took out the box of beads and gems Cindrea had acquired for her. Ember pointed out the unique characteristics of each. One of the only topics they didn't brooch was Jedoriah and her birth mom. Ember knew she would have to tell him about her condition, but she didn't want to bring it up just yet.

A knock sounded at the door.

"Come back in five minutes," Noor called from their bed, jumping up to sit cross-legged on the sheets. A sound of agreement came from the door. Ember couldn't tell who from the distance.

"We have some kissing to do, princess," Noor said to Ember as if speaking about some other necessary thing.

"Oh really?" she questioned with a quirked brow before immediately lowering it. She did not think she was good at flirting. She threw the covers over her head, hiding the reddening of her face.

"Nope, this isn't the time for hiding. I'm here to woo you!" He pulled himself under the covers as well and tickled Ember's sides, who squeaked and tried to shuffle away.

"Alright! Alright!" she squealed.

"Alright, what?" he asked, his hands settling on her hips. His face lay only a few inches from hers, both of them hot beneath the covers after the sun had risen.

"I do want to kiss you," Ember whispered to him, her chest heating. She absently scratched her scales. Ember realized they had yet to talk about her scales. She immediately pulled down her hand. He glanced at them but didn't comment. Ember realized that may have only been the second time he glanced at them. Was he purposely ignoring them? Did they disgust him?

Ember dropped the covers from her face and sat up. Her hair was a fluff of volume and tangles from last night, but she was glad she took a moment to wash her face before laying down. Her arms, however, she hadn't cleaned last night, so she was still decorated in gold shimmering powder. Gold dust was all over the sheets.

He scooted closer and Ember felt his warmth surround her. He leaned into her.

"Is it okay?" Ember asked, scared to bring up the part of herself that she feared for so long.

His eyes found hers, confused.

"Is what okay?"

"That I'm deformed," Ember whispered, voice cracking.

She hadn't said those words aloud since she was a kid, crying at the fact that she had no friends. Her scales had made her identifiable to palace guards as the princess by sight. If it weren't for this unwanted birthright, she'd likely still be living life as a jewelry apprentice. Maybe she would have met Noor on his way to the castle. He could have come to Amlin's store to buy a necklace for his mother or bumped into her outside the bakery as Amir had.

But neither of those scenarios happened. Instead, she had been in the palace.

"You are not deformed, Ember. That is one thing I would never think about you," he said, reaching his hand behind her neck.

His thumb rubbed along her skin and inched up to her shorter hair.

"Is this okay?" he asked, mirroring her question and learning her boundaries.

"Yes," she whispered back. His hand tangled up in her hair as he pulled her forward.

His lips were soft and full, covering her thin lips with a delicate kiss. Ember's skin sung at the contact. He pulled back to look into her eyes for a reaction. He found joy there, and he smiled before pulling their faces together again.

Ember didn't know what to do with her hands. Should they be on his shoulders? His waist? She fumbled for a second as she lost her breath and wits; she put them around his neck.

She didn't want it to stop, but Noor pulled away only seconds later. His absence felt like a loss, and she hoped he would never pull away again. So this time, she reached forward and their lips lapped together. Her whole body hummed in his arms, and she knew that if she had ever felt the sea like Noor's father had, it would feel like this kiss. A cascade of waves, salt, and hunger.

"I never want to leave this bedroom," Noor said huskily to her, and she found herself nodding into his neck, burrowing herself in his warmth as they fell back onto the bed. If only they could lock themselves up in this tower, away from the world around them. No responsibilities, only breath. Or at the very least—bread, honesty, beads, and sleep.

A knock sounded at the door again, a hesitant tap tap. Ember closed her eyes, and Noor groaned. His curls tickled Ember's face.

"Dragon Daughter?" Amir called from the door. "We need to go over security measures with Noorworth Knight."

Cindrea's voice echoed afterward.

"We need to get you two ready for breakfast with your family and some officials from the ball."

Noor kissed her nose lightly and mustered the will to get up first. He extended his hand to pull her up, the rumpled shirt and pants from the night before making Ember smile.

"I can't wait to get to know you," Ember said as she removed herself from the bed.

"Me too," he said sincerely. Ember pulled on her robe and they walked hand in hand outside of the bedroom and through the living and dining area. Behind the door stood the three people she expected; Cindrea, Amir, and Wally.

"What a weird week this has been," Noor commented absently before addressing the two guards.

"Do you guys have any spare clothes?" Noor asked.

<hr>

"CAN I ASK YOU A QUESTION?" Ember asked her lady in waiting, staring into the fire instead of her eyes. They would be leaving with Noor to breakfast shortly, but first more security briefing. Being a knight started immediately. Good thing he had training as a guard to fall back on.

"Of course," Cindrea said as she finished brushing Ember's hair. The shorter length didn't seem to change how much time it took to detangle each morning.

Ember opened her mouth and hesitated. Her face flushed, and she curled her legs under each other on the couch.

"I promise not to repeat whatever it is you want to ask me," Cindrea responded, seeing the change in color to Ember's cheeks. Cindrea put down the comb and sat down beside her, looking her in the eyes.

"The consummation of the fating, does it usually happen right away?" Ember asked, wondering if she was strange for wanting a little more time to get to know him. She trusted Cindrea. While she wasn't yet fated, she was observant and wise. Ember knew she could trust her with this question. Though now that she was bringing it up, Ember hoped it wasn't something that would hurt her. Being unpaired at her age wasn't as common. At least, it hadn't been before the Fateless. Now she wasn't sure about the averages.

"No, the timeline is up to you and Noor," Cindrea assured. "Not every fated pair is intimate in that way. Not if they don't want to be. It's like the blessing. Mutrien doesn't punish those that don't want children. Aaleia would never punish anyone that did or did not want to be physically intimate. Noor can be your life partner, your closest friend, and nothing more if that is what you both want."

Ember nodded. She knew she did want that step but was glad it didn't need to be right away.

"Everything is okay, Ember, whatever does or does not happen between you two," Cindrea said, grabbing her hand for a gentle squeeze.

"Thank you, Cindrea."

The door creaked open and Noorworth came in, wearing a uniform slightly too big with a smile just as wide.

"Are you ready to go?" he asked.

"Yes," Ember replied happily. While she was dressed, she did not feel ready at all to go outside the confines of her room.

Official training would now begin, and she would have less time than ever to just...be.

Cindrea pulled out a paper from her pocket.

"I have your schedule for the week," she said.

Noor put his hand out for the paper, his face not leaving Ember's. He quirked an eyebrow at her as if asking why she was still sitting. Ember stood up and joined him.

Walking hand in hand, two half hearts came together as one and approached the day together.

"Oh look," Noor joked in the hall as he glanced over the paper.

"It seems like we get to spend the whole day together."

"Why do I have a feeling that isn't what it says?" Ember asked. They walked down the narrow stairs.

"Because it doesn't say that," Noor admitted, "but I think we'll get an exception so that you can show me around."

FOURTEEN

WISDOM OF SCRIBES

"I told you I could get us out of lessons today," Noor boasted. He was proud to have already delivered some peace to his pair. For the rest of her life, he would help her rule. She found herself not minding the companionship. She wouldn't have been able to say that a few days ago. Today would be a day to reorient herself and talk to Noor about one particularly important bit of information. She wasn't looking forward to the later.

"Here we are," Ember said as Noor continued to swing their arms back and forth. She enjoyed his playful banter. He smiled as he observed the stables around him.

"Which one is yours?" he asked.

Ember pointed to the black horse at the end. His coat shimmered in the light that bounced off the white and brown stable house. Stone and wood blended together to house the combination of anchoris and horses. Her own horse was only partly so. Oma had brought him from her own stables in Cruelindime.

"He is part unicorn, one of a kind like you."

She pet the anchoris as she passed each of their stalls.

"What's his name?" he asked, reaching the tall and slim

horse-beast first. He had a subtle, almost unnoticeable mark on his forehead where the horn would have been had he been full unicorn. Ember wondered if she would ever see one, if there would ever be a time to cross these walls.

"I haven't decided. We haven't been able to interact much yet."

Ember stopped before him, and the horse looked quizzically at her. When she first saw him, she felt like he could help take her away. He wanted to fly as well. But there was no way she could do that now. She had a bigger role to play.

"Noor, before we go, I need to tell you something." Ember fiddled with the hem of her cream linen pants. She couldn't look him in the eye.

"What is it?" he asked, his hands immediately moving around her waist. She dared to look up and his eyes spoke to her that he wanted to hear her. Every day, he would want to hear what she had to say. She'd never be able to keep a secret again, not with the care she saw reflected back at her.

"The queen," she hesitated, her mouth drying up, "is Fateless."

Noor's eyes widened and breath rushed into his lungs. His hands gripped her waist tighter.

"How?" he whispered.

"It was before I was born. The merfolk. Oma thinks they did this to her. That they started this, somehow." Ember brought her arms onto Noor's shoulders.

"But she has a pair. She was blessed with you," he said, his face leaning closer to hers for fear of being overheard. Wally and Amir were getting horses ready on the other end of the stables, still far enough to not hear them. Though she wondered, as she often did, how much they knew after years of service.

"She may have been the first. Or the fact that she is part dragon impacts her differently. We are not sure."

Ember shook her head, upset that she didn't have more answers to give him. Or even, more answers for herself. Despite the cruelty of it, she understood now why Jedoriah stated the news to her so simply before walking away.

His eyes glanced down to her scales, peeking up from her lower collared shirt. They held the same thought as he kissed her lips.

If the queen, someone of dragon decent, could become Fateless after being paired and blessed—then so could Ember. She was not safe. Maybe no one was.

"Thank you for trusting me with this," Noor whispered on her lips, one of his bouncy curls unleashed from behind his ear. Ember smiled and closed her eyes, feeling a lift from her chest. One day he would know everything about her, and she'd know everything about him.

"Are you guys done kissing yet?" Wally asked as he trotted to them on a sugar white mare, interrupting what they had yet to say.

"We've barely started," Noor joked, lightly pecking Ember on the nose before he asked the stable hand to assist them with her horse.

Ember knew that in the times before a heart was fated to another, men and women were meant to navigate finding and committing to that one person on their own. Conception was even different, determined by how your bodies reacted to one another rather than a divine gift from Mutrien. It seemed chaotic, to be torn and never sure if your love was true. Love was different now, a term used only for family. For your pair, it was more than love.

She felt those distinctions now. Noor sat behind her on her horse, whispering at different intervals as Ember steered them down the path that led to Azororion's marketplace. Wally and a few other guards led the way, Amir Captain and more behind her.

When they arrived and tied up the horses, intermittent hushes of quiet and excitement pulled them forward. Men and women bowed as they passed and Ember felt immediately overwhelmed, wishing she had something to hide her appearance. It was easier to see the crowds from the balcony the night before, but in the daylight, it was a lot harder to bare her scales. The last time she was in a market, she was running for her life.

Sensing her discomfort, Noor suggested, "How about a scribe shop?"

He pointed to one not too far away, red-curtained windows fluttering inside.

"Yes," came Ember's quick reply.

Amir and Wally followed them into the small room, other guardsmen and women waited outside to keep other shoppers from entering. The room smelled like musty books, old paper, and pine—Ember's favorite scents. She took a deep breath upon entering, Noor inches in front of her.

An older man, hunchbacked with a kind smile, shuffled forward from behind a book stack. He started speaking before he looked up to greet them.

"Hello, welcome—Oh, Embrence Dragon Daughter. What an honor! Welcome to Mangriole's Book Shop! I'm Jardano Scribe. Let me know if you need help finding anything. We have a great selection on dragon lore in the back if you'd like."

"Thank you, I'd enjoy that," Ember replied.

Ember and Noor followed behind the man. Noor tucked a hair behind Ember's ear, and she blushed.

"Oh, a recent fating, yes? How lovely. I heard a rumor. Happy to see it's true." The wizened man said, glancing back as he brought them to the dragon book display.

"Here you are, might I recommend this book?" Jardano pulled one out from the shelf, a book with a cracked spine that read *Mysteries of the Dragon King*. Ember accepted the book and started leafing through.

"It's very interesting, very interesting, all garbage and hearsay, but interesting to read." He chuckled. Ember decided she liked this man.

"I appreciate someone with humor," Noor said. "Hi, I'm Noorworth Guard. Sorry, Noorworth Knight."

Noor stretched out his hand and Jardano shook it.

"A pleasure! How lovely, a fating at the debut ball. The last time that happened was with Omanox Dragon Matron." He nodded, his hands clasped together. Ember made a note to ask Oma about that, so little was discussed about her grandmother's deceased pair.

A rustling sound was heard further in the shop. Jardano glanced back but resumed talking quickly.

"You'd probably also like to read this," he handed her another book. "This one..." Another was added to the pile. "And this one is great for information on our gods."

The third book was heavier than the rest. Ember rearranged them in her arms.

"Why thank you, Jardano. I've always been one to appreciate the guidance of the scribes," Noor said, nonchalant as he took the heavy book to hold for Ember.

Jardano blinked, staring at Noor as if he didn't expect the compliment.

"Of course, it is my purpose. Blessed may you reign," he replied, his eyes darting between the two. A book fell, and Wally stammered an apology behind them.

After a few minutes of conversations and many more suggested books later, Noor and Ember exited the store.

"We'll meet again, I'm sure," Noor commented and Jardano nodded his head enthusiastically. Amir gave him a pat on the back and exchanged a few words on the way out.

Noor reached for her hand and lead her down the u-shaped market. Knowing the layout, Ember quickly realized they were getting closer to the jewelry stalls. A giddy feeling built in her chest.

He made a big show of picking up pieces and bringing them up to Ember's face to see how they would look against her skin. She laughed at the serious expression his features took on as he compared different pieces. The shopkeeper laughed as well.

After several minutes, Noor pretended to throw up his hands in frustration.

"Luciana, you must help me. I need a piece of jewelry as unique and rare as my queen. Have you any suggestions?"

The crowd oohed at the near treasonous term of endearment. Ember blushed, the red spreading across her face and chest. She hid under his shoulder, both enjoying and worrying over the attention.

The white-haired and dark skinned woman took a moment to look pensive, playing up the act. She stared at Ember with slitted eyes before she had a eureka moment.

"I have just the thing," she exclaimed, running into the back room.

"You are silly, I don't need anything," Ember said to Noor when the woman disappeared. Though she was happily thrilled about someone picking jewelry for her. This was her first gift from her pair.

"I am, thank you. That's my favorite thing about myself." His smile was almost crooked in its glee.

He took a long bow, grasping her fingers and kissing up her arm as he rose with loud wet smacks of his lips.

Ember giggled loudly, almost squeaking as he tickled her ear.

"I have found the perfect item for our dragon daughter," the woman exclaimed as she pushed through the tent flap with an air of importance. No doubt her shop would see an uptick in sales after today.

"What do you think, Noorworth Knight?" she asked conspiratorially, tilting the box so that only he and the gathering crowd could see. Ember heard a few surprised exclamations.

Noor's eyes widened. "Why Luciana Jeweler, you've outdone yourself. May I?" he asked, putting out his hand for the box.

"But of course, it is my purpose."

Noor took the box and pointed its open end to Ember. "My queen, what do you think?"

In the box was a small golden ring. It swirled intriguingly upward like a spiraling fire to host a rainbow pearl. This was indeed special. This piece was passed on to the shop for repurposing when the previous owner joined Aaleia in the after.

"To commemorate our meeting," he said. He hugged Ember to him and slipped the ring on her finger. The crowd applauded, and their guards encourage them to push back.

"We should be on our way, Dragon Daughter, Knight," Amir called, more people joining the crowd to see them. The opening of the shop overflowed with the spectacle. The shopkeeper stood waiting, her apprentices behind her.

"I agree." Noor followed, thanking Luciana for her hospitality after paying for the ring.

The crowd parted to let them pass. Several hands reached out to try and touch her as she moved. "The Dragon..." they whispered, and it made Ember uncomfortable. She felt the world turning around her, felt the stars move in the sky, and a rumbling in her chest.

That night, Ember turned over in her bed and reached out her ringed hand to Noor's side. She found only cold sheets.

FIFTEEN

MORE LIES

Ember had awoken in the middle of the night to a cold bed four days out of the past seven.

"I'm adjusting to new duties, like this one," Noor would say, kissing her on the lips and distracting her thoughts. Even as she let him kiss her, she knew it was a lie. He was not out exercising with Wally or training with Amir at sunrise. He was not wandering the grounds because he couldn't sleep. Every excuse came out of his mouth easily, but if those things were true she wouldn't need to ask for answers. If it were true, he wouldn't be distracting her a moment later.

Ember stared at the closed door that she knew Noor had exited. Amir's voice whispered behind it. Their shadows passed under the door and Ember watched them leave. Should she be doing this? Following him wasn't something that pointed to a trusting relationship. But if he didn't answer her questions truthfully, how else was she going to find out what was going on?

Ember didn't know how to feel. Shouldn't your fated pair tell you everything? Why would he and Amir have anything to hide from her?

She followed behind them, timing her steps and turning corners while she was far enough away to be unnoticeable, but still close enough that she could see their path. It lead her to duck behind statues and hide in alcoves, but soon they stopped and a third man joined them. She recognized Wally as he left Jedoriah and the queen's tower. Zhieve's bed must be as cold as her own. Together, the three of them walked to the gardens and entered one of its many doors.

Ember trailed behind them, pulling her robe tighter around her body in the chill air. She walked along the edge of the garden, eyes widening as she tried to take in more light. The bushes that lined the walls glimmered with small firebugs and torches, creating a low glow. If she weren't attempted to be sneaky, this would have been a nice stroll.

There it was, a whisper of voices ahead of her. She slowed down until she turned around a bend to find three figures crowded together in the dark. Crouching low behind a tree, Ember stared at the three men that have become pivotal figures in her short life at the palace.

Amir, Noor, and Wally were all out of uniform in outfits of brown and black, softly arguing about something Ember could not hear. They looked like civilians. Wally continued to speak as he bent down, lifting something from the ground. A groan was heard and the bush lined wall behind them opened up. She crept a little closer, her dark robe helping to hide her figure in the trees.

Ember's heart skipped a beat. What could her pair and two main protectors be doing in the middle of the night that would involve a secret entrance?

She rushed forward just as Noor closed the door behind him. Ember put her hand into the foliage, scratching her arm as she looked for any sort of knob or latch. She felt nothing but the sting of thorns.

Thinking for a moment, she looked down. In the darkness,

she couldn't make out much. She bent to the ground, trying to feel around where Wally had stood.

That's it! A small stone was latched to the ground, but when lifted a certain way...

The hidden door pushed inward with a small creak. Slightly open, their voices filtered in a few feet from the door. If she wanted to turn back, now would be the time. If she wanted to go in and look into the door when she knew they had already moved on. She could do that without them knowing. But then she'd have no way of figuring out where they went next. What if she got lost in her own explorations? Ember knew that if she wanted to get to the truth, she'd have to go now while the courage was with her. She pushed at the crack that formed within the foliage and her eyes were hit with the lights from within. Steeling her breath, she walked through the door.

"Ember, what are you doing here?" Noor asked, his eyes as wide as Ember's as she took in the passageway before her. Noor, Wally, and Amir stood ten feet from the door, half turned towards their direction. Every few feet there was a blazing torch, and she could see the outline of what must be other hidden doors. It was a narrow space, but long. Ember turned around and saw that it continued in both directions. The room smelled of stale air. Few people must know of this hidden hall between the castle and the gardens.

"Dragon Daughter, is everything alright? Why are you here?" Amir asked her, as if she were interrupting them in her bedroom hallway rather than a secret passageway she needed a lift a fake rock to enter. His hand reached for her shoulder. Ember stepped back. Wally didn't say a word, the least calm of the three of them as he wrung his hands.

"I think," Ember began, "I could ask the same of you all. If you could explain to me why my guards, including my knight, left their post and are now in *a secret passageway?*"

Ember pushed her short strands of hair behind her ears and

crossed her arms in an attempt to fight the urge to scratch her scales. She hated the way she felt in that moment, the nerves pulling her back into her past life.

The three of them looked to each other, unsure what to say. Noor stepped forward first.

"We should go back to your room and talk."

"I'd like to know where you've been sneaking away to first," Ember said.

"That's a long story," he hedged, putting his hands in the pockets of his linen pants.

"No, it's quite simple. Where does this hallway lead too?"

Ember's chest flared, and her heart filled with heat. She needed to know. She had to know now. She looked at Amir and Wally.

"Well?"

"We were going into the city to meet with friends," Wally volunteered. Amir glared daggers at him. So it led to the city. Ember stored that information away.

"In a secret tunnel?" Ember threw up her arms and turned to where the door had been.

"Can we speak privately?" Noor asked her, asking for her attention. She felt her personal bubble of safety pop around her. The fragile acceptance of her new life was thrown out of balance.

"How do I get out?" she asked, pushing the center of where the door had been. The outline was visible on the beige walls, but there was no doorknob. She frantically pushed it again, kicking out her foot as her mind whirled and emotions flared in her chest. The air was too thin. Her thoughts began to spiral around her like they did the morning she met her mother and began to learn the truth.

"Ember, stop! Let me help you," Noor exclaimed, pulling her back from the door. She growled at his touch, feeling anger build in her with each second. She had never felt this much anger before. Never pulled into such emotion. They were lying. They were keeping things from her, and she wanted to get away from them as soon as possible. She did not want to talk to Noor in private. She did not want to talk to Noor at all.

Noor pushed the top right corner of the outline and the door sprung open again. Ember ran through it, scratching her arms on the bush as she passed through the door. Was the gardener in on this secret? How did the bush not grow into its neighbors? Was this door opened frequently enough that the plant couldn't expand to join the other foliage on the wall?

There were liars everywhere, and Ember felt unreasonably upset that the gardener was likely in on it too.

"Ember, wait," Noor called, following after her. Amir and Wally stayed back.

"Why should I?" Ember replied, walking faster.

"I will tell you everything. Let's get to the room first, okay?" Noor pleaded. From the side of her eye Ember glared at him, not saying a word. She had wanted to be wrong. She did not want to find out they were actually doing something behind her back. Part of her wanted to take it all back and live in the ignorance that Noor had tried to wrap her in.

What were they doing in the city that she couldn't know about? Did he drink too often? Was he in a fight ring? She'd heard rumors of that, but no that didn't fit. She never smelled alcohol or spotted bruises on him. Her legs pumped faster, and Noor worked to match Ember's pace as she sped through the castle. She became more harried by the second.

Outside the stairs that lead to her tower was a guard. She vaguely remembered his name was Coralie. Ember glared at him as they passed, letting her anger bleed into her other actions. Why wasn't he there earlier? Was he in on the secret too?

Noor closed the door behind them after they ascended the stairs single-file. Ember stood in the middle of the room, waiting expectedly. Her face was set into a hard line as she waited for him to talk.

"My parents joined the resistance when I was only two years old," Noor began.

The floor fell from beneath her. Her moms...were Noor's parents involved in the attack that killed them? Ember's body tensed in defense.

"After the wall had gone up, they lost their purpose. It wasn't easy for traders and fishermen to adjust to life after that. How can you take away the sea from someone? They lost faith in the kingdom and joined with a group of people they heard were trying to fight back." He stopped, gathering additional memory strands from his mind.

"They weren't even considered a resistance yet. It was a group of people that wanted to have their voices heard. When the Fateless became more widespread that changed. They wanted to take action, not petition."

Ember knew that he must be thinking of his sister. How old was he when she began to lose her mind?

"When it was a more formed rebellion and you were older, did you join them?" Ember asked, trying not to jump to conclusions.

"I have joined them," he said. Noor walked to the couch, sitting down and putting his head in his hands.

All steam left Ember's body, and she plopped into a chair. Aaleia had fated her to a rebel. A rebel and a future queen. Why would she do this to her? How did this go with Ahnika's lessons, that all pairs were meant to help each other reach their potential? A thought came to her. The way he phrased his confession...

"When exactly did you join?" she held her breath.

"When I met you," he whispered.

Ember pulled her cloak tighter and exhaled a quaking breath. She wanted to hide. She didn't want to talk about this at all. Why did she have to follow him? Her position had given her new confidence. She had been more assertive in this month than she had her whole life. On some days, she thrived on it. Tonight, she wished she had never gotten up from that bed.

Ember stayed silent, waiting to see what he would volunteer. She could barely think, let alone speak.

His head still in his hands, curls spilling over the side of his face, Noor spoke.

"I never wanted to join them. I even became a guard more to piss my parents off, rather than for any passion for it. I didn't know what I wanted to do, and there were always positions available for guard training. After Naomi, my sister, became unrecognizable...I figured, two wraiths with one stone. I would get away and upset the parents that cared more about the mission than their family."

He pulled his body back, leaning against the couch as he turned to look at her.

"Then I was actually good at it. I was recruited not for province work, but asked to join the extended Cruelindime guards that would be going to assist the debut ball."

Noor laughed a little at the upward trajectory his purpose path became.

"I didn't expect to meet you. I figured I'd be in the perimeter duty. I was so confident that I'd go back to my normal life after the ball, that I didn't even tell my parents I was coming here."

Ember's eyes widened. "And then you were announced as the knight."

He nodded. She could only imagine what kind of letter he received from them.

"Did they pressure you to join?" She hoped his answer was yes, that he didn't join that group that probably hated her for existing. She tried to remember if any letters arrived for him from his parents, but she couldn't recall. Ember realized suddenly she hadn't heard from Hasley since her short note about the ball either.

"No." His voice cracked and Ember didn't know what to do.

"Why?" Ember whispered, thinking of the day she found her moms were killed. They had gone ahead to scout for their next home. They were due to be home in a week. Ember stayed behind as she always did. One week became two then a third. Ember packed up her stuff and went to the next province over to look for them. Out of her comfort zone, she asked people if they had seen them. She found out about the attack within moments. The guards had already burned the bodies, not able to locate a next of kin. That made sense to Ember now, but it didn't then. There was likely no record of her even existing.

"Because I realized my parents were right. When you told me about the queen, I knew that the royal family knew more about the Fateless than they let on. The people need to know this information."

At the mention of her blessed mother, Ember felt a renewed terror that clenched her heart. The anarchy that would reign if the whole of Ashkadance found out was unimaginable.

"Did you tell the rebels about my mother?" she asked slowly.

"No. I wanted to do some exploring, see what I could learn, then share it with you. I haven't said anything..."

The unspoken *yet* lingered in Ember's mind.

"I have no idea what to think right now," Ember replied honestly. Where did the line draw? Where were his loyalties?

He stood up from the couch and walked towards her, his eyes asked for permission and she nodded yes. He bent his knees to the floor and hugged her. Her head leaned on his chest, level with him from her position in her chair and his height. A tear fell from her eyes, splashing on his wrinkled shirt.

"What do they know about me?" she whispered.

"Nothing. Nothing at all. I gave them a fake name. I'm a nobody guard in the palace."

The squeeze on her heart lessened a little.

"What are they like?" she asked next. Ember lifted her head from his chest, and he pushed away a tear from her eyes. He looked into them and spoke with deep sincerity.

"They are not what you've been told. They want to help the kingdom. They just don't agree with the way it is right now. They care. They are a lot like you."

She ignored the comparison.

"And my moms? What about what happened to them?" Her voice quavered. The bite and pain of their death leaked into her words. And was the violence they committed a lie? She couldn't see how.

"I haven't been able to ask them. I can't tell them who your parents were without revealing I know you. No one else has that information. I promise we can find out. We can find out together."

"I need some time to think about this," Ember whispered, unsure how else to close the conversation and be with her thoughts.

"I understand," Noor said with a sad shake of his head. "Can...can we lie down?" he hedged.

She nodded her assent and followed him to the bedroom. Dawn would soon approach, and they needed rest. She felt hurt that he had jumped into this, became part of an unspoken conflict that she had seen to be violent. But it was his family. He had been part of this for years, even before he officially joined through the connections of his parents. She told herself that it made sense he would have considered being part of them. She told herself that his family had been dealt a rough card, purposes taken from them and then their daughter succumbing to the Fateless.

But that didn't mean he had to stay. She'd work with him and get to know this group. She would find out what happened to her moms and what was done to them. Then she would decide what to do. As heir, she'd have to decide whether or not to reveal the secrets she learned from them. If they proved to be violent like she had been led to believe, then no motivation made them justified.

She laid on top of the soul thread, her coat discarded at the foot of the bed. Noor's arm draped around her, his head rested in the crook of her neck. Within moments, he was asleep like he always was. Her mind whirled, tears fell, and eventually, Ember felt her thoughts fade away into the sky.

PART 3
EMAIRY WAITING

SIXTEEN

KARIANA'S TEARS

When Ember asked Wally to go on a walk with her the next day, she had no idea what she wanted to say or ask. Ember tried to chase down her thoughts as Wally kept a constant stream of commentary about each plant and different palace gossip. He didn't seem to mind her silence, letting her think as she strolled. Finally, she gave up on being coherent. She left the path and sat in the grass of a wide tree, her long cobalt dress pooling around her.

"What's wrong, princess?" Wally asked as he sat beside her.

"Can I not be the dragon daughter for a minute?" she mumbled back as she moved her chest to her knees. Her body felt like a cave in collapse and while she knew she should not be on the floor right now, she could not keep herself upright any longer.

"Okay. What's wrong, Ember?" he rephrased. His soft hands ran a circle down her back, she appreciated the gesture and took in deep inhales.

"What's it like to be paired to Zhieve?"

His hand paused.

"Why do you ask that?"

Without looking at him, she spoke in a rush. She needed to ask, but was scared she'd lose her nerve.

"Because I feel like I am paired to this palace, this future that I didn't ask for, and not just Noor and his... affiliation. I have little control and the exact opposite life I had wanted. I wondered if you feel the same about Zhieve and if that's why you, uh, joined the same group too. So you have more control. An escape." It was a blunt thing to say, but her thoughts returned to the murderous man her friend was paired too and the words came far too easy to her lips.

"Because in my scenario, Zhieve is the dreary and cold stone I cannot escape?" he asked with tense shoulders, but not an unkind face. He understood how others saw his pair, but he did retract his hand.

"Yes," she said, feeling guilty immediately for bringing it up. Ember didn't understand why Aaelia would have thought their hearts matched. Was Zhieve once a kind man? Was he different in private? Would joining the rebellion change Noor?

Wally leaned back in the grass, resting on his elbows before pointing to a flowering patch in the distance.

"You see those purple flowers?" he asked.

The bush held different patches of flowers. They seemed to glow, their purple hue cascading around all the other more subdued white flowers around them. This flower patch was lined with small round stones, and the soil within the stone border appeared leached of color.

"Yes, what about them?" she asked, not taking her eyes away. Was he not going to answer her question? The flowers swayed lightly as a breeze blew past them, but their stocks were stiffer than the rest. The other flowers waved dramatically in the wind, not having that same control. The purple was stead-ier. Stronger.

"Those flowers are growing out of soot created from a dragon's fire breath or the remains of an object burned into ash by blood fire."

Ember's whole body startled, her eyes widened as she stared at the flowers.

"Really?" she asked, what a peculiar thing to bring up and a strange thing to even exist. Who would plant a flower seed in the destruction of fire?

"That is Zhieve and me. We are the purple flowers. We don't know why were chosen to be together, but we know we love each other. We know we can make each other a better person and we are working on finding that balance. He is rough, sometimes unsympathetic, but I soften him. I show him kindness, and he shows me strength. He shows me order, and I bring him serendipity," he said as a way of explanation. Ember understood immediately his message.

"For good to grow, sometimes bad has to burn down. For beauty to flourish, it is often after a struggle," Wally said, plopping completely down into the grass. His eyes closed and Ember was reminded of the night the Fateless man died. Seconds before, they were laying like this in the grass. But then, they were lit by moonlight.

"What about the white flowers?" Ember asked curiously as they moved in the breeze.

"Purging. Parts they no longer need. The flowers that become white instead of purple eventually crumble, become part of the soot. It's part of life. They are called Kariana's Tears."

Struck by the thought of the flowers crumbling into ash, Ember laid down next to Wally in the grass. No doubt, her dress would be stained and Cindrea would be angry when cleaning her clothes that night.

Kariana's Tears...she must have been a strong queen. Paired to a dragon, daughter of an over 100 year war, rebuilding from the ash.

"Am I a purple flower or a white one?" Ember asked out loud, looking up at the sun through the trees.

"That's a question only you can answer," Wally replied back, eyes still closed.

"Thank you," Ember said. She knew that this conversation was something she would replay again and again for the rest of her life.

"I will meet them," Ember said to Noor that night. Her arms were crossed, and she couldn't look him in the eye. She was scared, felt wide-open in her fear, but she knew that this was something they needed to do together. She could uncover who killed her parents and maybe even some insight into the other kingdoms and merfolk from the traders. Aaleia could have brought them together for this exact reason.

"Thank you, Em, you won't regret this. I promise."

She hoped for the sake of her own sanity that she did not.

THEY HAD DEBATED for several days on her disguise, cover story, and the inner workings of the rebels. Tonight was finally the night she would meet them under a false identity.

Noor's cover story wasn't as elaborate as hers. When Amir introduced him to the group, he suggested a fake name and to wear a hat. His face wasn't as recognizable yet. She glanced at him, the circular shape of his fabric hat poking out from his back pocket. Shouldn't her captain and knight of the guard have done a better job at hiding their identity? It was laughable.

Ember glanced in the dressing mirror. She experimented with kohl liner. Cindrea was happy to teach her some makeup skills. While Cindrea had used makeup to look more youthful, Ember aimed to do the opposite. She needed more practice. She had never used makeup before the palace, but discovered she actually enjoyed it. A masquerade. It gave her more license to feel confident going into a situation even more beyond her control.

She pinned back the shorter front sections of her hair, adding a ribbon to her braid and twisting it into a bun, mimicking the appearance of longer and fuller hair. It would do. At least at first glance, she appeared like a different person. At least strangers wouldn't recognize her right away. If someone from the palace was also a rebel, they'd likely do a double-take.

Noor put his hands in his pockets and rocked his feet back and forth. The nerves of getting to this meeting had weighed on them. She wasn't going to pretend that it was okay, that his involvement in something so large was not a shock. But she owed it to him, her moms, and herself to learn more. The silence stretched until a knock sounded at the door. Amir popped his head in.

"Are you two ready?"

Ember and Noor walked into the living room, following the voice, two feet lay between them.

"Here it is," Amir said, handing to Ember a small pin similar to his captain pin. She thanked him and pinned it on her sweater.

"Hi!" Wally sang happily as he came in unannounced. He saw the space between Ember and Noor and said bluntly, "Wow, it's awkward in here."

"Everything's fine, let's get going," Noor redirected. She didn't reply to him, instead directing to Wally.

"And Cindrea is asleep?"

"Yes, not a peep from her room."

"Good," she nodded, her nerves hammering her chest as they left. There was still a few hours to sunrise, but not a lot of time for dawdling.

Following the same path they had a few nights prior, Ember saw how Amir dismissed or distracted every guard as he walked ahead of them.

"He doesn't do this every night," Wally said, "Sometimes I do it and other times we just sneak around or say we are on the way to train. As long as nobody sees our actual direction."

She didn't think they'd believe she was training too. She also had no idea how they were getting away with this for so long when she was able to trail them easily. But then again, people don't see what's right in front of them unless they are told to look.

The hidden passageway was longer and more connected than she expected. They circled the perimeter of the garden with hidden doors at each corner to transport people wherever they wanted to go. After two turns down the long hallway, there was a break in the path where you could continue along the other side of the garden and then down under the castle. Ember felt the cold leak into her as they walked. Noor gripped her hand and chatted amiably along the way. She didn't hear a word, barely feeling the hand she let him hold.

When the tunnel began to warm again and the air freshened, Ember knew they must be close to their destination. She never wanted to go underground again, but she was sure it would soon become a regular torture. If she had wings, they would ruffle.

Amir stopped in front of a door, outlined similarly to the one they entered. He pressed the top corner and it sprung open to reveal stairs and a top latch.

"This is where I leave you all," Wally said with a wave and a kiss on Ember's cheek.

"Good luck," he whispered, he turned back down the tunnel to the castle. She took a deep breath and climbed with her remaining companions to the surface.

It took Ember a few minutes to adjust to their surroundings. They had climbed up from the ground to a secluded area beyond the gates close to the surrounding perimeter wall. Trees surrounded them, and in the distance the home districts were visible with lanterns lit in their windows. Fear began creeping in again as they followed Amir through the trees and into an alley between two inns.

Amir and Noor appeared more casual than Ember felt, seamlessly walking to the sidewalk as if nothing were suspicious about them at all. They walked half a block to the space between the market and the residence, where delivery carriages would bring in food from the farmlands and other goods for shopkeepers. It was a barren dark road at this hour, the glow of a few homes peeking between alleyways.

"There are several different entry points," Noor whispered to her. "This one is the closest to the palace." Before them was a fenced-in home.

"Here we are," Amir said.

It looked like a regular home on the block, one of the many structures that lay in identical rows. Simple homes in grey and various tans, brown fences with small patches of green between.

Noor looked behind them and waved briefly at a faraway figure walking from the Scribe delivery area. In the dark of the delivery road, no one would be able to see them go into this home except for anyone also heading in the same path. Ember couldn't tell who it was at this distance, and Noor pulled her through the fence before the figure could catch up.

Ember wasn't sure what she expected, but walking into someone's backyard wasn't it. Especially an empty yard, no torches or seating area. Just grass.

"What are—"

Amir cut her off with a finger to his mouth, signaling her to be quiet. He gestured for her to follow and led her to a cellar door. They climbed down the stairs and Ember stopped dead, almost tripping Noor.

It was not a cellar at all, but rather a hidden city beneath the city. It was wide, almost as wide as the road in the market and extended farther then she could see. The space was filled with light, torches and fire pits created all along the walls and between divided camps. She was underground again and it made her squirm, despite the mystery of what was around her.

All around her were divisions she did not yet understand. Areas with many tables and seating, long and small couches where people were talking out in the open. Sections that were packed with tents for private meetings or sleeping arrangements. Other sections of open beds in an infirmary setting. A clearly defined kitchen area was close by, the smell of cooked vegetables wafting between them. And men and women all throughout. Smiling, laughing, and some sparing in a training formation. And children. There were more children in this hidden world then she had seen in the market on a regular day.

Who were all these people? This was not the disorganized rebellions she was lead to believe. This was a way of living. How had this stayed hidden? Who built this place? Children ran around them, weaving between legs and bodies.

"It's a lot to take in, isn't it?" Noor asked, smiling brightly.

Not the first time, all that Ember had known was thrown on its head. There was more to this than Noor had said. Could this all have come together since the wall was constructed seventeen years ago? Given all that had happened just in the past few weeks of Ember's life, she reasoned that yes, it could. Her family was not telling her everything. The rebellion held more for her to learn. She hoped that would mean answers.

They walked and Ember noticed other entry points at different intervals. And in some corners, suits of armor with the family crest from before the First Fating, like what guarded the entry to her tower.

In one corner were large chains that signaled the history of what this place could have been. Teenagers sat on the chains, wrist cufflets the size of sofas that fit many lounging people. Some of them even seemed familiar to her. Regular people that she may have passed during her many moves. But the majority were strangers, wearing clothing that looked weathered and used. Behind them was a claw-like scratch into the wall that extended deep. Ember shivered and looked away before the other teens spotted her.

Dragons had been trapped here before the First Fating. Possibly even a relative of hers. She understood then why she didn't feel comfortable. A lingering fight or flight swirled her blood. She was part dragon. Dragons cannot survive underground.

If dragons had been kept here against their will, there was a small list of uses this hidden makeshift city could have been created out of. Torture was one likely case. Torture and war planning. Beneath them all the time.

Ember glanced around her, unsure where Noor and Amir were leading her. She guessed the tunnel must be at least a mile or two in each direction. Enough for many people to come together, enough room for a tight-knit community to expand. Did every province have a place like this or was this the equivalent of a rebel capital? She heard whispers of conversation as they navigated where Amir pointed, to a tall tent several divisions away. The whispers she heard as they walked held a common theme.

"Her scales are purple and her skin is green," one little boy conspiratorially whispered.

"She carried a Fateless girl out of a burning building without getting hurt," a small blue haired girl claimed.

"I think it's cool. She's a real dragon!" Another said.

Noor smiled at Ember and squeezed her hand, but they did not slow their walk. Ember didn't smile back; the hair on her arms rose.

They reached the larger of the tents. A woman outside appeared to be guarding the entrance with a stiff posture and ill-fitting attire. She nodded at Amir, recognizing them, and announced his entrance before opening the red tent flap.

Amir, Noor, and Ember walked inside to see a tall woman standing over a desk. She shuffled paperwork without looking up and Ember noticed a knife strapped to her side. Her muscles were lean and taut as she looked down over the scatter of papers around her. Other people were in the room, handing the woman tea and more papers. She had on one wrist a traditional fating bracelet.

The woman looked up, a shock of bright green eyes reflected back at her. She grazed over Ember briefly before turning to the men she came with.

"Hello Amir, Brookworth." It took Ember a minute to remember the fake name Noor had told her he claimed in the rebellion.

"Who is this?" she asked and Ember answered quickly, bringing out her hand for this stranger to shake.

"I'm Emairy Waiting and yourself?"

"Jade," she replied and shook her hand firmly. Ember inclined her head to her, noting that Jade did not share her purpose name. Jade's plump lips pursed as she turned back to Amir and Noor.

"And she is here because..." Jade gestured between the two of them, expecting an answer. Jade had a natural suspicion about her, understandable for her current situation.

"Emairy is my pair," Noor said, reaching to bring a hand around Ember's shoulders. "We met this week when she joined the dragon daughter's tower."

He parroted the cover story they put together. Emairy was a person of wealth, someone who could gain power, but not threatening. An unassuming girl with potential. Pairs don't go against each other. That was something she repeated to herself in this strange scenario. It was an easy story. Emairy complimented Brookworth's life.

"Well, congratulations. A lady to the dragon daughter...." Jade's eyes squinted but her mouth tugged into a small smile.

"Amir and Brook haven't been able to get close enough to her to share any useful information about our long lost dragon daughter." Jade glared sidelong at Amir and Noor. The confirmation that they haven't shared anything about her warmed Ember's chest.

"We told you, Jade. She has a special guard from Jedoriah. No one can get near her," Amir reminded Jade, covertly looping Ember into the story.

"What impressions do you have of her?" Jade asked. She gestured to a small seating area and they sat. A pale man nodded to Jade before vacating the space.

"She is quiet and observant. She doesn't like being helped in and out of clothes or being assisted much at all. Not in the ways that ladies would normally help," Ember said. She acted as if this was an inconvenience, while also subtly pointing out that the future queen wasn't used to wealth.

"She takes classes most of the day, learning about palace traditions and history," Ember added. "I see her as kind. She treats the other servants in the palace well and isn't as quick to anger as Jedoriah Knight."

"Good, I'm glad to hear that. And what of Embrence's knight?" Jade asked, leaning forward with clasped hands.

"He is devoted to her, a guard from Cruelindime. Funny, handsome. Wherever she sides on a conflict, he is likely to follow." She could almost feel the laugh that Noor was holding in from beside her. That had not yet proven to be true, or they wouldn't be here.

"Anything else?" Jade asked as she leaned back to extract a small bull-leather-bound notebook and pencil from her trouser pocket.

This was the card that Ember knew would cause murmuring across the rebel fleet. She'd be an asset now. Given all that she had seen as she came into this base, Ember needed to get accepted into the group to be able to get the information she needed.

"Her scales..." Ember started, waiting for Jade's reaction. Jade paused her scribblings and looked up.

"Everyone out!" Jade called, keeping her eyes on Ember. A good precaution, Ember appreciated the discretion. The few guests left in the tent left, exchanging sidelong glances.

"What about them?" Jade asked when the room was quiet once more.

"They are only on her chest. They are not growing like the rumors suggest." In truth, Ember didn't know if that was a rumor, but the guess seemed to work as Jade's attention wrapped around her like a moth to a flame.

"They are a family trait. The daughter of Kariana and Drakul had them. It was not public knowledge," Ember finished explaining. "There was still a lot of prejudice against beasts in those early days, so it was kept quiet. When she was born with the same markings and then was kidnapped, I think they kept her scales quiet so they could identify her easily, weed out fakes."

Oma had explained so in vague terms to Ember in their many conversations since they met. It explained enough, but Ember still felt like she was a missing piece in a puzzle.

"Why would she share this with you?" Jade asked skeptically, eyes squinting in her direction.

"She didn't. There are portraits of the child in her private quarters. As for whether they are growing, I stole her medical files." Ember trained her face into a smirk, hoping she had positioned herself as valuable.

"Are you telling me," Jade said as she turned to Amir, "that this girl could gain all this information in one week and you couldn't get anything in a month."

He shrugged as if this didn't surprise him.

"I'm not allowed in her rooms unless she calls for help. Emairy is," he said by way of explanation.

"There is one thing that she did tell me," Ember hedged. Noor glanced at her. They hadn't talked about this prior. Ember prayed she didn't overstep a boundary.

"Her kidnappers," Ember began, glancing again that they were alone. Using the word kidnappers was more painful than she expected.

"Yes?" Jade prompted.

"They were killed. Embrence," she said, referring to herself by her formal name, "said the rebellion is responsible."

Jade's face paled a degree. "What?"

Ember nodded solemnly.

"Get me their names. I'll look into it. This could be a problem."

"I agree." Ember said, jotting them down on Jade's notepad. She exhaled, glad that Jade didn't pry into this personal bit of information. The sooner they answered the question of Julimore and Echoris' death, the sooner she could decide what to do next.

"Welcome to the resistance," Jade said as she stood, pulling Ember up with her and shaking her hand. Noor and Amir clapped her on the back in congratulations and shook Jade's hand in return.

SEVENTEEN

A SECRET

oor sat on the edge of Ember's tub while she used
the assortment of oils left near her sink. She had to
get all of the makeup off of her face before she
became too tired. Honestly, she was already too tired. Cindrea
would have too many questions if she saw Ember covered in
black when she had left her with a clean face and ready for bed.

"What did you think of them?" Noor asked, looking down
at his shoes rather than at her eyes. She could feel that this was
an important question to him. She thought as she rubbed the
oily substance over her eyeliner.

"I think that there is a lot I don't know about our kingdom,"
she began saying. The idea that the kingdom was hers as
foreign as the thought that she was part of a pair.

"And they will help me learn that information," Ember
said.

Her mind drifted to the running children and to the group
her age, sitting beside that large gouge in the wall. Claws.
Ember pulled off the sweater so that her scales were free.
Someone had to know what happened to them. As soon as the

thought struck her, she wasn't sure who she was talking about—the dragons, or her moms.

"How come no one recognizes you?" Ember asked him.

"What do you mean?"

"If your parents have been involved for so many years, shouldn't they know you?" Ember questioned, rubbing the oil again on her lids. She turned to him and leaned against the sink.

"The resistance isn't as organized as they seem. The scribe-masters speak to all factions, but there isn't a set system or organization structure. Most of the time, the groups across the provinces don't speak," Noor explained and sighed.

Then he burst into laughter.

"What?" Ember asked, momentarily anxious at the outburst.

She looked back at her reflection and laughed too, the oil had smeared black all over her eyelids and into her brows. Well, at least he wasn't laughing at her the next day when the black was not only on her face, but on their pillows and blankets.

She quickly dabbed her small towel back into the oil and worked to get the rest of the makeup off her face.

"I can see why you like it down there. It's...different from the castle, different from any place I've been," Ember added as his laughter died down.

And that was true. Ember knew it. The closest she had ever been to that much companionship was when she was with her moms, but that life felt so removed from who she was now that sometimes she felt like it was a dream. Had it actually been only two years ago that she was eating dinner at the family table alone, wondering why her moms weren't home yet? Her eyes drifted to the door briefly, imagining them helping Karwyn get ready in the same room that she now slept.

Noor's face lightened, as if the gravity of Aaleia was lifted from him. He stood behind her and smiled into her now-clean face, oblivious to the tilt of her thoughts.

"Noor, I need to ask you something," she said. Her tone changed, and his light face sobered. When she saw she had his full attention, she asked a question. The only question that she needed answered for them to move on.

She had not forgiven him for the lies. She would not forget that he didn't bring this to her first, but she could move on if he agreed.

"I am in this now. I will hear out the rebels," he winced a little at the term, "but if they did kill my moms in cold blood, if I find out they hurt people intentionally or are involved in some other danger that I don't agree with, I will make them pay for it. If that happens, I need you to leave them behind and not look back. Will you do that?"

Noor stood from the edge of the tub and held both her hands. "I promise you, Embrence Dragon Daughter. I will leave with you and help you take out whatever punishment you see fit if that were to happen. You can trust me."

"How do I know I can trust you, Noor? You've already lied and went behind my back," Ember whispered to him.

"Because, Em, I have one more secret to tell you. It could mean someone's death, this secret." His eyes watered and his voice cracked. This was not the answer Ember expected.

"Are you sure you want to tell it to me?" Ember asked. She feared what this could be, but knew that if someone's life was on the line it should be shared without care.

"Yes," he said. Noor edged closer to her, a hair's breadth from her face. In a whisper, Noor told her the one thing he had not told anyone.

"My sister, Naomi, is alive. She is Fateless and has been in hiding for years. She was not killed, like I let you and everyone else believe."

Tears streamed down his face, a constant flow as he

confessed. Naomi had always cared for him as a child, stepping in when his parents hadn't. When she went mad, he took care of her instead.

"I don't trust the community homes," he said. "Not yet, anyway. I think there is something more to it. Something Jedoriah Knight hasn't revealed yet. I want to keep her in hiding. Will you keep my secret?"

Ember felt the trust he was giving to her, the torch he now asked her heart to bear too.

For her birth mother, Ember said yes. Because if the queen was granted life in madness, then it should be available to all. If all went to plan with the community homes, maybe Naomi could join later. For now, she would ease this pain for Noor.

"I promise to keep your secret," Ember whispered back. The trust that they had the moment of their fating began to flow back into place.

They had a lot to learn together, but they would do it —together.

He nuzzled his face into her neck. She leaned into his touch, feeling the scruff of his unshaved facial hair coming through.

Kissing her neck, his own arms snaked out from around her waist and went up to her hair. He lifted his face away and gently undid the black scarf that wrapped in with her braid.

Her short hair fell down into waves, very unlike their usual straightness. He unpinned her bangs and ruffled them.

"The day you are in charge is the day I will feel at peace," Noor said, his arms on Ember's shoulders. Ember's breath halted. "Why?" she asked. She wasn't at peace with the idea at all. Her? Responsible for the well-being of the whole kingdom? And a *baby*? She only just got used to the idea of thinking of herself as more than a dirty secret.

"Because you listen, you try, you give everyone a chance. Not many people would do that," he answered.

Ember held herself closer to him, enamored that he felt that way.

"I grew up hiding," she whispered to him, inches from his lips. Something she now knew his sister had in common.

"I don't want other people to have to hide too." She was surprised that it rang true. Surprised that she had quickly identified something she needed to believe in and fight for. It clicked into place today. Her moms. The Fateless. Naomi. Karwyn. And she welcomed it.

"I can respect that. I respect you," he said, leaning down to kiss her lips. She shivered, but not from the cold. She felt a quivering in her heart, a pull like when they first met. Ember brought her own arms up to run her fingers through his hair, standing on her tiptoes and pulling closer to him.

In their short week together, they had fallen into each other's arms often. To hug, kiss, sleep. To feel. But in this way, they hadn't yet crossed. At first, Ember wasn't sure why they had prolonged it. Their love was inevitable, a soul matching a soul. Aaleia guaranteed that with their fating. But she knew, instinctually, the pull to complete their bond was happening now because she had learned more about him and his desires. She knew now this other part of him, the hero and little brother in him that complemented his position as knight.

Noor groaned into her mouth, and she felt his body rise against her. Heat exploded from her chest, and she moaned back, his arms inched lower.

As Noor pulled her closer, she fumbled with the buttons on the linen shirt he wore, eventually giving up and untucking it from his pants to pull it off. Noor loosened his grip on her body to let her take the shirt off. He pulled back and flew out of his trousers. He began walking them backwards until they were falling backward onto the furs and soul-thread that lay across her bed. Ember pulled her undershirt off. All that was left between them was her pants and his underwear.

"Are you sure?" Noor asked Ember, panting in between a kiss.

"Yes," Ember gasped out as Noor's hand dipped to take off his underwear and her own pants. They didn't stop touching each other, hands groping and lips kissing wherever their skin could touch. Their bodies burned together in a slow rhythmic dance. Feeling each atom between them collide, they sighed into each other.

She felt whole and lost, perfect and broken, at home and both in another world while in his arms. She wouldn't have it any other way.

"Em," Noor said in the dark. He ran his hand along the soft skin of her back.

"Hm?" she said groggily, cracking open an eye. Sunlight streamed into their room. The soul-thread refracted subtle light.

"When my sister started getting sick, she could tell it was happening. Because of that, my family wrote down what we each would do if we too became Fateless. We discussed as a family what our wishes would be. She said she'd want to stay with us. If something were to happen to you—" Noor choked, having trouble continuing the thought.

"You want to know what I'd want for myself, if I were sick like Karwyn?" she pressed, the seriousness of the conversation waking her. He nodded.

If dragon blood allowed her birth mom to gain a pair and a child, while Fateless? The same thing could happen to her, even with Noor in her life, Ember wasn't sure what she would do. But as she opened her mouth to say so, she knew the truth of it. A hard truth to say aloud.

"If Oma and Jedoriah are alive, I do not want to be trapped and played up like a puppet. Not like the queen. I would rather die. If they aren't with us, I would like you to decide how to care for me,"

The line between Noor's eyes grew tight and he reached to hug Ember. She held him back and was reminded again why no one could know the queen was sick. If the Fateless evolved in a way that anyone could become sick, if it progressed past this dragon blood exception, she didn't know what the people of Ashkadance would do.

"When your family asked, what did you say you would want?" Ember asked him, her head tucked into his neck.

"I left it up to whoever survived me. If I am gone, mentally unaware and not myself, I'd want you to do what would give you the most peace."

Her scales pressed against him, chest to chest, and heart to heart.

EIGHTEEN

NOT OF YOUR CONCERN

Zhieve knocked on her bedroom door an hour later.

"Have a good time," Noor said as he kissed her cheek. "I can't wait to hear all about it." He joined Wally and left the tower.

Ember felt giddy as they left the castle and walked down the drive towards the stables and carriages. When she was Ember Julimore, daughter to Julimore Instructor and Echoris Guider, she had seen the royal family as people that ruled with fear. Now that she was one of them, she didn't know what to think. She had faith that her purpose was doing good, after years of hoping to just persevere, it was nice to feel like she suffered for a cause all along.

Even if her relationship with her family, Jedoriah and Karwyn in particular, was strained—it was worth it. To do this for Karwyn, prove it could work for Noor's sister, and for the people that would need it.

In echoing steps behind her, she and her entourage met Jedoriah and his men in the main entranceway. Amir nodded to Zhieve. The man barely glanced at him. The beautiful face that matched his red hair shared a mask of indifference.

"Are you ready, Embrence?" the head knight asked as the carriage doors opened before them. He wore his usual black suit with gold accents.

"Yes, Jedoriah Knight," she answered, looking around them for her grandmother. If he kept insisting on calling her Embrence, she would call him by his full name. He seemed to enjoy his full name. His wide smile left her uncomfortable.

She looked away, wondering what it would have been like to grow up in the castle. Would he'd have taught her how to ride beasts in the garden? Time could have brought them together, but right now he was a somewhat cold and overbearing influence. Karwyn, while someone she felt bonded to, wasn't much better. Ember wished she knew what their relationship would have been without the pressure of a foreboding madness and missing years.

"We should be on our way then," Jedoriah murmured as he took her arm and helped her up the step of the carriage. It must be a shorter distance then, a few hours maximum if they didn't need one of the beasts built for endurance to pull them on their journey.

Once settled in the carriage, Ember asked, "Where is Oma?"

"She had other concerns to attend to today," Jedoriah responded as the door clicked closed. The red soft interior of the seating stood out compared to the blue dress Ember wore.

"Is it anything that I can help with?" Ember asked, worrying how much Oma had to take on without the kingdom knowing. Jedoriah didn't seem to mind the extra duties. Maybe she could lessen some of that load too if they would let her.

"Work to fight the rebels, not for your concern," he responded flippantly. Ember's face twitched quickly before she could stop it. She wished Noor was here. Or that at least Cindrea was sitting in here with her, rather than riding with guardsmen in the carriage beside them. This space was too big for the two of them to sit alone.

"Shouldn't Noor be involved in anything related to the rebels? He is my knight," Ember asked. Noor was head of her security, and he should be involved in anything related to the rebels—plus, he was one. Ember paused, realizing that she too was one now. They'd have to find out what was said.

"He's not suitable," he said with a slight sneer to his lips, as if acknowledging him was a bad taste in his mouth. Maybe it was. When Ember was queen, Noor would be head knight. Jedoriah would no longer be in charge of much of anything.

"What about him is unsuitable?" Ember asked incredulously. She crossed her arms and the carriage began to move forward.

"He does not understand what it takes to be a knight. What sacrifices are required," Jedoriah's face went up to the covered sky before turning to Ember. His face became stillness as he added, "don't push the subject."

But she would. Once she spoke with Oma to see her plans for the rebels, she would bring up this conversation.

"Aaleia thought he was suitable," Ember pressed.

"And Aaleia is not all-knowing," Jedoriah countered. Ember was aghast, how could a divinely chosen ruler disagree with the will of the gods?

Just as much as he liked praise, he disliked questions.

The rest of the ride to the community home was uncomfortable. Ember tried to focus on the sights around her, as Azororion was one of the two provinces that she and her moms had never lived, but each quiet moment had Ember replaying the conversation in her head.

Jedoriah made decisions quickly and without consultation of others, he was comfortable with the death of their people, only deciding to change their Fateless policies when the people began to change opinion and rebellions grew. He had no problem hiding away the queen, his pair, and taking on as much of her role as possible. What snap decision had he made about Noor?

"He's not suitable," echoed in Ember's consciousness.

At their first rest stop, Ember insisted that Cindrea join their carriage. The two girls maintained quiet conversation until they arrived. Cindrea found it much easier to ignore Jedoriah Knight.

THE COMMUNITY HOME was not what Ember expected from their early conversations. At least, it didn't appear like the comfortable facility she had imagined from the outside.

Standing in front of it, the building appeared cold and overbearing. It was a tall building of cracked peiradoone stone. She didn't even know the material could crack. Feather-black lines marred its surface and the color of the stone itself. Well, it was as grey as soot. Not the blinding white she was used too.

"Why does the building look damaged?" Ember whispered as her eyes trailed around the mass of it.

"Because it's almost as old as the First Fating," Jedoriah answered. His tone showed more appreciation than the apprehension Ember felt.

"Why are we using such an old structure?" Ember questioned.

"We needed a building that could hold several dozen people and staff, and these are old war buildings. It would have been wasteful to not utilize it when it worked well for our needs. There are four of them across the kingdom. That should hold those newly inflicted with room to grow."

His voice took on a lecturing tone that she did not appreciate.

The phrase *newly inflicted* reminded Ember that the Fateless were murdered until recently. The dead eyes of that nameless man flew into her memory unbidden. She couldn't think about that now.

Knowing that the building was made for war and soldiers, the tall enclosure with small windows seemed appropriate. The thick door, opened before them with two guards in place, must have helped protect them from a siege.

Attempting optimism, Ember said, "then I'm excited to see how the inside is being renovated."

"They better re-do the sidewalk at least. This is a tripping hazard," Cindrea said as they walked up the drive.

The inside did appear cleaner to Ember's relief. There was something like a reception area with seating upon entering. Beyond that, she could not see, as an in-progress doorway blocked her vision. Men and women worked around them, filing paperwork behind the counter and taking in supplies.

"Welcome," a timid voice said.

Ember smiled as the short woman came into view from behind the construction. "Hello."

"A pleasure to meet you, Embrence Dragon Daughter. I am Farlein Doctor. I will be studying the Fateless." She spoke in soft but punctuated syllables.

"A pleasure to meet you," Ember said as Cindrea and Jedoriah shook the doctor's hands.

"Let's give the dragon daughter a tour," Jedoriah said as he gestured towards the door and the construction beyond. Farlein's small stature walked ahead of them.

"One benefit to the prior structure is the way the rooms are laid out. Each door leads into another room, and they all connect together. We are keeping that layout, with only a few additional divisions to create small guard and doctor stations," Farlein said. She tucked a strand of her brown hair behind her ear as she led them from one room to another. The space turned them around in a circle.

"And in the back of the building, there will be a recreational yard. We would like to study the effects of physical activity on the patients," she continued.

Ember stared at the door, imagining the queen walking through it and into another garden. Trapped in one building of stone to another, with greenery. If her biological mother came here, her life might be better. More people to interact with. Less seclusion. But also, chaos on the streets. She shook herself as Cindrea put her hand behind Ember's back, "pay attention," the older woman hissed quietly.

"Come this way," Farlein said as she walked with a construction team member. Amir appeared behind them, having gone on his own private tour. He had said it was to check the security of the building. She knew it was to gather information for the rebellion. Or both. He was exceptionally good at his job. They followed as Farlein explained, "Through this door, we have the quarantine area."

"Why would someone need quarantine?" Ember asked.

"When new patients come in we need to keep them separate from the others to confirm the plague. We anticipate some families may drop people off who are inflicted with other diseases besides being Fateless. Here we will weed out other possible contagions.

"Through these doors are the stairs to the dorms. We'll have three floors of dorm rooms for the sick," Farlein said as they continued on the tour. Most of the first foundation floor was complete, but the upper levels weren't yet ready for use. Seeing the rooms for the Fateless would have to wait for the next visit in a month's time.

"There is much still to do," Jedoriah commented.

"I agree," Ember said. She realized it was one of the first things she remembered agreeing with him on. But it was a promising list of to-dos. Farlein, at her advice, was going to check in with some local scribes for their records on the Fateless. With their studies, it could help gain any other information that would help get them started.

On the way out the doors, one of Jedoriah's guards gasped.

One of the more quiet guards, Moniker, glowed gold, as did a woman at the end of the hall. She started to cry, running towards Moniker.

"I thought I'd never find you," she said, wrapping her arms around his wide torso. He held her back, kissing her hair and face. Gold sparks erupted around them, encircling them. She let go, shock spreading across her face.

The sparkle began to transform into purple. She looked down at her middle and swelled, a small pop to bring their blessing into being. Barely a bump, but a life. Blessings and fatings didn't often come together. In fact, this was the first time Ember herself had seen Aaleia and Mutrien work in tandem at first sight. It was beautiful. Moniker's hands came to sit atop the nurse's stomach.

"Hello," he spoke to her stomach.

"Hi," she whispered back, her hand covering his own.

Jedoriah chuckled. "See you tomorrow, Moniker Guard."

As the only man fated to someone who was Fateless, Ember wondered if seeing that special moment hurt him.

"Congratulations," Ember said to them both as she passed with Amir and Cindrea. They nodded to her absently, more preoccupied with their lives coming together than speaking to the heir.

Walking up the drive a few hours later, Amir followed closely behind. Cindrea lingered to speak with the driver, a man Ember hadn't had the chance to know yet.

"Did you get what you needed?" she asked, knowing Amir was in earshot.

"Yes," he responded simply.

He's not suitable.

"There is something else I need for you to do," she said,

unsure if this new fear in her chest was warranted. But after what Jedoriah said and Oma attending to a mysterious rebel matter, they had to be cautious. Ember was not going to let her new-found purpose become a jail, not like the queen.

"Whatever you need," he replied sincerely. His boots clicked on the floor in rhythm with her own.

"We need to have emergency bags packed. All of us," she declared. He knew she meant themselves, Noor, and Wally. The core group in her life. Rebels.

"I'll see to it," he said. Ember smiled at the pride in his voice.

NINETEEN

WITHOUT SECRETS

The weeks that followed brought Ember to heights unknown. While the conversation with Jedoriah had caused her to worry, no action had come from it. In fact, Jedoriah had begun to distance himself further from her even more than before. Other than in their weekly history lessons on Aaleia, Mutrien, and the two foreign kingdoms across the sea, she saw him only during mealtime. Oma kept him busy, pulling him into meetings and seeing he took on extra tasks like the new filtration system for Ashkadance's water supply.

Life with Noor had never been better. Without secrets, each day they got to learn the little details that made each other special. They had spent the morning getting to know each other particularly well, and in the afterglow, they came together for breakfast with her family. Some days, they didn't make it down to breakfast at all. Today was not one of those days.

"I have something to discuss with you all," Oma said around the table that morning. She folded her hands together before her food, steam curling upward from the mug to her left.

"Is everything alright?" Ember asked, unconsciously

mirroring her movements. She reasoned that everything had to be fine, if not this conversation wouldn't happen in public. Her heart didn't typically follow logic. Karwyn cleared her throat at the end of her table. The gurgling sound from her mouth lingered too long as her eye was drawn away by a wraith sitting atop a tree.

"Fireheart, I don't have much time left here," Oma answered. A stray wind picked up her white hair.

"What a delight!" Karwyn called with a jump from her seat, her cream dress wild with the movement. She ran from the table towards the sitting dragon-relative with her arms splayed open. Guards ran after the mad queen, while Ember turned back to the dragon matron. She was used to it. At least her mother wasn't violent like many of the other Fateless she had met as the homes began to take on guests.

Noor squeezed her hand before he too left to help Karwyn. Her voice drifted farther and farther away. Only Jedoriah, Oma, and Ember remained seated at the thick glass table. There were vines similar to her debut ball in the center of the table, dried out and curling.

"What do you mean when you say you don't have much time left?" Ember coached her voice to speak in a level tone. Was she sick? Dread pooled in Ember's chest quickly and irrationally.

"This is not my home, I came to meet you and help you get acclimated, but you don't need that anymore. I have to go back to Cruelindime and reassert our presence on the other side of Ashkadance. The Mutrien ball is coming soon," Oma explained.

Breath exhaled in a rush, Ember almost laughed for having immediately thought Oma was dying. Then the words hit home.

"You're leaving?"

Her voice creaked like the door of the last home she held with her moms.

———

"THE LAST KNOWN dragon known to fly over Ashkadance was sixty years ago when the dragon matron was only twelve," Ahnika lectured. Ember barely heard her above the roaring in her head. Minutes went by without notice.

"Embrence, really, it is as if you aren't even trying," Ahnika scolded. Ember blinked, the haze of her thoughts dissipating. She re-drew her focus, reminded briefly of Amlin Jeweler's lectures.

"Yes, Drakul died a mortal death," she blurted when her eyes cleared enough to see the expectant look on Ahnika's face.

"Right, that would have been relevant to the conversation twenty minutes ago. It is not, however, relevant to the disappearance of dragons altogether."

"Well, maybe it is," Ember attempted to argue, trying to bring back favor of her teacher.

"Why would that be?" Ahnika questioned, leaning back against the desk next to Ember's.

"Well, Drakul died because he began to live a human life. His dragon life would outlive Kariana's, so he stopped transforming so they could age and die together..." A lightbulb went off in Ember's mind.

"And?" Ahnika prodded, leaning forward to hear the theory.

"Maybe something happened to the dragons that were left, shortening their lives similar to how Drakul's timespan changed in this environment, but we wouldn't be able to know what it was since our line is no longer able to talk to dragons. Maybe they stopped coming here because we couldn't help them anymore?"

Ember felt proud for the sudden idea, thinking it might actually prove interesting to her instructor. Echoris would have been proud.

"If that were true, then you are saying all dragons, everywhere, are dead or dying from some life-shortening illness or condition with no one to help them," Ahnika commented somberly.

"If they aren't dead, where else would they be?" Ember hadn't even realized what she was theorizing, but the thought of all dragons in the world as dead hadn't even crossed her mind before. There would have to be less dragons, for sure, but all gone? She absently grazed her hand over her scales, now more a part of her than she ever would have thought months ago. In her heart, dragons were just not here.

"Well you did mention one thing we know for sure," Ahnika said as she stood up again.

"What was that?"

"The royal family no longer has the ability to talk to dragons and other beasts. If the queen, or you," Ahnika gestured to Ember, "saw one miraculously, you wouldn't be able to ask them where they have been for sixty years."

She sat at her desk. "Anyone would leave if they couldn't communicate."

Could the merfolk speak to dragons, Ember wondered, if their claim to speak to the gods was true?

Two hours later and still charged by the conversation with Ahnika, Ember knocked on Jedoriah's office.

"Who is it?" his muffled voice asked.

"Ember," she called.

A shuffling sounded within and the door unlocked. Taking it as a sign that she should come in, Ember cautiously entered. Jedoriah sat behind stacks of papers, organizing them into piles. Several also lay crumbled on the floor.

"What is it, Embrence?"

"I had some thoughts I'd like to run by you," Ember said. She sat in front of his long desk hesitantly. The candlestick flickered at her movement. She glanced at the other lights sources in the room, none of them shared the calm steadiness of the bloodfire that surrounded her tower.

He looked up from his stacks, his grey-blue hair uncharacteristically messy.

"What's on your mind?" Jedoriah asked.

"The wall..." she began, unsure how to even bring about her thoughts.

"What about it?" His posture straightened.

"If we are unable to communicate with the other two kingdoms, how do we know that the dragons are gone? What if they came back to Grydagia and Faeinto instead? How do we know that the other kingdoms don't already have *a cure for the Fateless?*"

Ember's thoughts pushed out in a rush. She had meant to lead with dragons and then bring in the idea of a cure, but her heart jumped ahead of her. A cure. A mother. Oma will still leave, but the idea of getting to know her mother? She couldn't shake it.

"They don't have a cure."

His voice was clipped and defiant.

"How do you know?" Ember gripped the clawed hands of her chair.

"Karwyn became Fateless because of them and their lack of help with the merfolk. We put up the walls to keep this from happening to anyone else. If the same happened to the other kingdoms, and they didn't create their own wall, then the merfolk have destroyed them by now."

At each mention of the merfolk, his body became tense.

"But we have more Fateless than ever before. Every year there are more. We have to be able to communicate. We have no way of knowing it is any different out there, right?"

Ember tried to temper her anger, heat flared in bursts through her heart, but she pushed it down. She didn't know everything about their resources yet, for all she knew there was more to this.

"I know that it is different, end of story." He stood, walking out from behind his desk. His dark cloak moved with him, causing the candles on his desk to flicker once more in the waving movement.

"There is unrest from former tradesmen and sailors. We can't import any goods. Do you know how much peiradoone we have left? The Fateless aren't getting better. What is this wall solving anymore?" Ember said defiantly.

His hand rested on the door handle, looking towards where Ember now stood.

"This is the way things are now. We are walled in. It is all that we can do to protect our kingdom. Now leave," he seemed forlorn, defeated, his face weary.

"We need help. We need resources," she pleaded, thinking of all the suffering she had witnessed from the rebels.

Jedoriah opened the door, gesturing for her to walk out of his office.

"Why are you so unwilling to discuss anything?" Ember asked him, exasperated.

"I'm the only help you are ever going to have, Ember, and there is only so much I can give you an answer for," he said, ignoring the question.

Feeling braver than she ever had in his presence before, she said, "I will be queen one day. I may have never wanted it, dreamed of it, but it is a fact. It is my *purpose*. When that happens, these half-baked answers aren't going to work anymore."

She walked through the door into the light of the hallway.

"The wall is coming down," Ember declared defiantly, the door still open behind her.

Karwyn stepped forward from the end of the hall, guards and her lady in waiting in her tow. Jedoriah's office stood only feet away from the queen's tower. On the opposite side of the hallway stood Cindrea, pushing a tray of tea. All that was missing was Noor.

"You don't know what sacrifices are being made for this kingdom every day," Jedoriah said, looking between all the parties present and closed the door.

Karwyn's giggle startled Ember out of her shock.

"And what do you have to add about the Fateless, the dragons, and the wall, my queen?" Ember asked cruelly, knowing it was inappropriate and biting. She wanted to take it back the second the words were out, seeing a shadow pass over the queen's face. Ember felt hopeless. Her only royal ally, her Oma, was leaving, and she would be left with a mom that had told her she didn't belong and a knight that didn't see reason or speak to her with any sort of fondness.

"If only you knew how often my thoughts spiraled on the subject. Gone, gone, gone," Karwyn repeated, her sing-song tone helping to carry her voice across the hall as she walked closer to Ember. She flittered her fingers into the air, creating a pattern.

"I'd very much like to know your thoughts," Ember whispered as the queen passed.

"Always listen to your father!" Karwyn yelled as she passed. The guards guided her farther out of the way, towards the passage that would lead her up into the tower that mirrored her own. Cindrea turned as the queen passed, watching her back as Ember did the same.

She turned and smiled somberly to Ember.

"Can I help you with anything?" Cindrea asked as she wheeled the tea cart forward.

Ignoring the question, Ember asked instead, "why are you bringing Jedoriah Knight tea?"

"I made tea for him and Karwyn when I was her lady in waiting. Now Jedoriah doesn't like how the new girl does it," she shrugged as if there was nothing else she can do about it. Nodding to Ember, she added "I'll head back to your rooms shortly."

Cindrea knocked on his door and then turned the knob, entering without waiting for his reply. Ember turned back the way she came, disappointed, weary, and alone.

Behind her she heard a crash and a gasp, the tea set falling behind a closed door.

"No, not now!" Jedoriah's voice sounded through the door.

Whether the tea fell onto his papers or Jedoriah decided throwing tea was better than drinking it, Ember did not care. She'd check on Cindrea later, but this was the last she wanted to see of Jedoriah for a while.

TWENTY

STRUCTURAL DAMAGES

The light of the stars lit their pathway between the trees.

"Did Jade say what this was about?" Ember asked as she adjusted her scarf, dropping Noor's hand. Her few shirts that hid her scales were being laundered. The quality and shape of her clothes changed dramatically since joining the castle. Now there were decadent materials and a variety of cuts, most showing what she had kept hidden her whole life. Not having something to wear, when her clothes had quadrupled, was a surprise.

"No, she just said there was news," he shrugged as if it were a normal occurrence. For all she knew it was. She hadn't been a rebel for long.

"But why us and not everyone else?" she questioned nervously.

"You know all four of us shouldn't attend the same meetings, it isn't safe," Noor assured her.

Logically she knew that was the truth, but having Amir or Wally with them calmed her nerves. Noor could protect her, but she wasn't confident that she could protect him if anything were to happen. But she did her best to keep those fears hidden. Noor was her knight, and she could trust his judgment.

They settled into camp in the same way they had the previous meetings. However, this time the tent held more people than an average meeting. Noor introduced her to a few people she hadn't met yet and they all sat down together to hear Jade's news. Her energy was palpable the second she walked into the tent.

"We've found them!" Jade declared to the group of seated men and women in front of her. Her skin glowed brightly in the firelight. Ember re-crossed her legs with difficulty. This floor was not meant for the long dress of a lady in waiting. She glanced at her scarf and pin, making sure it was still in place.

"Found what?" a man called impatiently. "Why did you call us here?" Another asked. If they were concerned too, maybe this wasn't a normal occurrence. Ember absently bit off one of her nails.

"I have called you all here tonight because the inventory on the wall's defenses is complete," Jade said. Her eyes tracked the room as she spoke.

A hush stole through the seated crowd. Ember's hand gripped Noor's as he smiled encouragingly to her. Did he know about this project already?

"What did you find out?" an older woman asked near the front.

"I have brought in the scribemaster to discuss our findings," Jade said. She turned to her left and Ember noticed the figure seated at Jade's desk.

"Hello," he replied with a nod to the crowd. They all seemed to know him well and Ember realized moments later that she did too.

"Isn't that—"

"Yes, he is the scribe from the market. He is one of the scribemasters," Noor whispered in her ear.

"What is a scribemaster? Should we be worried that he knows us?" Ember asked quietly.

"I'll explain after. We're safe with him, don't worry," Noor assured her.

"There are weak points in the wall all across the kingdom. Dozens of them, in fact," Jardano answered the crowd, a wheeze escaping him. He inhaled deeply before speaking again.

"We have found structural inconsistencies that we may be able to exploit. Not even peiradoone is impenetrable. It couldn't be when the wall was created in a rush. Many different craftsmen and different standards of work coming together. We are lucky, very lucky, that speed was needed those almost seventeen years ago," he said. The crowd murmured their agreement, edging closer and coming to a stand.

Could this be true? Ember's heart beat faster. An opportunity. This was opportunity knocking for her to meet her promise to Jedoriah during their argument. When it was her turn, she could remove the wall. Or at the least, create a door. Ember felt the urge to free her scales right then, to lift her heart to these people and assert that she would do this for them. But not yet, it wasn't safe. She had questions that needed answers first.

Murmurs rose in the crowd and questions of when, where, and how began to build until everyone was standing. They were excited, crying, and hopeful as they hugged their neighbors. They spoke of their dreams and a change of purpose, giddy that opportunity was possible for them too.

"I can go back to the sea," the woman in the front row said. Noor hugged her then, feeling the energy all around them.

"I feel like I was waiting for this," Ember whispered to Noor. He leaned in to hear her above the noise and celebration. People began leaving the tent to tell their families, while others came to pile in and hear what was happening. A movement of mirrored emotions surrounded them, but Ember only had eyes for Noor. He looked back at her, understanding instantly what she wanted to say before she even said it out loud.

"We have some work to do," she said.

"It is my purpose," he responded back, eyes twinkling with mischief.

Their lips met with a promise.

An hour later, as the meeting began to come to a close, Ember pulled Noor to the side to speak as they waited.

"Tell me about the scribemaster," she requested.

"A scribemaster is a leader among the scribes, someone that brings together information across different provinces. They are vital to the cause," Noor explained quickly. They whispered in the corner of the tent, waiting for the crowd to dissipate so they could have their chance with Jardano.

"And how do you know him?"

"He got me in the resistance here. Well, Amir did, but remember when we spoke to him the first time in the market?"

Ember nodded her head.

"I said a resistance code phrase, something only current members and family of them would know. Jardano told Amir what I said so that he could keep an eye on me and get me into the group."

The conversation came flittering back to Ember.

"*I've always been one to appreciate the guidance of the scribes,*" she quoted back to him.

"Yes! That is the phrase. Most scribes are connected somehow to the resistance. Many aren't active members, mostly relaying information to the scribemaster as needed. You know, it's natural for scribes to question what's going on around them." Noor beamed as he explained, happy to bring Ember into more of the world he knew.

"Brook, Emairy," Jade called, gesturing they join her and the Scribemaster.

"Would you two be willing to escort Jardano home? Emairy, he has some info on your princess's concern."

"Really?" Ember asked, hope and fear blossoming in her chest. Jardano smiled at Ember.

"A pleasure to meet you." He waited for her to introduce herself.

"Emairy," Ember replied, shaking his outstretched hand. He smiled mischievously, a twinkle in his eye at their little secret.

"Emairy, a pleasure. Will you escort me back to my book shop?"

"We'd love to," Noor answered for her.

"It is lovely to see you again, Embrence Dragon Daughter," Jardano said as he, Noor, and Ember walked across the loading area to his shop. Even after the resistance wore out his voice with questions, he was still in a spirited mood. She smiled back at him.

"Thank you for letting us walk you back to your shop," Ember said, "I wish you would let us walk you to your home." She didn't like the idea of him being at his purpose so late.

"I actually sleep in the back room," he commented with some hesitation.

"Why is that?" Noor asked, treading delicately as he looped his hand through the weathered man's arm. His hunched form straightened slightly with the assistance.

"It's easier to get around that way, stay close to where I'm needed."

"That makes sense," she told him, understanding why he may want to remain close. It couldn't be comfortable to travel this often at his age.

Once settled inside the store, Ember began overcome with jitteriness. If Jardano knew both the resistance and her true identity, he had to have the answers. Noor and Ember sat on the two seats before his desk, Jardano shuffled to get some tea.

Books surrounded all surfaces of his desk. One spot lay

empty, mug rings littered its space from repeated use. If she weren't so nervous, she would have found the stains cute. He placed two steaming tea cups in front of them before he too sat down. Ember felt like her heart was exploding out of her chest.

"I was raised by Echoris Guider and Julimore Instructor before coming to find myself in the castle," Ember began. Sweat pooled around her neck and she fiddled with the loop. Unable to handle the droplet that was seconds away from dripping onto her scales, Ember pulled the scarf off and dropped the fabric to her lap. Her body shivered at the freedom and she opened her mouth to start again.

"I was told they died in a rebel attack. What do you know of their deaths?" Ember started again in an even tone. Her eyes stared straight into the hazel of Jardano's.

He took a sip of tea, his hands trembling as he brought the cup to his mouth. He seemed to save his breath, waiting a moment to plan what he said. Ember began to feel choked up, unable to move or breathe. What was she about to hear?

Tears began to line her eyes, and Ember pushed them back. She had to be present right now. She couldn't let her feelings cloud what information he could share with her.

The look she found on Jardano's face was not a comfort.

"What do you know?" Noor asked, his body going taut with attention. Her hands gripped harder on the scarf in her lap.

"They weren't killed in the resistance attack, my dear," he addressed to Ember. "They were murdered by castle guards. Given what we know now, the guards might have found out about you, and they died defending the secret." His eyes softened as he delivered the blow, reaching forward to reach for her hand across the cluttered desk.

Noor's sharp inhale drew her eyes away. Her horror reflected back at her.

"As covert members of the scribes, they gathered information and reported it to members across Ashkadance. They were researchers for the cause. Guards had been on their tail. They told me in our last meeting," Jardano confessed.

"You knew them personally?" Noor asked.

"Yes, but I did not know you, my dear," Jardano said to Ember. "You were a treasure they were hiding. I had worked with them for four years, and they never mentioned a daughter. They got information on their travels and reported back. Their loss hurt me greatly."

His voice drifted off as he looked from her face to the visible scales on her chest.

Ember's breath came back to her in bursts, her chest jumping up and down as she gulped in more and more. She jumped from her chair turning away from Noor and Jardano.

Was anything in her life what it seemed? Did she have any bits of truth to fall back on? Ember feared the answer was no.

"Ember, it'll be okay," Noor reached for her waist, trying to pull her close to him.

"No!" Ember screamed, pushing farther into the bookstore and away from him. Her life, her heart, her name, purpose, family, none of it was her own. Control belonged to everyone but her and she didn't have a home. Shoots of pain ran up her arms and she held them, rubbing her skin violently to push away the shivers of fire.

She collapsed to the floor, holding onto the leg of the table that held religious texts.

Sobs racked her body, the truth a crushing blow to what was left of her memories. Her moms, murdered for information on her and the scribes. They were part of the keepers of this world, the researchers and readers that uncovered all secrets. Jardano said he only worked with them for four years. Had they worked with someone else before? Were they working for the scribes before they became maids in the castle? Was it all part of a plan?

They had chosen Ember, decided she was theirs. It was not

from the divine blessing of Mutrien, but because they loved her purely. It meant more to Ember that they chose her. But did they, or was she a means to learn more? She'd never know what they felt. She could only hope that they loved her the way she loved them.

Guards had killed her moms. Who? By whose command? There was one obvious suspect.

Salty tears warmed Ember's skin, mingling with the heat of her broken heart and the shaking of her limbs.

"What's happening in here?" Jade's voice rang out from the door, concern, and confusion dripped from her.

Ember froze on the floor, fear stifling her anger and sadness. Her scarf lay on the chair ten feet away. Ember couldn't move without risk of being discovered. She had to keep her back turned.

"It was an emotional evening for the dear, all the talk about the wall, you know," Jardano said, side-stepping any mention of her moms. "Come, let's give them some privacy." Jardano stood and attempted to usher her aside.

Jade stood still in the doorway, but Noor did not. Quickly he was at Ember's side, his body crouched over hers. "It's going to be okay," he whispered. He leaned down to hug her and when he did, Ember could feel the scarf he wedged between them. She ducked into the embrace of his wide shoulders, looping her scarf around her neck.

"Emairy, Brook, my favorite lovebird spies. Are you okay?" Jade questioned again, ignoring Jardano's suggestions. She walked through and closed the door.

Ember tried to laugh, but it didn't sound as airy as she had hoped. Instead, she clung to Noor's side. Her scales were covered, as was their cover story. But did she want that? Noor had given her an out; she was still safe. Life had ideas to the contrary. She would no longer be pulled to the whim of others. It was time to forge her own path.

Her heart catapulted into a gallop, she knew what she had to do. Noor wasn't going to like it.

"Actually, I'm not okay," Ember answered honestly. Noor's arm around her waist tightened.

"What's wrong?" Jade asked with concern. She walked towards them, weaving around stacks of books.

"I will be queen one day," Ember stated. Jade's face went from shock to disbelief, her eyes widening and then narrowing again as she decided it was a joke. She opened her mouth to laugh.

The laughter died before it could gain steam as Ember pulled the scarf back off of her neck.

"You—you—" Jade stuttered.

"I am Embrence Dragon Daughter. You have my ear and dedication," she stated. Her moms worked for the scribes and their scribemaster. The scribes worked with the resistance. This was their mission, she was part of that mission. She had to follow it through. For them, but also for herself.

Noor smiled at her, and she felt the pride he felt through his smile. But he was also a knight. His hand left her waist to instead sit on his hip, inches from his knife.

"Flaming stars, Brook you are a dragon turd for not telling me this!" Her voice was mystified, staring wide-eyed at Ember's purple and green scales.

"I'm Noorworth Knight, by the way," Noor said as he walked passed the shocked resistance leader.

"We have a lot of work to do. Sit down," Ember said, gesturing to the chair she had exited moments ago.

TWENTY-ONE

TWO WRAITHS, ONE STONE

"Fireheart, I have some bad news," Oma said the next morning. Cindrea excused herself, leaving Ember alone with the dragon matron in her bedroom. Oma's hair was tied in intricate braids, looping around her hair to mimic a crown. It reminded Ember of the hairstyle she wore to her debut, a subtle way to remind the people of her standing.

"Is everything okay?" Ember asked, turning away from the mirror and the jar of moisturizing oil at her vanity. Her eyes and face were swollen from the late night spent talking and crying. Noor walked into the room as Cindrea left. His training clothes were damp with sweat from his morning session with the other guards, he hadn't wanted to miss the opportunity to exert some of his nervous energy. When he sat on the bed with folded hands in his lap, however, Ember saw that instead of feeling better Noor too was feeling more remorse. What had Oma told him?

"We received this in the post today. The guards read the letters before they come up to the rooms. I asked Noor to join me to share this one with you." Oma's lips pressed into a line, hand angled down as she spoke.

Ember looked at Noor and saw the pain in his eyes as he looked back at her. What could this mean? The soul-thread sheets creased where he sat. She began to shake, nerves clouding her senses as she felt more paranoid.

"Please, just tell me what it says," Ember pleaded. She remained seated, rooted to the spot as she waited. She couldn't take more bad news. There wasn't any more space for her heart to mourn.

Oma handed over the letter and with shaky hands, Ember uncurled the parchment.

Embrence Dragon Daughter,

Your letters to Hasley Jeweler have gone unanswered because she is missing. I went to her parents' house to find her; she hadn't been to her purpose in days. They haven't seen her. They fear her to be Fateless.

Please send guards to locate her. I am running the shop alone. For all that I have done for you as my apprentice, I implore you to help me now.

Your former mentor,
Amlin Jeweler

"Hasley." Her first friend's name escaped her mouth in a whimper. Noor stood from the bed and knelt to hug her on the vanity stool. She held onto him and let guilt and shame overcome her. She should have known, should have thought to send someone to check on her when the letters stopped. She was the heir; she had the resources. She could have packed up and left to go to her or demanded some sort of search party. She should do that now.

"We-we have to help," Ember said as she pushed back her tears.

Noor rubbed a circle on her back and said, "Of course we will, Amir is already putting together a group to look for her."

"No," Ember said, untangling herself from him. That was not enough.

"Oma," she addressed her grandmother.

"Yes, Fireheart?" Oma's dark blue dress reflected on her hair in the low morning light. Her grey hair almost looked blue, reminding Ember of Jedoriah.

"We should leave early for the Mutrien ball. Rather than leaving in a week or so and going straight to Cruelindime, we'll treat it like a tour and spend a day in each province. Me and Noor," she hoped he'd agree, "will follow you to your home and then travel back the opposite way to see the other side of the kingdom, including Firetop."

"Yes, that's a great idea," Noor said.

"We have yet to meet the people outside of Azororion, other than at the ball," Ember said, gesturing between herself and Noor.

"We could get to know the citizens and the keyholders better while we look for Hasley," Noor added, going along with the idea. She felt unbelievably grateful that he understood immediately how this could work.

Oma appeared pensive, looking at her granddaughter and her pair. She tapped a finger to her chin before nodding.

"We could use this as an opportunity to kill two wraiths with one stone," Oma said. She tapped her chin again and the strength seemed to drain from her. She leaned down onto Ember's bed, heaving a sigh and her shoulder's slouched.

"Are you okay, Oma?" Ember asked.

"Yes, yes. I'm thinking through our needs. With the number of people we'd need to keep you safe and the preparations we'd need once we got to each province, it would take about two weeks to reach Cruelindime stopping at each province instead of going straight through, then the ball...no, it wouldn't do to go to both sides. Karwyn and Jedoriah would go on one side of the kingdom then you and Noor with me on the other."

Ember could practically see the mental checklist forming in the dragon matron's mind. She was forming one of her own. But would she trust her sick mother and the malicious man she refused to call father to look for Hasley? An idea struck her. Zhieve would be with Karwyn and Jedoriah. He could hurt Hasley like the nameless man in the woods if he found her first. She could send Wally with Zhieve. The wheels were turning, and soon she was making her own list. She eyed Noor, who was looking at her with cautious eyes. What was on his list?

"I'll send wraiths, Cindrea, and a few of the guards ahead of us to prepare the way and make sure all the rooms are ready in the castle. She can also prepare notices so people know to look out for your friend," Oma decided. She nodded her head as if reaffirming her own idea.

"I have preparations to attend to. We leave in three days," Oma said and stood back up from the bed. She gripped the sofa, balancing momentarily for additional strength on the way out.

"What's the real plan?" Noor asked when the door was shut a few moments.

"Jade said we needed to decide how to tell the rest of the resistance, right? How about we visit each of the factions? They can also help search for Hasley, and we'll start to organize them. Bring the different factions together. She may be hiding with one of the groups, like the people we are sheltering." Ember's smile widened. This would work. She'd have every side looking for her friend. Once they found her, she could bring her to the community home and help her.

Ember had never wanted to save someone before, never imagined herself as much of a heroine, but she had also never imagined herself as a princess and that didn't make her reality any less true. Her moms were gone; her new family was either insane or misguided by hatred for those on the outside of their walls. She would do what she could for her people. She would bring together each faction under her banner. They would save the Fateless, Hasley and Karwyn included. They would remove the wall. Together, they would greet the beasts and kingdoms outside it.

"We have to speak with Jade and Jardano again tonight. In fact, every night until we leave. If we're going to each faction, we should let them know exactly where the weak points in the wall are across the kingdom," Ember said.

"How will we use these weak points?" Noor questioned as he grabbed his jacket.

"That part of the plan is still in progress," Ember admitted. Because honestly, they had no idea how to break through those weak points without being stopped. It would have to be quick, across the kingdom all at the same time. She took out another piece of parchment and scribbled a note.

We'll tell them tonight. Be ready.

TWENTY-TWO

RUN

Day fell into night in a blink. Noor, Ember, and Amir were back at the resistance base for the third time that week. While it was likely their final time visiting the hidden city under the market before their trip, it would not be her last late night. For the next few weeks, Ember wasn't sure when she was going to sleep. She had to meet every base she could. She would take one half with Noor, while Wally would visit the other while accompanying the other half of her family on their tour. She needed her own troops, her own resistance members working the problem with royal support. Well, her support anyway.

She could only hope that these next few visits would involve less emotional turmoil. She wasn't sure what to do with the information Jardano gave her the night before. Could it have been only hours ago she had learned the royal guard was responsible for the death of her moms? And even less time since she was told her best friend has fallen ill to the disease that also inflicted her mother. Continuing as if nothing were wrong was not something she could do. Uncovering irrefutable proof, beyond that of the word of the resistant members, was her next step. If Jedoriah was going to pay for what he had done, she'd need to learn which guards took out the orders to kill her moms.

She took a deep breath as the clamor around her died down. Her scales stood out in the open for the first time in this underground city. It was harder than she expected to tell them the truth after being a smaller figure in the crowd the past few weeks. It reminded her of what her life could have been if she weren't the princess. If she had met Noor before Amir had found her, would that have been what her life was like? Would she have ever even found out she was the princess?

"I am Embrence Dragon Daughter." It was the obvious place to start.

The time for hiding was over. While those that were privy to the news about the wall was a shorter list, that was not the truth for this announcement.

It was a risk, but one Ember wanted to make. Everyone would know she was here. Amir stood at attention near the tent flap; he couldn't avoid his unease. They were vulnerable now, her position no longer hidden, and his and Noor's secret identities revealed.

She resisted the urge to scratch her scales under the pressure of the underground. Having everyone know about her scales had advantages. Her identity was undeniable. The rush of conversation did not die for several minutes. Fear, anger, confusion rung through Ember like a snake crawling beneath her skin. By the time she was able to speak to the men, women, and children around the meeting tent, she was shaking.

"I am here today as a friend. I am trusting you with this secret in the hope that you'll also trust me," Ember began. She thought of her moms and their involvement with the scribes. She thought about Noor and his family's involvement. No matter what, she likely would have found herself here. There was peace in knowing that.

"I have a friend in Firetop named Hasley Jeweler. She is missing and presumed Fateless."

The crowd seemed to hold its breath. Everyone knew the impact of the Fateless. They all had lost people. Ember looked to Noor, thinking of her birth mother and the companionship Noor couldn't have with his Fateless sister.

"I'd like your help to find her and bring her home."

"Why not use your own resources? Why were you even here?" a woman in the front asked.

"Not everyone agrees with my policy to save the Fateless. The community homes are new and not everyone believes in the mission yet. We can't wait for that to happen before we take action. There are people that would hurt her if we don't find Hasley first. It's the only way to guarantee her safety," Ember said.

"As for why I am here..." She smiled at Noor. "My fate led me here, my family, and my hopes did."

"Dragon Daughter, how is the search for one Fateless girl going to help us?" one older man asked with a creased brow and hunched back. Despite the tired appearance of his body, she could see the determination and will of his expression. Ember couldn't imagine all he must have seen in his lifetime, life where Oma was queen. What would that have been like?

Ember considered lying. She thought to say that Hasley had answers they all needed. That she somehow was the answer to all their problems. But in truth, she was just a girl looking for a friend and calling in any favor she had under her belt. She hadn't taken care of Hasley. She had to do that now.

"Because that girl could be your daughter. She could be your cousin," Ember replied.

"This girl, Hasley, is the best friend I do not deserve. She is the kind of person that would have made a great princess. She is part of us. I want to treat all of the Fateless and all citizens in the way that she would, with tremendous care, patience, and respect."

Ember's eyes moistened as she spoke, imagining what Hasley would have done if she had been in Ember's place. Her heart hurt for her lost friend. For Hasley's parents. For Ember's mothers, all three of them. This was what she could do: fight for one and then for all.

"We've made so much progress with the Fateless through the building of the community home and our new policy against their harm. These safe places for them will be ready any day now. But we can only do so much without making a stand," Noor added, "we have to be their advocates. It starts with how we care for even one person."

Ember smiled at Noor, gripping his hand in solidarity. That he would even say that warmed her heart.

"I have one final question for you, Dragon Daughter," the same man asked. His thin lips grew thinner as he considered. She looked him in the eye and nodded, prompting him to ask it.

"What is your stance on the wall?"

The room was silent, her public opinion resting on the top of a pin.

Ember smiled, thankful they asked the one question she had an answer too.

"I am looking for an opportunity to remove it. If you or anyone in this room—" She lifted her head to the crowd. "—have any information or tools that can help me on that quest, I welcome you to speak with me."

"Thank you," the man replied with a smile and nod. She nodded back to him as the whispers resumed.

Glancing between Ember and Noor, Jade interjected. She stood from her desk as Amir pulled away from the tent flap and to their side.

"I think we've asked our Dragon Daughter enough questions for today," Jade interrupted.

The little girl interrupted with a bounce to her feet and swaying pigtails, "but I haven't asked where the dragons are yet!"

Ember was glad they hadn't.

"We can talk about that with the princess at another time," Jade promised the bouncing five-year-old. She responded with a pout before her mother apologetically pulled her back down to her lap.

"For now, know that we are protected by the heir of the throne herself. Embrence Dragon Daughter is still Emairy Waiting, the same girl we've gotten to know. She has a special request and as a friend, we will help her." She gave a cursory stare at the group before she located Amir.

"Amir, hand over the descriptor of Hasley, and we'll start circulating it. Now, let's move on to updates," she concluded. Jade gestured to one of her own personal guards to gather extra seating. Noor and Ember sat beside her as they listened to updates from their teammates.

Ember heard a rushing of steps in the distance. Heads turned. It grew louder, and a man pulled back the tent with a pant.

To her surprise, it was Zhieve, Wally's pair. His blue eyes roamed the room, his breath stilted from his quick movements. She knew that Wally had told him about the resistance, but had no idea he'd know where they were. When Zhieve's eyes found hers, his yell shattered the room.

"They're here! Run!"

"Zhieve, what are you doing here?" Noor exclaimed.

But Ember grasped the truth before Noor could, jumping up from her honorary seat before the confused men and women. She yelled, "The royal guard is here! Run!"

Zhieve barreled towards them as the crowd began to panic. Many stood frozen in their spot, fear paralyzing them, while Ember saw the little girl that asked about the dragons get swept up and carried out the tent before most of the crowd could decide their path.

Zhieve grabbed Ember's arm and pulled her with him to the back of the tent. Noor and Amir followed without question. Jade called those around them to run and hide. The sound of feet began to stampede towards them, whether they be other scared resistors or the guards closing in, Ember couldn't tell. Amir pulled up the back of the tent, pulling up the edges to go through as the crowd bottlenecked out the opening flap.

"Where to now?" Noor asked in the low light behind the tent. He gripped Ember's arm, bringing her closer to him than Zhieve. Despite being Wally's pair, trusting him was a gamble. How did he know they would be here tonight? Did Wally tell him? Did Zhieve tell Jedoriah Knight she was here?

They stood sandwiched between the tent and the wall, shadows, and lights flickering on and off as other parties became aware of the chaos around them. More people than Ember had seen at one time in the underground city were moving around them.

"Follow me!" Amir responded, taking them back around the other side of the tent ahead of Zhieve. People ran scattered, finding the different entrance points around the province. Amir went in the opposite direction of the crowds, down towards the large shackles that once held dragons. Screams echoed around them, and Ember cried out as she tripped on her full skirt, her feet unable to keep up with the pace. Noor pulled Ember up, sweeping her into his arms as he ran.

Turning the corner behind the large dragon irons, Amir stood in front of an empty wall. A few bits of trash lay in uncleaned sections, but the space was mostly clear. Did he want them to hide in a corner?

"Why are we here?" Ember asked, rushed and out of breath. Noor held her tighter in his arms. Amir turned in circles around them, looking for something. Noor looked too, both of them seeming to know something she and Zhieve did not.

"In here!" Amir exclaimed in excitement, having found his intended target. He braced his two hands against a seemingly random bit of wall. A groan escaped the space and it opened inward like a hidden door. It blended into the grey and low light.

"Get in!" Amir called and Noor walked in, still holding onto Ember. She wiggled, forcing him to let go of her. On the floor around them and the small shelves against the back of the room, Ember saw small baskets of shimmering blankets and smaller shackles. They shined like the large irons outside the hall. Wait.

Ember bent down and ignored the sounds of Zhieve and Amir arguing outside the door. The blankets were soul-thread. Seeing the two items beside each other, Ember could see the similarities between the soft blanket and the hard material meant to constrain outside. Were they made of the same material? She picked up one of the blankets, seeing several of them in a pile in the hidden closet. Why would they be in here? She looked behind them and saw more shelving with other mysterious objects shadowed around them. It was difficult to see what they were in the dark, they did not shine like the blanket in her arms.

"Guys, get in, stop this!" Noor called. Ember looked up, holding one of the blankets with her. She felt calm despite the circumstance, happy to have found such an interesting clue to the dragon captures of the hidden underground.

"I've got somewhere else to be," Amir replied, looking straight into Zhieve's eyes as he said, "Thank you for the warning."

"Don't you dare," Zhieve growled at his fellow captain. They were both bound to the crown. Bound to a job that meant being the first line of defense, protectors of their knights and the descendants of dragons that rule the kingdom and their hearts. Amir shook his head at him, a look of resignation crossed his features.

"No," Zhieve whispered.

"Take care of them," Amir responded back, shaking Zhieve before turning him forcibly around. The screams grew louder, feet marching towards their direction. The sound of tent flaps forced open in the distance and personal belongings clashed to the floor filtered their way. The royal guards were searching everything in their path, getting closer to their hideout.

Amir pushed Zhieve Captain into the closet with Ember and Noor with urgency. Zhieve fell into them, his strong and broad body blocking the view of one of Ember's only friends.

"Goodbye, Zhieve Captain. Tell Wally. Tell him it's not his fault. I'm choosing my purpose. And Zhieve, choose your pair. Always choose your pair." Amir closed the door, a captain weighing the risks.

"NO!" Zhieve called again, hitting the door as Amir somehow locked it from the outside. A sliver of movement caught her eye, and Ember saw the small hole to the bottom left of the door. It must be the locking mechanism. How would they get out? What was his plan? Ember tried to push past Noor, but the space was too tight and he was too strong. The four of them would not have fit.

"I don't understand," Ember protested to herself. She dropped the shimmering blanket, and her heart began to clamor in her chest. The darkness seemed to grow; only a small crack below their feet brought in light outside of the small hole. There was no way to open the door from the inside. Zhieve hadn't come to that conclusion, didn't realize yet they were trapped. He banged at the door, occupying almost the entire mystery closet with his figure.

Noor took command. Keeping Ember behind him, he covered Zhieve's mouth with his hand.

"Everyone, be quiet," he scolded in a whisper, pulling the taller man back with more ease than Ember anticipated.

Zhieve's eyes began to moisten, his hands shaking at his sides. The space was cramped, Ember could feel the heat of the two muscular men surrounding her. This was the most vulnerable Ember had ever seen Zhieve. The most he had ever spoken in front of her too. It would have never occurred to her he had this bond with Amir, just as his relationship with Wally had seemed foreign.

"Do you think everyone else got away okay?" Ember whispered. They had been at the back of the underground structure, Zhieve must have run past many people before reaching them. Were there other closets, or panic rooms, like this one where people could hide? Or other hidden doors they could escape from? Her thoughts swarmed back and forth between Amir and the other resistors.

"Everything is going to be okay." He nodded while saying the statement, but she noted that wasn't the answer to her question. She took comfort in the fact that she didn't know about this room. That must mean there could be others. It was a difficult to move as cramped as they were, but Noor was able to bring his arms up so that they hovered on top of her shoulders.

Zhieve leaned against the door, blocking the little light they had. But then from the corner of her eye, another bit of light came into her sight. It was a hidden lookout hole, confirming her thought that this was indeed a panic room.

Zhieve noticed it first and his eye peered into the small slit. Feet pounded in the distance, as did the screams. Ember lay her head on Noor's chest, squeezing her eyes shut. Shouldn't she stop this? She gripped Noor tighter, and he held onto her. Doubt crept through her. Was keeping her identity worth these lives? Would they kill all the resistors or only a few to leave a lesson? Was Jedoriah here with them bringing what he thought was justice? If Zhieve knew with enough notice to get here,

Jedoriah had to be the instigator. More blood she could blame on his distorted perspectives. What justification did he have for the death of the moms that raised her?

The cries and commotion in the camp continued. What was better, Ember wondered, for the screams to keep going or to stop? It grew silent and Ember looked back up at Noor, tears streaking down her face. She was letting her people down. She opened her mouth to demand Noor break open the door of their hiding place when she heard it.

She closed her mouth with an audible snap and Noor's eyes grew wider. Familiar voices were approaching them, closer and distinguishable from the screams due to the echo of their lesser-used hall. Noor shivered, bringing Ember closer to his body. They held each other, waiting.

"It's disgusting down here," a raspy female's voice said. Her tone dripped of venom. Ember felt she knew her, but she wasn't sure how.

"What were they thinking? They might as well have hidden in a cage," the man replied. She knew him immediately, the man she refused to call father.

"Which way did he go? Are you sure it was the guard?" The woman inquired, her tenure gravelly and deep. On the second listen, she knew that voice too. She didn't want to admit that she knew that voice. A tear that had nothing to do with the potential death of her friends peaked out of Ember's eyes, dripping down onto her scales. They were tears of betrayal, sticky and hot. Noor gripped her harder, and she knew that he recognized her as well. Ember pulled away from him and crouched quietly to the floor. She put her eye to the small hole from the lock. Zhieve hadn't moved an inch from the taller peephole. Only Noor was left without a view.

"Yes, I'd recognize Embrence's captain anywhere," Jedoriah said.

"I would agree, but your competence has been in question

as of late." Oma sneered back to him. Ember watched as she came into view. Oma was no longer the picture of a tired elder queen she was familiar with, rather she stood rod straight. An act. So much had been a lie. She shuddered in the dark.

"Don't test me," Jedoriah said. He stood behind Oma, staring daggers into her back.

"Oh, I most certainly will," Oma said. She turned around and mirrored his glare. A hatred was shining between them, one Ember had never seen before. In her presence, Jedoriah had always seemed to bow to the dragon matron's will. In private, it seemed to be a different matter. Or had something changed?

Ember couldn't believe her ears. Zhieve backed away, shaking his head and pulling at his face and hair. She saw the panic in him. If he was caught, what would become of him and Wally? Would he be tortured for more information on the resistance? Or just killed in spite? The risks he took to get here first, to warn them...

Zhieve's backward step pushed Noor against the shelves. Noor held his lips shut with a grimace, keeping in the pain. The wall, however, disagreed with the need to be quiet.

Ember turned her eye to the lookout hole Zhieve vacated just as Jedoriah and Oma turned towards the hiding spot. They inched closer, aiming a torch in the general direction of the hidden door. Just as Ember feared they were about to be caught, a clear voice ten feet away called, "You've found me."

Amir moved into the light, smiling gravely at the pair. His eyes ignored where he knew his princess and friends stood.

"I knew it was you," Jedoriah said, his triumphant look as vain as his disposition.

"And you are always right, aren't you? It's one of the things I hate about you," Amir said with a laugh. Not a laugh of joy, a tone she had never expected of him.

Oma snorted at the comment and Amir's eyes turned

to her.

"I've been in the castle for ten years, *ten years* working on my purpose and learning how to be a good guard. You know what I learned in those ten years, Jedoriah Knight and Omanox Dragon Matron?"

Amir didn't wait for an answer. He walked in a circle around them, forcing his body between Ember and the other members of the royal family. He pointed his finger at Jedoriah and spoke again.

"You are not my knight. Who I follow is of my choosing. I follow Embrence Dragon Daughter. I follow Noorworth Knight. I do not follow you. I do not follow Omanox Dragon Matron. And I do not follow the queen you keep hidden away. Ember is our true queen and Mutrien is going to make it official soon enough."

"I think you've been around long enough," Oma replied coldly. She pulled a dagger from the folds of her black dress. It held a blue gem at the handle. On the other side of the door, Ember held her breath, unsure what her birth family would do. She wished she could see more, see the expressions on their faces more closely and know what they were thinking. Instead, she heard the muffled cackle of her grandmother. She felt Noor beside her as he looked from the other peep hole. Zhieve had switched positions, shaking behind them.

"You know what to do about this insolence, Jedoriah," she said. Nothing was heard for several moments beyond the breathing of her, Noor, and Zhieve.

"Well, you have guaranteed you won't be in the castle any longer. How about you join the community homes? Who is going to tell me that I am wrong, that you aren't Fateless? No one," Jedoriah spoke the threat easily, while Oma shook her head.

"No, we can do better than that, Jedoriah," she called. He looked back at her, face weary.

"Him or *her?*" she asked him with an arched brow. The long braids of her silver hair shone brightly in the firelight of her torch. He stared at the dagger in her hands as she tilted the blue gem hilt to reflect in the firelight.

His face turned up away from the dagger and to the dragon matron again. He nodded before turning back to Amir. As if on command, his face turned to malice. He reached backward and accepted the dagger in Oma's outstretched hand.

"Or better yet, how about I kill you?" Jedoriah asked Amir.

Zhieve sat on the floor, taking up more space seated than when he stood. He rocked, head on his knees. They were powerless. Reveal themselves and possibly live the same fate or accept Amir's willing sacrifice. Honor what he gave them. Those were the choices.

She couldn't do it. Ember raised her hands, about to push and bang the door and reveal their hideout. This was her friend. She couldn't watch him die for her sake.

Before her hands could make their strike, Noor's reached in front of her and held her arms down. She kicked backward, protesting against him but he was too strong. He held her back with one arm snaked around her chest and arms and the other over her mouth. Ember screamed into it. Frustrated, afraid, and helpless. She heard the physical signs of their fight. Blows hit skin and feet scuffling on the floor resonated as their bodies pushed together in battle.

Her pair held her back, keeping her from watching as her Captain fought the head knight. Blows were hit, but she didn't know who. Fear circulated in and out of her quickening breath. Helpless again. Helpless to help Amir. Helpless to help Hasley. Helpless to save her moms, birth mother, and Noor's sister. There was so much out of this bubble of control. Lack of control felt like the only constant in her life.

Amir cried out in pain, a gurgling sound escaped from his throat. She knew it was too late before she even heard the thump against their hiding spot. Something heavy now leaned against the only door in or out. A body. It was silent for a moment.

Noor let her go and gently rubbed his hands over her shoulders and arms. She couldn't feel it. The heat was rising in her. She looked through the hole, but Amir was not visible, laying below the lookout hole. She could see Jedoriah and the look on his face did not appear to be one of pleasure. He stared in her direction, at the body that must be just beneath her eyesight. His expression was blank, motionless, and sweat dripped near his ponytail of blue hair.

"Hurry up, let's go," Oma said impatiently. Jedoriah re-animated, putting on a bravado so jarring from his expression mere seconds ago. Ember's eyes trailed to her grandmother. Oma glanced towards where Amir must be. Her eyes uncaring, she addressed Jedoriah again.

"There, problem solved. Didn't I tell you someone in her household was involved? We'll have to see how much our fireheart knew about it," she said.

"Your Fireheart, not mine," Jedoriah replied bluntly. He wiped the knife's blade on his dark pants. Ember hoped that meant her grandmother was not the same as Jedoriah, hoped beyond reason that she would defend her and damn Jedoriah for his actions.

"She is a dragon and deserves your respect, especially while we are still grooming her," Oma snapped back. They walked out of frame. All reason to hope splattered onto the ground. *Grooming.* She was a prized beast pulling their carriages.

Ember turned back to Noor. His broad shoulders a mere outline in the dark. He reached for her, and they held on tightly for several moments before their souls were rested enough to detach. She could sense Zhieve in the small room, quivering at their feet. Noor and Ember looked through both small holes in the door, double-checking the coast was clear.

She stepped aside as Noor pulled a key from his pocket, one she didn't know he had, and pushed open the paneling. He had a way out of the room the whole time, in sync with Amir and this plan, to her surprise and anger. A weight pushed on the door. Noor strained his muscles as he pushed it farther open and light began to fracture into their vision again. They were only able to open it far enough for them to squeeze out. Blood smeared where the door trailed.

As Ember emerged, her feet had to step over a red puddle. Beside it, the body of one of her only friends. His chest was still. Amir's lifeless eyes looked up at the three of them, as if he knew they would stare back into his face. Zhieve fell to his knees again, this time in the pooling blood. His voice croaked, a harrowing sound. What he meant to say wasn't clear. He laid his body over Amir's and sobs wracked him.

Ember didn't cry. She felt too dried up for that. Her whole body felt like it was constructed of salty flames. Dried up. Heated. She knelt before Amir and Zhieve. A stain grew on the fabric of her dress and on her mind, one she knew she would never be rid of. Without a word, she reached into his pocket to take out the pin that represented his captainhood. She smiled down on it, correctly guessing that even in civilian clothes he would not have left it behind. She held it gently in her palms.

"We have to get to your room. Jedoriah could come looking for us at any moment," Noor said from behind her. She could hear the tears in his voice. The regret.

She clipped the pin to the inside of her cloak, hidden and safe. She walked back to the hidden room, picked up the blankets and put the small iron chains in the inner pocket of her cloak. Detaching herself from the cries coming from around the camp, Ember held the blanket in one arm and Noor's hand in another. They ran, Noor leading the way back where they came.

A TEMPLE OF LIES

Noor pulled Zhieve behind him as he and Ember ran up the stairs of their tower. He prayed no blood dripped a trail. At the top of the stairs stood one solo guard.

"What's going on?" Wally called from above them. He pulled out his sword at the panicked pace of their steps.

"Zhieve!" Wally called in fear as they reached the landing. "Have you been stabbed?" He dropped the sword with a clang. His voice quavered as one arm curled around his lover's shoulders, the other checking his chest for wounds. Blood soaked his shirt where Zhieve had held Amir.

"There's no time to explain. Take Zhieve to your room, and don't come out until we tell you to! Clean him up as fast as possible," Noor said in a rush. As Wally opened the door to their room, he was already taking off Zhieve's blood-stained shirt.

Ember could still hear Zhieve's ragged breath as Wally closed the door to their room. Everything quieted besides their panicked disrobing. Her whole body shook as they moved and tried to detach herself from the event. The blankets lay on the bathroom floor, her dirty clothes on top.

"Are you sure he'll come here?" Ember whispered as she cleaned her hands in the sink. When the water ran clean, she stopped to inspect her hands. There was a spot of blood between the groves of the pearl ring Noor picked for her that first day in the market.

Ember ran her finger under the water but the spot did not budge between the silver casing. She pulled off the ring as she slipped into a clean sleep-dress. Before she jumped into bed, Ember hid the ring in her jewelry box. Noor was right behind her, shirtless and in linen pants. He reached under the bed before climbing in, checking for his dagger. He pulled it out from its hiding spot and tucked it into his pants pocket before settling in beside her. She shuddered.

"If I were head knight, I would. He'll be here," he affirmed.

Noor pulled her close to him, and she inhaled his sweet scent. His heart galloped beneath her head, and its glamour brought her own heart down to her stomach. She focused on the fast rhythm, pushing her fearful thoughts away. She hoped Jedoriah wouldn't come, that Noor was wrong. Maybe they should grab their bags and run away, live in Jardano's bookshop and never come out. She hoped Jardano escaped. She didn't remember seeing him in the crowd. Maybe he hadn't come tonight?

"I can't believe..." Ember began before her head snapped to the sound at the door. Jedoriah opened the door.

She sat up in the bed, too shaken to get up and pretend to be courteous.

Jedoriah stood twenty feet away, still in the living area of her tower rooms. He walked towards where they sat. As he passed into their room, she noticed he had also changed clothing. He did not wear his uniform or knight pin. He wore brown pants and a rough-spun white long sleeve shirt, colors and clothes she had never seen him in. If it weren't for the deep worry lines of his face and the tension in his shoulders, she would say he looked casual. Her chest tightened at his different appearance. Would Oma be walking through the door next?

"Embrence, I need to speak to you about a serious matter," he said solemnly.

"I'm listening," Ember said, still seated in her bed. She pulled the covers tighter around her lap. She felt Noor reach into his pocket from beneath the sheets.

"Your captain is dead," he said softly. His mouth pulled into a frown, part grimace and part fear.

A choked sob escaped Ember that was not faked. At least she could share her pain. Let out her grief. If she did that, she wouldn't have to act. Not like Noor would have to.

"How?" Noor asked as he stood. Amir's blood was on their clothes, the ones lying on their bathroom floor. They knew the answer to that question.

Jedoriah examined Ember's expression, his eyes trailed over her tears.

"Don't look at her," Noor growled. "Answer me, how?" Noor repeated firmly, anger tipping over. He moved to the front of the bed, putting himself between Ember and Jedoriah.

As if breaking from a trance, Jedoriah blinked several times and shook his head. He looked into Noor's dark brown eyes.

"You know how," Jedoriah said. "You saw me kill him."

Noor pulled his knife in a blink and Ember's tears ran cold. She stood up from the bed, and Noor angled to stay in front of her.

"I'm not going to hurt you," Jedoriah said. He did not move from the opening of the room. His body was as still as ice.

"Why are you here?" Ember asked, hesitant. Was he going to blackmail them? She tasted tears on her lips.

"Because I need your help," Jedoriah answered.

"Why would we help the murderer of our friend?" Noor asked.

"Because my pair was captured. The dragon matron has her, and if I did not kill Amir, her and my child would have been in danger."

My child echoed in Ember's mind.

"I...I don't understand. I have a sibling?" Ember whispered. There has never been an heir to the dragon throne with a sibling before.

"Do you know where Oma is keeping Karwyn?" Noor questioned more directly, already jumping into the problem.

"No, not Karwyn. The queen is not my pair." Jedoriah sat down on Ember's vanity stool with a bouncing knee.

"But you are the head knight," Noor protested, not grasping the truth. There could be only three knights, one for the queen, one for the dragon matron, and one for the dragon daughter. The pillar of lies that compelled Ember's life unraveled one by one.

"The family secret is not that the queen became Fateless while she had a pair. She was Fateless, pairless, and blessed..." His voice trailed as if it were the first time he was hearing of this as well.

"Explain," Ember deadpanned. She dropped back onto the corner of her bed, unable to stand any longer. Noor kept his knife out but lowered his fighting stance.

"I've known Omanox all my life. I knew her as Omanox Dragon Daughter when I was five years old and she was just paired. She was thirty years old before she met her heart twin, older than any other princess before her. She was forty when she had Karwyn. I served the family. First, doing favors for her around the castle while my mother ran the kitchens. Then, when I was old enough I was head of staff in Cruelindime palace for Omanox's mother. When your great-grandmother died, I moved to this palace and served your grandfather as a gentlemen in waiting. Not a guard, but his helper. I was part of the family. I was trusted," Jedoriah said with an air of wistfulness. He wanted to share this story.

"When your mother came back from the abduction, there was something wrong about her. The merfolk had done something to her, corrupted her somehow. We knew we had to protect her, she was under constant supervision. But as she sank into madness and her belly grew to house you..." He shook his head.

"Drastic measures were taken. To protect her and the kingdom, I was installed by Omanox as her pretend pair and as knight of the realm, sworn to secrecy. I was divinely picked to rule with Omanox. Karwyn became queen in name only." His puffed chest shared the pride he felt in his actions.

"Don't you see, Embrence? I was protecting you, your mother, and this kingdom. No one would have understood if they knew the truth. And when the Fateless spread, when we truly understood that all Fateless were without a fated pair like your mother, we knew we had to hide the truth further."

"So you executed them, as many of them as you could find," Noor whispered in horror. His sister flashed to mind.

"No, not executed," he pleaded. "We gave them mercy," Jedoriah insisted. "If your mother hadn't been queen, I don't know," he didn't say what he thought, but Ember knew. They would have killed her too.

She pushed her horror away. She had to keep him talking.

"Then why let us stop the killings? Why ask me to support the community homes?" Ember asked.

"Because you are here now. You can help me rule as soon as we've killed your grandmother."

He spoke it as if the idea were an easy favor.

"You want us to help you kill the queen's mother?" Noor questioned as the grip on his knife tightened. Hadn't enough blood been shed already?

"More death. Lies and death." Ember's heart clamored, hands sweaty with the reality before her. She pulled herself completely into her bed and covered her body with soul-thread. The thoughts quieted again. Her grandmother and not-father were abductors and murderers and more death was to come.

"My pair, she needs us," Jedoriah pleaded. "We can work something out. I had to do it, or it would have been my family."

"Did you kill my moms?" Ember asked, looking at her hands.

"Indirectly, yes," he said without hesitation.

"How?"

"Guards under my orders tortured them for information. They weren't supposed to take it that far. I killed the guards that committed the act."

She felt no comfort in knowing the answer.

Noor pointed his dagger at Jedoriah, punctuating his words.

"I am head knight now, you understand me? You will leave this room, and we will think about what you've said. Do not speak to us unless I seek you out. Understand?"

His reluctant assent was apparent as Jedoriah backed out of their room and closed the door behind him. Ember began to tremble, the adrenaline leaving her system now that they were alone again. She knew now why he pushed so hard to find her. Why her mothers were killed. He wanted out of his arrangement. He wanted his family safe. Anyone who got in his way was a byproduct, a justifiable byproduct. The death of her moms was part of his equation to find her. They were killed in his attempt to get out of the cage they too were trapped in.

She had never felt the blood on her hands as thickly as she did now. Waves of death, pain, and circumstance tumbled into her heart over and over again.

Noor held her in a heavy silence as she watched the sun rise again over her balcony.

TWENTY-FOUR

FOUR DEAD

"I'm here to say goodbye," Ember whispered as she stared through the frosted window. The days would get colder now leading up to the night of the Mutrien ball.

Ember knew the subject of her confession could not hear her. She shivered, looking at the mother she never got to know. The mother that was taken from her before she was even born. She sat barefoot in the grass and soot, next to the purple flowers Wally had shown Ember on the day she decided to meet the resistance. Kariana's Tears. She picked them from the ground as if they were just wildflowers and not the rare dragon-born blooms.

The kingdom, the scribes...they parroted that it was the merfolk. The mysterious people she had never even seen who had mysteriously infected the future queen and their kingdom. Ember no longer believed that. This was a punishment. It was a curse. As was everything else in their existence. They had fallen from Aaleia and Mutrien's grace, and one day soon, the other kingdoms would come to claim the crown she did not even want.

"I understand now," Ember said to the glass. "I know that my moms took me from you to save me. To save me from Oma," her voice cracked at the name, "and from a false knight."

"They were scared for me, and for the kingdom, I suppose. They took care of me because you couldn't."

Warmth spread through her chest, filling a hole in her heart. Her moms weren't using her for a rebellion. They weren't venomous kidnappers. They were friends of a queen that had gone mad, a queen kept alone and isolated. They saved what part of her they could. Ember had all the pieces of the puzzle now, and they painted a picture as clear as day.

This royal family was rotting and her moms tried to save what innocence was left.

Ember watched as the queen's guards came in closer to her, steering her away from a fountain. She gripped the flowers in her left palm, hands knuckling white.

"I wish I could talk to you alone. I wish that you'd hug me and tell me everything would be okay. I'd like to hug my mother right now."

Ember wrapped her own arms around her middle with black-gloved hands. She squeezed, and the tears began to come down again.

"Mother, so many people have died for me. How do I live with that? How did you accept this responsibility?" she whispered, curling tighter into herself.

All the Fateless that were murdered for her mother. All those that were killed so that it was easier and more convenient for the crown to keep up its lie. The people murdered to help find the heir. And a sickness that conveniently kept people preoccupied, eyes turned away from the slow siege of power at the palace. The fall from the gods-way. Despite everything that made their way of life possible, Ember had never considered herself very devout. The fating, blessing, the Fateless...it was what was. Were they being punished for the wall, for keeping their kingdom away from outsiders? Or were they cursed long before then? Would she ever be able to right these wrongs? Or would the pain of her family's decisions haunt what little chance she'd have? Could she find the cure or the exact cause, and right at least this one wrong?

Karwyn stood and lifted her head up into the open sky. She smiled with her eyes closed, her face warmed by the sun.

"Not again," one of her guards said, instinctually knowing what she was about to do. Karwyn giggled and ran, throwing herself between the two guards that weren't paying as much attention. She threw her hands up, flowers spraying everywhere. One comically landed on the taller guard, falling to the ground. They stumbled and tripped getting back up with dirt in their eyes and a pain in one's ankle.

The queen ran, faster and more intentional than she'd ever seen her. The smile on her face was wider than Ember had ever seen it. Ember let go of her body, eyes focused on her mother weaving in and out of the trees. She filled in the blank spots of time in her head, for the queen's path was blocked from where Ember stood to watch. Ember felt the pure joy of Karwyn's smile pierce her heart.

"I'll fly to you!" Karwyn yelled as she ran, circles growing wider and more determined, pushing away from the greenery and out to the path that circled this inner garden. The smile turned serious and then to rage as the running guards began to gain steam. Karwyn ran straight past the hidden door Ember herself had been using almost nightly.

Faster the queen ran and Ember began to understand why the guards had dreaded this. She was practiced. Karwyn did this regularly. Her hands splayed out like wings.

Ember gasped and the pit of her stomach dropped.

"I will find you!" the queen screamed as she threw her body outward in a leap. Her arms were spread wide in blind faith.

But the queen's fantasy was not true. She was not a dragon. She could not escape the grasp of this kingdom any more than Ember could. The queen fell, dirt and rocks tumbling with her as she landed sprawled on the ground.

Ember turned away as the guards helped her mother stand again. She could not watch the dejection cross her face. A dragon soul, trapped in a human body, unable to fly.

Ember knew the feeling well.

EMBER GRIPPED NOOR'S CHEST, her cheek leaning against his back as her horse jostled their movements. She had decided on a name for the horse-beast, after many weeks. He was now Carmain, and he seemed to take to the name well. Was it only weeks ago that Oma gifted him to her? All her life, she had no father, then a cruel one, and now she felt abandoned all over again. No relationship to mourn, but a potential one she didn't even think she wanted plucked away. And a grandmother she had loved, now fell into a cruelty that felt so sudden that she had no idea how she would cope.

"Why don't you come into the carriage, Fireheart?" Oma called from the curtained window of her anchoris-drawn carriage.

Ember turned to the other cheek, pushing away her bangs and staring instead to the wall. There was no family left for her here.

"She didn't sleep well. I believe the fresh air would do her good," Noor answered for her. His right hand held the reigns as his left covered her own on his chest. His fingers grazed over her pearl ring, cleaned and back on her hand. The ring would never be the same, just like her. She'd have to toughen up, to keep her feelings hidden again in front of the dragon matron, but she didn't know how. How do you bring back up years of repression and years of hiding after feeling free?

Karwyn and Jedoriah left the castle gates. While Ember and Noor would lead one side of the kingdom with Omanox, Karwyn and Jedoriah would visit the other. They'd converge at the end of Ashkadance in Oma's castle for the final ball of the year. Ember wondered if she'd get tired of all the balls, two a year for the rest of her life. That is, if she survived her family.

Her tutor, Ahnika, breezed past them on her horse. She appeared free and wild in a way Ember had never seen before. Her brown mare galloped around the party as it departed down the long drive of the castle. Her education would continue on this trip, Ahnika promising to take her to important sites of their history as they toured the provinces.

"Don't think you'll escape your lessons!" Ahnika said as she galloped past.

But they seemed to forget that Ember knew each province well. She had lived in every one of them but the two castle capitals. She had been everywhere and seen everything. That is, everything except for where her birth mother was kept and where her pair had been raised—the twin capitals, where the royal family lived. But all five other provinces? They were as familiar to her as breathing. Ember found herself missing Cindrea. When they reached Cruelindime, she'd want to tell her everything. She may be the only female friend in her life now, if they didn't find Hasley.

Their first stop on this kingdom-wide tour was, of course, their capital province and home of their castle, Azororion. The last time she had been into the city in the daytime was after her fating to Noor. The day she told him her birth mother was ill, and he bought her this ring. It was also the day he sent out the code word to join the resistance. Would Amir had died if he hadn't? Karwyn and Jedoriah would be part of this first visit, then they'd separate to their opposite directions.

From there, they would visit Faymader and Judcree, the two closest provinces to the west. When they reached Cruelindime, where Oma's castle lay, Ember would finally get to meet Noor's parents. She ignored that fact, as traveling with a now-known manipulator and murderer turned her veins to ice. Noor seemed to thrive on these new challenges, even telling her that he hoped to uncover where Oma was keeping Jedoriah's pair during this trip. Ember couldn't bear to think of it. She couldn't form words.

Oma's breath of deception had been so wide, Ember felt buried in it.

"Four other deaths," a voice whispered beside her.

Ember startled from her thoughts, looking up to see Wally beside them. He spoke casually, to not draw attention, as if he were speaking of the weather. His voice was low, mindful of the other people both ahead and behind.

"Who?" Noor asked shortly. Ember could feel his fear.

"Two children, one Scribe, and a local merchant. No one we know," he answered from the side of his mouth. His hair was shorter than yesterday, a fresh cut for the journey. The consolation did nothing to bury her pain.

In Amir's death, Wally took his place as captain. It had been a weird request, asking for her captain to not do the tour with her, but they agreed. Noor was enough security, she said. Ember played the romance card, saying she didn't want to separate him from Zhieve. Ember glanced down at his new pin, recalling that introductory conversation with Amir. He had planned for this. Planned for his death. Now Zhieve's pair was also a captain of the guard. Two men with a sacred duty that kept them in harm's way.

"They will be available to you if ever I am sick, help with shift changes, and would be my replacement if I were to die," Amir had said that first full day in the castle. Always the protector, always prepared.

Ember closed her eyes at the mention of children.

Her scales seemed to raise in the cold air, but thankfully she had worn her only dress that hid them today. The sleeves were fitted, long and grey, but as they would be riding—her skirts weren't as full today. Instead, she wore thick coverings on her legs for warmth beneath them. It made straddling the horse easier too, she did not want to worry about her clothing as she mourned and simultaneously met her people. They deserved a true queen. She feared meeting that standard.

"Jade and Jardano?" Ember asked quietly.

"Angry but unharmed," he said. He reigned his horse back, its anxious hooves trying to move on.

"We begin then," Noor responded.

"With what?" Ember asked behind his back. She gripped onto him harder, feeling the heartbeat beneath his chest.

"Our ascension," he replied with a promise.

Their ride to the market center was longer than Ember remembered. The trip she had originally put her whole faith in felt more like a death march now. With each gallop of the horse, she imagined Hasley dead beside Amir with twin stab wounds.

As dark as the thoughts and feelings were, she felt safe in the arms of Noor. He was the only part of her that felt settled and calm while the storm of her life swirled around her as if in a sea mist.

As the sounds of people started to build, Ember reopened her eyes and peered over Noor's shoulder. Crowds had gathered along the market, people streaming from each door as their precession grew closer. There were fewer people during their first trip, but that was a spontaneous outing. The people knew for days she would be coming.

As their eyes landed on her and Noor together, their voices climbed. Ember felt her heart tumble. It was as if it were her first day at the palace again, expectation and reverence over-whelming her senses.

Ember's hand gripped Noor's as he helped her off of Carmain. Her hands held his so tightly, he had to turn a wince into a smile as he detached from her grip. He instead cradled her with an arm over the shoulder. His white shirt was unbuttoned at the top. A single strand of gold circled close to his neck with one lone adornment, a crystalline fating bead. She was glad she had finally made it for him, ecstatic that the supplies came to the palace in time for one calming jewelry session before their trip.

It momentarily gave her hope.

Her smile faded as she remembered why they were here.

Oma left the carriage, joining Ember, Noor, and their guards. The carriages took a loop in the opposite direction through the inns to meet them at the end of the market's u-shape. Many of the horses stayed behind, held by the guards as an escape route. They formed a box around the two royals.

Ember shivered as Oma came beside her.

"Are you nervous, Fireheart?" Oma asked.

"Yes," she answered quietly, unable to look her grand-mother in the eye.

"You'll get used to the attention. Smile and wave, and we'll be moving on to the next province. As we already met most of the influential here during your ball, we can make a bit more progress early on in the journey."

Oma nodded to a few shopkeepers as they passed. Ember looked to them too, ready to mimic her movements when a familiar face caught her eye.

Jade stood apart in the crowd, an expression that mingled pain and rage. Her eyes barreled into the dragon matron like a snakebite. Her posture was tight, strong shoulders clothed in a black tunic and vest. Her eyes accused her, grey like steel. Then they blinked away to Ember's and she nodded.

She tried not to react, tried to pretend she didn't see the disrespect the rebel leader gave to the matriarch of the royal family. But Omanox did see it. Her hobbled rouse disintegrated as they walked and encountered more of the resistance members Ember had come to know.

Along each shop, around each corner, members stood in black. They ignored or raged at the dragon matron's appearance, then turned to acknowledge Ember with respect. It was a statement, an unignorable protest. Karwyn was farther back in the crowd, Ember couldn't see how they reacted to her. Was it the same as Omanox? She imaged so, as Karwyn traveled with her not-pair, Jedoriah.

Didn't they see this could implicate her? That their care and outright favoring could make some clues click in the dragon matron's mind like Jedoriah had uncovered the night before? Ember looked back into the crowd, unconsciously looking for the parents of the dead child. She didn't see them.

She could feel her grandmother grow angrier by the second. While the majority of those assembled along the drive were excited to see them, even reaching out for them, the angry and somber faces in black stood apparent no matter where they turned.

Noor stepped back from the front of the guards and put himself between Oma and Ember.

"A varied crowd today," he commented lightly.

"Yes, it seems our appearance brought in some rats," Oma replied with disdain. Ember nearly shivered at the memory.

"We should stop into one or two of the shops, split up and draw out the energy," Noor recommended. Ember could kiss him for it.

"Thank you, Noorworth Knight. The carriage is draftier than expected. I'll see to getting some extra blankets from the seamstresses," Oma said as her head turned to the store in question. She did not look at Ember.

The group split into two, the dragon matron's guards following behind her.

"Jardano's around the corner," Noor said hurriedly. Her hand gripped the crook of his arm as they walked quickly in the direction of his shop. The man that stood at the door barely resembled the man they met. His wrinkled and kind face was bruised, purple skin on both eyes, his cheek and peeking from his black shirt.

Noor and Ember rushed inside, Wally commanding the rest to remain with him at the perimeter.

"Jardano, I'm so sorry. Are you okay?" She reached for the side of his face hesitantly before letting her hand fall. Tears pooled at her eyes, blurring his face.

"I'm so sorry," she repeated from beneath the water and pit of her pain.

His small frame encircled her in a hug. "Ember we don't have much time. I will be fine. But before you leave, I have a message."

"What is it?" Noor asked with a hand to her back, making soft circles. His touch was comfort and she calmed enough to sit in the offered chair.

"This arrived for me last night, I was going to give it to you after the meeting but you know how that went."

His weathered hands reached into his desk and pulled out a small wraith scroll. He passed it over the clutter of books on his desk to Noor's outstretched hands.

He unfurled the small piece of paper and angled it for him and Ember to read at the same time.

I heard she is looking for answers about our predicament. I have something she must see. I can't share it in writing. Arrange a meeting.
-A.S.

"Who is A.S.?" Noor asked as he curled the message back into a size small enough for the mini dragons of stunted wings. They couldn't fly far, only about the stretch of the kingdom. Despite their wings, they weren't able to make it over the wall and to the next kingdoms above the sea.

"Amic Keyholder. He is a resistance scribemaster. The best one, in fact."

It took Ember a moment to comprehend the two sentences that Jardano spoke so freely. A keyholder, the protector of a province, was a rebel bookkeeper and studier of the realm? She was getting tired of the duplicity, whether it was in her favor or not.

He smiled at her bafflement.

"It surprised us all. He had been working in secret, gathering information for years before reaching out to us. When you get to Borderain, he'll have something to share with you, he must have heard your call for information about the wall. If he can't send it by messenger...well, we won't know what he has to share until you report back."

"Okay," Ember said weakly. She pulled her knees up on the chair. She began to sweat through the layers, a tremor rattling the shambles of her resolve.

Would they still nod their respect, rally for her, when she let them down? She knew she would soon find out.

Her moms, the murdered Fateless, Amir, the dead resistors, possibly Hasley. The bodies of the dead would bury her alive.

TWENTY-FIVE

COMING TOGETHER

Ember looked up into the darkness, swirls of clouds flittered in and out of her vision. This wasn't what she expected to feel. This wasn't who she wanted to be. The stars seemed to agree, twinkling between clouds like a nod of understanding.

She remembered the stories of the Unyielding War, of all the beasts that roamed their earth before man began to tear it all down. Before select creatures sat on thrones. Would the dragons have given her as much wonder as the stars and the sea? Would their world ever see a dragon again?

Ember leaned onto the edge of the balcony, looking down towards the first floor and out into the darkened streets. She barely felt the cold iron rails on her skin.

It was a lovely view, nothing like that of her tower, but she enjoyed having the outside air. They'd only be here for one night and one breakfast. Their official tour of the kingdom was on a schedule like the fating tours some families would send their older children on, in fact. Two weeks, every province, as many faces to gaze upon as possible.

But instead of the excitement those trips would bring,

Ember felt dread. The stars wouldn't stop turning for her to find comfort in their trip, nor would they help grant her confidence that they'd find Hasley. They had itineraries and meetings to keep.

"Is this a private brooding or can anyone join?"

Ember jumped and turned, finding her pair leaning against the balcony doorway. She smiled softly and nodded, unable to answer aloud. Noor walked to her and wrapped his arms around her middle, settling his face into her neck. She loved when he held her like that. Their bodies entwined around each other was calmer than her thoughts on past wars, but not less powerful.

"I didn't live that far from here," Ember murmured into the dark.

"Oh? When was that?" Noor asked from the crook of her neck. His breath tickled and she shivered.

"When I was fourteen. We moved about every year, to keep from settling. They didn't want me to make friends. She didn't want anyone to know me long enough, remember me well enough to answer questions if interrogated. I know that now. But before, they said it was because of these."

Ember's hand rested on top of her scales. They had healed, grown stronger since joining the royal family. Whether that be because of the better nutrition or the proximity to her birth mom, she didn't know.

"Did you like it here?" he asked. He already knew how the moves made her feel. They had discussed it at length. The isolation, pain, guilt, and shame of it. She couldn't be rid of them. But he asked anyway, inquiring more about the memory.

But here in Faymader, she actually did have some fond memories. In fact, her last memories. It was her move right after where Ember lost her family.

"It was the only year my parents let me go to the Aaleia festival. I couldn't go with the kids from school, but we went together as a family. I got to walk the streets with them, enjoy a hot meal and a show. It was one of my favorite family days," Ember said. She remembered the smell of the roasted corn and seasoned meat. There weren't that many places around Ashkadance that bred animals and served meat, at least not for a steep price. It was easier in Faymader. Many of the farmlands created the perfect environment for it.

"Wait, if you were fourteen then I was sixteen."

Noor stood up and turned Ember around. Her dress swished and smacked his legs with the movement. She could barely see his body in the dark; his clothing matched the sky.

"Yes, that's how age works," Ember teased, unsure about his abrupt statement. She couldn't keep the laughter from her voice.

"I was here during the Aaleia festival when I was sixteen. My sister, she wanted to visit a friend that had fated to a farmer. My parents let me come with her. I was here when you were," his voice took on a sense of wonder. A hidden discovery, a path where their future could have changed.

"What would have happened if we had fated then, at fourteen and sixteen?" Ember whispered back to him. His face grew closer to her, and she matched the movement. Ember felt the magic of what could have been at the fingertips of her mind. If she had this bond as a child, her whole life could have been different. Even if their intimacy wouldn't grow for a few years, they'd still feel the trust and support.

"I may never have discovered who I was. My moms may not have died. Or would they have died sooner? If I had been paired, would we have kept moving?" Ember's happiness dwindled and died. There were too many possibilities. Too many places their lives could have gone if they had found each other sooner.

"I wouldn't have been a guard," Noor said thoughtfully. He hadn't joined until he had an opportunity to make a difference.

If she hadn't found out her heritage, they may have never had become involved at all, despite Noor's parents' involvement.

Sensing her mood, Noor rubbed up and down her arms.

"It was meant to happen this way," he said. He pulled her closer to him, and their lips locked in a kiss. It was sweet and unhurried, a promise more than a sign of affection.

"You are part of me. I am part of you," Ember said. She felt safe in the circle of his arms. Would every night on this campaign be like this?

Within moments her thoughts told her no. Most of the provinces had resistance bases. Most nights they'd be awake, going off in the darkness to unknown destinations with strangers. This might be the only night, in fact, where they could just...be.

"I can't wait to hear more, to even see some of your life before I met you," Noor whispered to her.

"And I can't wait to share it," Ember whispered back. Because now, she didn't have to hide. Not with him, anyway. While the events of the past few weeks have shaken her to her core, scared her in ways she didn't think were possible, there was also peace and love. Even an acceptance of who she was.

She had never had that before.

But this acceptance came with the responsibility of her kingdom.

She didn't know how to survive it.

EMBER HELD Noor's hand under the table, his thumb rubbing back and forth over her skin. She smiled at the conversing keyholder of Faymader, trying to recall her name and hoping she caught enough of the conversation to add to any paused moments.

"The scribes are charging too much for their books,"

complained the keyholder. Ember's attention was drawn back to the conversation at their words.

"Why would that be, Midacle?" Oma asked politely from her end of the table. The blue of her soft dress brought out the white of her hair. It was early still and the sky held a cast of orange mixed with the blue.

"I have no clue. There are enough apprentices for them to have help," she spoke with a clipped tone, as if there was nothing for them to complain about.

The keyholder's daughter dropped her goblet down on the dark wood table a little harder than necessary. Her black hair bounced at the movement, ringlets springing on her shoulders.

"I have always appreciated the guidance of the scribes," she replied and crossed her arms. Her eyes briefly crossed over them, testing for recognition.

"As have we," Noor responded for them. "You apprentice for your mother, is that right Mina?" Noor asked before biting into the fresh fruit. A drizzle of liquid fell onto his chin. Ember smiled and reached to wipe it away. Noor caught her hand with a kiss.

"Yes, I am," Mina responded with a smile and a nod. Asserting herself as the next keeper of the province, a rebel ready and available to them and the cause.

"They are full of themselves if you ask me," the keyholder replied. She did not share the same affiliation as her daughter.

While Faymader did not seem to have a main base, probably less concentrated rebels in the farmlands, there were still people among them. There would always be people willing to jump into danger. Willing to take a stab wound for what they thought was right. Ember saw the cold eyes of Amir flash before her.

"Our dragon daughter is also here on a quest," Oma said with a sweet tone.

"Oh, do tell," The keyholder said, losing some of the venom

at the change of conversation. The idea peaked her curiosity, evidently.

"Yes," Ember chimed in, finding her voice. It cracked with the misuse, and she cleared her throat.

"An old friend of mine is missing. We'd like to share with your guard a description of her for circulation."

"Is this missing girl…Fateless?" Midacle asked with a curl of her thin lips. Ember felt the word *Fateless* like a brand on her heart. Most missing people were Fateless. The only exception she could think of had been herself.

"Yes," Noor replied quickly. He picked up the hint of disgust as well, and his distaste for it was obvious in the hard voice of his response.

"I don't understand why you want to help them. They are beyond that, a blight to our society," Midacle commented obliviously.

She emphasized *blight* and Ember wanted to hurl her glass in response.

"Is your daughter paired?" Ember asked the older woman. Mina must have been nineteen, not much older than Ember.

"No, why?"

"If she went missing, was Fateless, or both—how would you want me to handle that?" Ember asked her.

The table grew quiet for several moments, Midacle's lip tightening to a straight line until the daughter laughed outright.

"She doesn't want to admit it," Mina said between laughs, the deceptively happy sound turning into one of anger.

"She would want me dead," the daughter concluded, and the purple of her eyes shone bright with mischief.

"It was a pleasure to meet you, Ember and Noor," Mina said as she stood from the table. "Know that you have an ally in us."

She walked from the table with a nod to her mother and the

dragon matron. A servant bowed and picked up Mina's untouched food from the table.

"She's passionate, Midacle, I'm sure she'll make a fine keyholder one day," Oma said with a smile to the woman who stared back to her daughter. While being keyholder did not always pass down from parent to child, it often did. They grew up in the shadow of responsibility, just like the royals did. Or at least they did until Ember's kidnapping.

"Yes, she will," Midacle replied weakly as she turned back to her breakfast and scooped some porridge in her mouth.

IN THE WEEK THAT FOLLOWED, Ember and Noor met many resistors like Mina. Some with limited connections, others with an expansive network. But all of them had one thing in common. They knew about Ember. They knew a new queen was coming that heard their calls.

The needs of the few, those that were left with no purpose post-wall, they needed her. Resistors that had family in the kingdom of Grydagia and Faeinto, they needed to see them again. Those that have loved and lost; Family mourning their Fateless, murdered and swept away. The people have been neglected, forced to live day by day as if they weren't running out of resources and hope.

And the word was spreading. Their pains growing, a breathable and living thing. Those in the resistance were not just the youth. No one type of person was overflowing. It was distributed. Even. The old, the new, those fated and others not. Professionals. Keyholders. Their children. Guards.

Ember and Noor met dozens of people across the provinces, spending nights sleepless and days on the road in a makeshift bed in a private carriage.

If Oma noticed their behavior, she didn't comment on it,

but Ember could feel her stare as they ate breakfast each morning. Ember and Noor grew quieter in her presence with each sleepless night, the purple under her eyes growing larger.

Even separated, the resistance seemed to reorganize with each day. More sectors connected, asking their scribes for guidance and becoming one.

Hope followed her. She wished she had more of it herself. The longer they went without any sign of Hasley, the less motivation she had. She knew this wasn't only about her friend, but rather all of the Fateless, but her heart had a hard time remembering that.

They were only two days away from Borderain. Their next destination would come with some answers. It had to.

In their room that day, Ember lay in bed staring up at the ceiling.

"Are you worried?" she asked Noor, "about what we will find in Borderain with Amic?"

"Not at all," he replied, jumping into bed beside her.

"Why do you say that?" Ember asked.

"If we have a keyholder that is also a scribemaster, I can't imagine the resources and people he must have seen and interacted with. If he invited us to come, it must be for a good reason."

"That is a lot to assume from someone we know so little about." She stood up and adjusted her shirt. They had only met him for the briefest of moments at her debut ball. Today, she had decided against the usual skirts and dresses in favor of the outfit she wore the first day she met the resistance in Azororion. All black, scales covered, fitted pants and long boots. She even braided the scarf into her hair, which had grown close to three inches since her ball the month and a half prior.

"Don't you just love my observation skills?" Noor said with a grin. Ember stood up beside him, boots on and ready for their night. He didn't dress in purple, instead also choosing casual clothes. Other than his knight pin, he didn't wear his guard uniform much. Not after those initial few days. As a knight, he didn't need to.

"Really, you think you are observant? And what do you observe about me?" Ember flirted with him, wiggling his hips between her hands as she attempted to pass him. He didn't let her, grabbing her hand and twirling her to him like on the night of the Aaleian ball.

"I noticed your lips," he said pecking them lightly. She smiled against him and giggled.

"I observed your neck," he whispered as he trailed lingering kisses down her neck. His arms looped behind her back. Ember's breaths became rapid.

"I see your kindness," Noor whispered in her ear.

"I found a queen trapped in your mind," he said with a searching look at her eyes.

"You'll have to show me where because that part of me sounds very foreign," Ember said back. She let go of him, snapping the moment closed behind her. "Let's go," Ember told him, off to another late night visit.

PART 4
EMBRENCE DESTROYER

TWENTY-SIX

RIPPED APART

"This man is not trustworthy, Fireheart. Don't believe a word," Oma said as they departed the cabin together the next day. Oma's lips formed a line, the creases lining her face more apparent in the afternoon sun. Ember nodded as if she agreed, but her head spun at what awaited her.

Finally, they were to see Amic Keyholder, though now they knew his true name to be Amic Scribemaster. The first time they met had been the day of her debut ball, and to be frank, Ember barely remembered the brief conversation amidst all the events of that night. Now they met again, his letter to Jardano Scribemaster burning a hole in Noor's pocket.

Noor dismounted Carmain and stepped into stride beside Ember and Oma. Ember threw a glare his way for convincing her to ride with her grandmother instead of with him.

"She needs to believe we are on her side," Noor said the night before. She never wanted to be near her, but she knew his point. She couldn't completely separate herself from her, not yet.

They approached a tall tan building with a domed roof.

Unlike the usual grey of their structures, this province meeting center was painstakingly painted. It was a lot harder to paint peridoone stone, requiring many layers to adhere to any color. The cost of the effort was not lost on their traveling party as they took in the sight.

Ember remembered Borderain from her childhood. With its proximity to Cruelindime, Ember and her moms didn't stay long. Regardless, the tone of the province stayed with her.

There was a stronger military presence in Borderain, as with the other bordering provinces. This province held more diverse structures and decor than others, however. Ember was glad to explore it now, despite the dire occasion. With no leads on Hasley after a week of travel, Ember felt her thin layer of morale fall away with each passing hour.

"Hello there!" Came the loud and magnanimous voice of Amic, he strode out of their large open doors and bounced down the steps. Several companions trailed him, all seemingly as friendly with open smiles.

Amic walked straight towards them, his grey long-sleeve shirt was damp with a sheen of sweat but he paid no mind and bowed low. The rose twinge to his blonde hair shone brightly.

"A pleasure to see you again, Omanox Dragon Matron, and also you, Embrence Dragon Daughter. I hope your short months as dragon daughter have gone smoothly."

Images flashed across Ember's mind: the unnamed Fateless man, tears in the dark, the sound of Oma's betrayal, Amic's blood-stained cloak. Ember focused on the feel of Noor's presence beside her, forcing the thoughts down.

"Call me Ember," she said with a smile and gestured to Noor. "My pair, Noorworth Knight."

"Of course! Noorworth Knight, it is a pleasure to see you again. Some of our guards trained with you. They have regaled us with stories of your kindness from the second you were announced. They have yet to stop!" Amic winked at him before bowing again. A few of the surrounding guards chuckled, and Noor waved to a few of them.

"Amic, may we go inside?" Oma asked by way of greeting.

"Of course, of course, my apologies." He nodded and led them towards the steps. "Refreshments, Sandra," he called to a tall woman in red. She promptly turned and walked ahead of them.

The inside of the keyholder's home looked just as splendid. Columns bordered the room and small blue tiles covered the floor. In the center of the main room was a long table filled with food of various colors and sizes. Despite the elegant table settings of the clear table of the castle, it typically did not hold as much food. This setting was warmer and friendlier than she was used to. Ember couldn't help but smile when looking around.

There were no chairs, sofas, or recliners. Just a table, food, and citizens standing and speaking to each other as if they were the best of friends. The guests turned at their entrance, clapping in unison in greeting.

On either side of the room were two doors, one in which Sandra re-emerged with a tray of red liquid. She passed glasses to them and then the other guests, winking at Ember as she passed.

"A toast," Amic said with a raised glass, "to the future of Ashkadance!"

"To Ashkadance," Ember and Noor repeated.

"YOU HAVE A BEAUTIFUL HOME," Noor said as they walked out into the gardens.

"We at Borderain work hard to bring in the culture of the other kingdoms," Amic replied.

"How so?" Ember asked.

"See there," Amic gestured to the clay pots the marked the entrance to the intended trail. "They were based on designs from the capital of Grydagia."

The silhouette was long and uneven, mimicking two parallel wavy lines. Amic pointed out several other unique additives to his province as they walked. With each one, there was beauty and meaning. If they weren't here to address his mysterious letter, she would have turned around to invite Ahnika to study each piece. Little was discussed about Grydagia and Faeinto, Ember felt like she knew almost nothing of their culture and lives. Other than the occasional slur, she rarely heard about them in polite society.

"Why go through those efforts?" Ember asked curiously. She had always known that there was something special about Borderain from the first moment she stepped into the province as a child. It had a look and feel that was of comfort and color. A far cry from the grey and easier-to-manage appearance of many of the other provinces. For someone that cared enough to bring this to them, what did Amic think of the wall that kept back these cultures? It must not be a positive association as a secret scribemaster.

They'd soon find out, Ember realized, as the garden began to weave towards the outskirts of the province. Why build his home so close to the wall? Wouldn't the center of the province make more sense for his goals?

"Why did you call us to you, Amic Scribemaster?" she asked, addressing him by his true name for the first time. Who knew how long Omanox would be distracted. The local theater company said their performance was inspired by her rule, something she knew Amic must have planned. It worked to get them away, but they had been walking for fifteen minutes already.

"Because of her," Amic said and gestured right off the path. The trees began to grow denser.

Noor stepped off the path curiously, walking ahead of his pair and into the shaded trees. Ember followed behind, glancing at Amic again. Were they meeting a new rebel?

Ember stopped mid-step, her foot hanging in the air before her instincts dropped the heel. Joy exploded inside her, and her whole body filled with warmth.

Despite her blue messy hair and frail body, a spark of Ember's best friend was before her. Hasley smiled briefly before breaking into wailing sobs. Haunted eyes looked back at Ember.

"Hasley," Ember called. She ran to the quivering form of her best friend. They collapsed together onto the floor, arms wrapped around each other.

"I'm sorry," Hasley said between hacking breaths. She buried her face into Ember's neck.

"Why would you be sorry, Hasley? You have done nothing wrong. I'm the one that is sorry. I failed you," Ember whispered. She held tighter to her best friend, brushing her dirty hair with soft fingers.

"I knew. I knew I was sick. I couldn't tell you. I...I..." Her words fumbled, and Hasley pushed away. Her legs stumbled backward in the grass, dirt collecting on the few clean spots of Hasley's legs.

"It'll be okay," Noor said. He inched closer to them. "We can help you."

"If we take down the wall, we can," Amic added. Ember turned, forgetting he was even there. "What do you mean?"

"Her pair is outside that wall, right now," Amic said matter-of-factly. He pointed to the spot right behind Hasley's head, as if her pair was actually there this moment.

Ember felt lightning strike her heart. She jumped to her feet.

"I'm sorry," Hasley whispered again, this time to herself. She pushed her back flat to the wall.

"How can you know that?" Noor asked, his hand hovered nervously near the knife on his hip.

A wraith flew down from above their heads. It landed onto Hasley's shoulder. He nuzzled her bowed head like a pet, scales meeting blue hair, and Hasley looked to him with a smile. She reached for his leg to take the letter tied and opened the small scroll of paper greedily. Her skin seemed to brighten from the inside out as she read. A soft yellow cast seeming to bring her to life as she absorbed the words.

"What's happening?" Ember whispered. Amic pushed closer to them, a hand resting on each Ember and Noor's back. It resembled...she couldn't even think it. What does this mean?

"Come closer and see," he said. The three sat before Hasley on the ground. She fished for a pencil from her dress pocket and began writing on the opposite side of the letter. The wraith hopped down, his long thin tail brushing the grass. As Hasley finished her scribbles, he stuck out his leg and accepted the letter. The wraith readjusted his stance and with a proud chirp flew fast into the sky. They tilted their heads up to watch the small dragon disappeared over the wall.

"But wraiths can't fly over the wall to deliver letters," Noor said in disbelief. They were told this fact their whole life.

"Oh, but they can," Amic said. "You just have to have someone at exactly that spot on the other side waiting. If no one is there, they circle back. The water is too far for them to cross, but they can visit the eroding coast and old docs on the other side if they have a reason to."

"Someone is out there," Ember echoed his meaning, staring at Hasley. Her friend's face was upturned, eyes bright and smile wide with the golden glow. But the more seconds that passed, the more the shadow of the Fating faded. Hasley's skin lost its glow quickly, and her smile turned to a frown. As if the light never appeared to her, tears welled up, and she looked back to the ground. Her long arms wrapped around her legs, and she lay her head down on her knees.

"Who are you speaking to, Hasley?" Ember asked quietly, scared to disturb her.

"Arsenio," Hasley said between tears, her body quivered at the mention of his name.

"My son," Amic answered back. "She and my son experience bursts of the fating every day, then they feel it ripped from them."

"Help us," Hasley whispered.

TWENTY-SEVEN

STRANGE

ELEVEN YEARS AGO

"Hi, my name is Hasley," a small voice said behind her. Ember froze, wringing her hands as she turned to the voice.

"Hi," Ember squeaked. She looked around her, making sure Hasley was speaking to her. Ember's heart pounded in her small body, unsure how to react when spoken to. If her moms were here, they'd say hello back and usher her away. They were good at that kind of thing, being polite but not welcoming. Ember had yet to learn that skill. At seven, she only felt fear. Friendship was forbidden.

"You are new, right?" the blue-haired and sweet-faced child asked. Hasley bounced side to side, her bright yellow dress swaying like a bell. Ember looked around again at the playground of the small school in Firetop.

"Yes," she answered softly and immediately covered her mouth. She was not supposed to speak to her. Mother Julimore would be mad. Ember yelled afterward, "don't talk to me" and turned around. She pretended to go back to her task, organizing a few rocks before her by size and shape, while the sounds of laughter flittered by from the swing set.

"But I like to talk," Hasley protested, a pout crossing her lips.

"Well, I'm not supposed to," Ember grumbled, shifting one rock to the third position.

"Not supposed to talk or not supposed to like to talk?" she asked with a plop, sand crashing over some of Ember's rocks as Hasley sat down beside her.

"Both," Ember admitted, wondering why that was.

"Aren't you hot in that shirt?" Hasley asked, pointing at Ember's long-sleeves and rounded collar.

"Yes," she replied shortly, a weary excitement to have spoken for this long.

"You're strange," Hasley said and stood again. The girl walked off, and Ember felt hot tears build in her eyes. The threatened to spill as the heat rose through her chest and up her neck. She was embarrassed to have been such poor company and ashamed to have even entertained speaking to Hasley for a few moments. She scratched her chest, feeling a prick of pain on her scales beneath it. The rocks on the ground before her became unfocused as the gush of tears grew.

"Here you go," the same kind voice said. Hasley's black shoes walked into her line of sight. Ember looked up to see her holding an arm-full of rocks of many sizes. Hasley sat next to her again, displaying her bounty from other areas of the park.

Ember's tears came down harder. She covered her face and the blanket of her long hair became a curtain around her.

"Why are you crying?" Hasley asked, her face turning to the side in question.

"You came back even though I'm strange," Ember spoke between her hands.

"Don't be silly, it's good to be strange. Let's play with rocks now. Though I don't know how to play," Hasley replied honestly, putting her head on her hands to study Ember's pile.

"I don't get it," she said as she stared at them. Ember said, "I don't either. I just like them."

"You are *very* strange," Hasley amended with a smile.

They had two months together before they moved on to their next home, Ember not given the chance to say goodbye to her secret friend. When they met again, Ember's family was gone.

"Hi, I'm Ember," she said when walking down the market on her first day back at Firetop.

"I remember," Hasley replied and pulled her into a hug.

TWENTY-EIGHT

FREE

"I don't know what to do," Ember said to herself as she stared at her friend. Noor reached out to squeeze her hand.

"I do. Follow me," Amic said and stood.

"We can't leave Hasley here."

"She has been in these woods for weeks now," Amic said. He seemed rushed, already a few feet away from them. As he paused, his feet shuffled from side to side.

"We'll come right back, Ember," Noor said as he stood. He too felt the sense of urgency. How much time had passed already?

"Don't leave, Hasley. I'll be right back, okay?" Ember asked, stroking blue hair from Hasley tear-stained face.

Hasley nodded without moving her head from her knees. She stared at the earth.

Reluctantly, Ember stood up to follow. Whether they could make it back immediately or tonight when Oma went to sleep, they would do it. She would not leave Hasley here to suffer alone. She could feel her heart tearing as she walked farther and farther from her friend. She just found her, how could she leave? Noor pushed her on. He was right, they couldn't be caught with Hasley. Who knew what Oma would do if she knew. It was better to come back when she knew there was more time.

"Where are we going?" Noor asked Amic as they followed him out of the trees.

"You'll see," he commented vaguely.

"No," Ember spat angrily.

Noor and Amic stopped and turned. They now stood at the edge of the trees, Hasley no longer in view.

"You called us here without saying why. If I had known Hasley was here, we'd have come straight away. I don't appreciate the deception and will not tolerate it. If there is something that can help her, say it. I will not be led blindly," Ember said. She crossed her arms and stared into Amic Scribemaster's brown eyes. He clicked his tongue and sighed.

"You are right. I should have told you she was here," Amic conceded, "but there was something else developing at the same time that I could not describe in a letter. If I had, and that letter had been found, I would have been murdered for treason."

Noor walked backward, keeping his eyes on Amic until he was beside Ember again. He gripped the knife on his belt.

"Where are you leading us, Amic Scribemaster?" Noor asked in a cold voice. Ember held her breath, unsure of what to think. She couldn't look away from Amic's eyes. They bore down on her, alight with secrets he had been dying to spill.

"To show you how we break down the wall," was his reply.

EMBER AND NOOR looked down into the cavern, glowing red lights sparkled from within. Voices whispered in the dark spaces they could not yet see. Borderain too had their hidden secrets. And if what he said was right, there was another underground city just like the one in Azororion. A city of weapons and destruction, rather than hope and acceptance.

Ember gripped the railing until her knuckles grew white.

"Tonight I will show you, Embrence Dragon Daughter, what my son has brought us from the other kingdoms." His pride shown through, a smile wide in the shadows.

Amic led them down the steep stairs with Noor behind him, Wally on the end, and Ember between them. Noor kept his steps slow, ready to take any action needed to protect them. The whispers clamored, halting for a moment as they came in view before coming back up again.

Ember surveyed the room before them. The stone floors were similar to that of the Azororion base, but in place of the sea of tents were long tables and assembly lines of people. Sitting on the floor to the left of the tables were large silver barrels of liquid with attached spouts. On the tables beside it lay lines of clear glass canisters. After that, special insulations to put the canisters in. An assembly line.

Each person in the group was moving the liquid from the barrels into the canisters, then the canisters into the insulation. On the opposite end of the barrel were wheeled carts. All enclosed canisters were slowly placed into the carts in neat stacked lines. One of the tables filled a cart as they silently watched. A volunteer pushed it away from the table to a long line of completed carts beneath the stairs. The cart pusher smiled at Ember before moving back to his station with an empty cart for them to fill next.

The liquid they were carefully distributing was a deep red. In fact, the red was so deep that it appeared as if it were glimmering darkness with a hint of red sparkle beneath. The red liquid glowed faintly, filling the whole glass container she saw it pour into with a firelight.

Pure dragon blood. This was not the same thing as the

diluted blood fire, a drop of dragon blood in water that could breed eternal fire. This was real. Where was the dragon the blood belonged to?

Ember's eyes clouded over as she stared into the glimmering dark. Part of her was aware of Noor asking Amic questions, gaining answers that she should hear. But she couldn't rip her eyes away. She felt a stirring, awakening, her scales warmed.

Ember walked to the line of barrels. The assembled workers stopped moving, their gloved hands moving away from the materials.

"Dragon Daughter It may be synthetic dragon blood, but it is not any less potent," Amic cautioned. Wally and Noor walked away from him to shadow her.

"This is not synthetic," she declared with a shaking voice.

"How do you know?" Noor asked her. He didn't get closer, seeming more on edge than she was near the undiluted blood of her ancestors. Her fingers reached out, aiming to touch the barrel.

"Wait!" the boy closest to her yelled. He couldn't have been older than thirteen given the pitch of his voice.

"Dragon Daughter, please take my gloves." The boy handed the black gloves to her. The light caught Noor's eye as he accepted them from the boy and watched Ember put them on. The gloves were lined with a silver-white thread. Ember barely registered it as she put them over her fingers.

"I feel it," Ember said to Noor and Amic, insistent. One of her gloved hands brushing over the scales that covered her chest. Ember swore they flared in response.

"I assure you," Amic repeated, "it looks real but it is not. The dragons have not been seen in the other kingdoms either. No one has seen them in sixty years."

"Your supplier is lying or ignorant," Ember re-affirmed. If they were receiving these shipments from the other side of the wall? The implications swirled through Ember's mind. There was much to discuss this night.

She carefully held one of the clear glass canisters to her face, the liquid within sloshing with the movement. Red glowed on Ember's skin. She felt calmer than she ever had, a smile tugged up her face.

Dragons were alive, somewhere. They were out there. And their blood would set her people free.

NOOR GRIPPED HER HAND, a thumb grazing over the top of her hand. The purpose of a knight was always to protect, as well as to love, but not everyone was suited to it. She could only imagine what that must mean for some of the former knights. What it means even for Jedoriah, who took the knightship without being paired to the queen. Becoming paired to the heir of Ashkadance came with a purpose. It was chosen for you and not the other way around. Like Ember, Noor was wrapped into something bigger them herself.

And now Hasley was too.

She would not leave her alone in the night.

As Ember snuck away with Noor that night. As they approached, Hasley's face glowed golden. Her eyes wide and happy as she stared down at scribbled words. Ember sat next to her on the forest floor, her head resting on Hasley's shoulder. Noor leaned against a tree close by, his flashlight surveying the area. As Hasley's tears dried up and she began to fall asleep in Ember's embrace, the little hopping wraith flew back down. There was no letter on his feet, only comfort. He sat on Hasley's lap, curling into a ball.

Ember wondered, looking down at the miniature beast, if it took turns sleeping on the lap of Hasley and Arsenio each night.

CALAMITY

"You know that Hasley couldn't have left with us, not when she knew her pair was there waiting for her," Noor tried to reason with Ember the next morning.

"I know," Ember said underneath a blanket of tears. "I just can't believe I am letting her go." Ember felt torn in two.

"Don't think that way, it is only temporary. Amic is putting the plan together. It will all be over within a fortnight. She'll be safe."

"Then why does it hurt so much?" Ember's heart cracked. She found her best friend and couldn't tell anyone. If she had, she'd be taken away from her letters. She wouldn't have been able to stay at the wall. She'd be forced to stay in the community homes that Ember herself had created. They meant to help, but for Hasley they would take away all semblances of her humanity. She'd have no choice in the matter. Or worse, Oma could take her life. Attention to the wall was a threat.

One Ember planned to exploit.

Ember boarded their carriage with Oma and Noor. The dragon matron on her side of the anchoris-drawn carriage, and Ember and Noor cuddled together on the opposite side. With plush velvet black wide benches, it felt like they were still in the comfortable quarters of Borderain's guest rooms. The main difference was that Ember was moving away from her best friend rather than within walking distance of her. Ember pulled a few small bags from a case, intending to pretend her Oma was not there at all and focus on jewelry.

"How was your evening?" Oma asked the two and plastered on a serene smile. Ember didn't believe it for a moment as she thumbed through supplies. She didn't know what she would do with her growing jewelry collection. She didn't need or wear most of it. The act of creation was mostly for joy, for collecting, and for distraction.

"Quiet," Noor said.

"Making necklaces again?" Oma asked, a slight twitch to her hand.

"As always," Ember answered. Beads and reading was all she did with her spare time. Well, that and rebel meetings. Not that she'd volunteer that new hobby.

"It seems like a waste of your time," Oma answered. "There are many better things to learn." Her wrinkling fingers grazed over the curtains, a flutter of light crossing her withered face and silver hair.

"Like what?" Ember asked. She didn't like her tone, her implication that Ember's hobby was a waste of time. This was the first time Oma had outwardly disagreed with something she did. In fact, it was the only time that Ember could recall her breaking away from the strong but loving grandmother facade while in front of her.

"The weaknesses of the beasts," she commented.

"I can find that in history," Ember mused. What better way to learn of strengths and weaknesses than the past?

"Genealogy determines your weakness. Too much of a mother's genes. Too much of a father's. Not enough of this or that. You are determined by *your* parents and all before them."

The subtle emphasis on *your* gave Ember pause. Oma did not know Jedoriah revealed his falsehoods to them. Did she? For Ember was all Karwyn. Maybe that was why the veneer started to fall. For love, kindness, and acceptance did not commonly come in one package. The dragon matron loved her daughter, but a kindness nor acceptance of the Fateless queen did not seem likely. How much of her patience for her daughter was a ruse for Ember's sake?

Unwilling to discuss the narrow-minded view, Ember turned her face away to her beads. Noor was tense; his body barely moved with each breath. Oma turned away, looking out the window again. They were approaching her home, Cruelindime—their final destination on the first half of their tour. Karwyn and Jedoriah would meet them at the palace tonight, and Noor's parents were visiting tomorrow so they could meet.

Mutrien's ball, the celebration of the longest night and the god that brought to them the blessing, was only two weeks away.

CINDREA REACHED for Ember the second she exited the carriage. Her face was bright and full, a glow over her that Ember wasn't used to seeing. Her blonde hair had even seemed to grow, as if the few weeks away had actually been months. The night twinkled above them, arriving just in time for dinner.

"My dragonia, I missed you," Cindrea said with an extra squeeze. Ember inhaled deeply, happy that there was someone kind waiting for her in her grandmother's palace. After seeing Hasley for two days, being ushered right into her only other female friend was necessary.

Ember brushed her hand over her horses dark mane as she

passed. Carmain neighed and rubbed his face into Ember's cropped hair.

The walkway up to the palace was wide like Azororion's. On either side of the walk stood the staff. Ember felt as if she were in a mirror, reflecting back to her a similar scene to her first introduction to royal life. The uniformed men and women were less stiff than at Azororion, some better at hiding their excitement than others. The difference here, however, was there were many older staff members than in the main castle. Some were almost as old as Omanox. Were they here when she was crowned, loyal previously to her mother?

Oma took time to address each person by name, shaking their hands and insisting they don't bow. Ember studied the interactions, working to memorize their energy. She hoped her people would come to view her with respect as well, even if in this aspect it was a lie. A carefully constructed facade to show both strength, wisdom, and frailty. Ember followed behind her grandmother, working to speak with each of them as well. It took longer to finally make it inside the dark palace and into the dining room, but the effort was worth it. She felt energized by the time they were done, all the weariness of their journey soaking away. Noor had a spring in his step as well.

Cindrea chatted amiably as they walked together up the drive about little things, like meeting the different keyholders ahead of them to prepare their rooms, coming here to Cruelindime a few days prior to help oversee some of the preparations for the ball in two weeks' time. Karwyn and Jedoriah would join them later in the day, having made the same trip on opposite sides of the kingdom. They would spend the rest of the time together in Cruelindime, asserting that both castles represented the power of the royal family.

That was the reason this castle too had the runway strip for Drakul between the two spiraling towers. While not an exact replica, this castle was similar to that of Azororion, with a garden in the front rather than center. Despite being slightly smaller, it was still an imposing visage. This castle was not made of light grey stone. Instead, it was almost black.

THE GARDENS of Cruelindime's palace were the most beautiful Ember had ever seen. Each plant seemed to have a spirit. Spots of glowing purple, green, and blue wiggled across the night landscape. These were star flowers, happily blooming in the night air. With Noor holding her hand, and her other hand reached out to touch the effervescent plants, Ember felt peaceful. For a moment, she was not thinking of Hasley and the weight of her world.

"It's beautiful," Ember commented. She couldn't think of anything to say that accurately described the plants before her. Interestingly, there weren't any Kariana's Tears in the garden.

Noor reached down and plucked a purple glowing blossom, placing it behind her ear. She smiled up at her pair.

"As are you," Ember said, wrapping her arms around his torso.

"I'm nervous about meeting your parents," Ember admitted. Noor kissed the top of Ember's nose playfully. Her scales lightly leaned against his chest, something that used to make her feel self-conscious, but he never commented on them. Never flinched away. It was almost as if they were normal to him, and she loved him more for it.

"Don't be," he said. They'd be there the next day; a lunch feast was planned for the parents of Ashkadance's knight. The kingdom's only true knight, but that secret was cocooning in Ember's chest. It drilled holes where needed, adding to the web of lies that surrounded the royal family.

"But they are resistance, why would they like me? They could hate me just for being born." She almost twitched at the thought. A normal fear, she realized. Not being liked felt so normal compared to the other thoughts that had swirled through her mind the last few weeks.

"That's impossible. We're fated. That proves already you are nothing like the other royals. Once they hear you speak, hear how you think and what you want to accomplish, they'll be allies, and we can take advantage of those connections to reach the resistance on the East side. They'll work well with Amic. His arrogance suits them," Noor joked.

Ember laid her head on his broad chest. "I hope they like me," she whispered. At her core, she still felt like the hidden girl, forbidden to make friends. That girl was nobody, told to remain alone. That vulnerability made this new meeting an anxious thought, one she wouldn't be rid of until it was over.

Future queen or no, Ember wanted her new extended family to care for her. When a tear streamed down her cheek, Noor lifted her chin and kissed her.

This kiss was softer than their usual passion. A sweet kiss of assurances and hope. A lingering tickle that fluttered in her chest as well as her mouth.

"You are my kind of calamity," he whispered on her cheek as they separated, his breath caressing her skin.

Ember's laugh erupted from her without permission, falling into his chest in a fit of giggles.

"Is that a compliment?" she asked breathily.

"Yes," Noor answered. "A hidden orphan turned future queen. A woman that runs to the aid of those that can't help themselves. A liar on a quest for truth and for good. Someone that sees all outcomes for what they can do for the whole and not what they can do for themselves. Perfectly imperfect in body and in spirit. My chaotic queen of improbability, don't ever stop being that."

Ember reached up, and gripped his face in both hands.

"I swear to always listen to what you have to say, hear your side of the story. I swear to put your needs only second to that of our people. You are my jokester, my heart, the only person that truly understands me for who I am and what I need. The only person who sees past the scales and into my soul," Ember pledged.

"And I promise to always think about what you need, even when you are all wrapped up in what you can do for others. I promise to guarantee you bathe regularly and eat right. I care too much about your hygiene to do anything else," Noor jokingly vowed before adding, "and I promise to hold your heart in my own, to be its shield, and help you find what you need that is wholly for you and not anyone else."

And while she didn't intend on this garden visit to turn into an exchange of vows, that was what it became.

"Well, thank you," Ember said with a smile through her tears.

"Anytime," he said.

"Dinner is ready. Karwyn and Jedoriah have also arrived," Cindrea called from the open garden door.

They turned from the garden and entered their home for the next two weeks.

THIRTY

"WE HAVE HER."

"Are you sure I look okay?" Ember asked for the third time, adjusting the feather-light sweater she wore over her black pants. She had tried to keep her look casual that morning, wearing clothing she would have liked to wear before she knew she was heir. Well, Ember knew that wasn't exactly the truth. If she could have afforded the materials and had more confidence, she may have worn this jewel-toned sweater. But otherwise, she would have kept to the rough-spun grey and brown tunics. This is the kind of sweater Hasley would have liked, and that may have factored into her decision to wear it today.

"Embrence Dragon Daughter, no matter what, you look amazing. They'll prefer you over me in no time. In fact, I already prefer you over me. Over them too," Noor said flippantly as he tied the laces of his boots, a curl plopping over his brow. If Noor's family were part of the resistance, odds were their opinion of the royal family was not favorable, and Ember hoped to show this other side of her. She was not raised royal, and she hoped that difference would mean they'd give her a chance.

"Why do you act so nonchalant about them?" Ember asked curiously. He'd been saying similar things for weeks, cracking jokes whenever his parents were mentioned.

"My sister raised me. My parents are nice, but they've always put the resistance first. I don't like to think about their opinions often." And with his shrug, Ember understood why he held quick answers to every question Ember asked about his parents. It was his sister's opinion that mattered...and she was Fateless.

Hand in hand, Ember and Noor followed Cindrea into the dining room. The room practically glowed in white light, a stark contrast to the darker tones of the castle's exterior. It held more lanterns and torches than she'd typically see in a single room, making sure every crevice of the space had perfect lighting. Oma looked almost ghostly in the brightness. But Ember's eyes weren't looking at her, they drew to those in the room she had not known. Stopping short, Ember saw two people sitting at the table already.

She looked at Noor and knew immediately who they were. Her stomach dropped. She thought she'd have a few more hours to think about what she'd say to them until they arrived.

"Mother, Father, I wasn't expecting you until lunch. What a nice surprise," Noor said. His cheeriness rang false in the stale air. Some extra time ordinarily wouldn't be a grave concern, but the slowly growing smile on Oma's face set Ember's heart to flip-flop.

"Isn't it a happy surprise, Nori? The queen matron invited us to stay at Cruelindime with her," Noor's mom said with an erratic bob of her head. Her short curls held the same bounce as Noor, but their deep pink and white strands reflected the light.

There was a missing piece of the conversation here, something his mother was trying to convey to him. Ember could only imagine what Noor's mother was actually thinking, a rebel asked to live in the palace of the former queen. It was an information goldmine.

"They'll be living here indefinitely, Noorworth," Oma elaborated, taking a sip of tea.

"Did your knight's parents live with your matron, Oma?" Ember asked, cautiously hoping it was a tradition. She should have known not to hope.

"No, they did not," was her cold reply. Noor's father coughed suddenly and dropped his fork on his plate. It clanged loudly, and he waved his hands as if to say he was okay. The blonde of his hair reminded her of Amir.

A threat then. What did she know? Why now?

"Noor, are you going to introduce us to your pair?" his father hedged, working to break the tension.

Ember and Noor lingered before them. She squeezed his hand again, jolting him out of his spiraling thoughts.

"Of course, I'm sorry," Noor said. He rolled his shoulders back and let go of Ember's hand. He gestured to her and said, "Mother, Father, this is Embrence Dragon Daughter."

"It's nice to finally meet you, Embrence. Especially since Noor didn't mention he was even going to the palace until after he was fated. I am Drae Owner," Noor's mother said, sucking her teeth.

Drae gave Noor a pointed look as she stood up from her chair and moved to hug Ember. It was a stiff and unwelcoming hug that Ember hoped to never repeat, despite it lasting half a second. Ember could practically feel the disdain roll off of the woman.

"Please, call me Ember," she replied automatically, already regretting giving this cold woman the power of a nickname. How could someone with such immediate distaste for someone, based on their birthright alone and no other facts, raise such a beautiful being?

"It's a delight, Ember. My name is Cane Builder," Noor's

father said, ruffling Noor's hair as he passed him to give her a hug that felt opposite of his pair. Ember took an immediate liking to him. He must be the key to Noor's sweet nature. Thank Aaleia.

"Sit," Oma demanded quietly. Cindrea did so as well, moving from the corner of the dining room to take the opposite chair to Oma. Ember glanced, confused. She'd never seen one of the staff sit with Oma before. Ember felt a tremor move through her. An intuitive moment telling her to fear.

Cane pulled Drae to the table and they sat back in their earlier spots. He put his arm protectively around his wife. She did not seem to feel the impact of the situation as they did.

Noor held his breathe as he sat beside Ember. There was something unreadable in him, a distance Ember hadn't felt before. She held his hand and stared her grandmother in the eye. Oma was a murderer. Oma was a manipulator, installing a fake knight to the people and kidnapping that knight's pair and child to keep him compliant. This odd behavior after over a week together was not good. She knew something.

Jedoriah walked into the room, the heel of his black shiny shoes clicking on the floor.

"And my daughter?" Omanox asked him, keeping her eyes on Noor.

"Asleep still," Jedoriah answered. He surveyed the table and its occupants, seeing the tension in their stances. He sat beside Cindrea, giving her a sideways glance as if to ask why she was at the head of the table. She remained silent.

"Good, we can begin then," Oma said and stood from her chair. She dismissed the servants bringing in food and one of Oma's guards closed the door behind them. Ember surveyed the room. Wally and Zhieve were nowhere to be seen.

Oma cleared her throat and looked each individual in the eye.

"Every single one of you has betrayed me," Oma said flatly,

clasping her fingers together as if in prayer. She shook those clasped hands and pursued her lips.

Noor was rock still, staring across the table at his parents. Ember's heart began to beat erratically.

"Is everything okay, Oma? What happened?" Ember said and stood up again, feigning innocence. Her legs quivered, but she hoped Oma wouldn't notice.

"I am surrounded by rebels. Even my heir is a rebel. This will not do." Oma's voice came out in a sing-song.

Jedoriah stood too, glancing between Ember and Oma.

"There are no rebels here, Omanox. Come, let's discuss without company," he said. He pushed back his chair and walked towards her head of the table.

"Sit down, Jedoriah," Cindrea said from the opposite end of the table. He blinked in surprise at the outburst and turned back to sit down, looking to her. Was Cindrea also a secret rebel? Ember wondered, trying to piece together her reason for being summoned to this occasion. How had she betrayed Oma, and why would Jedoriah listen to her?

"You too," Cindrea said in warning to Ember. Jedoriah nodded to her and given his recent confessions, she sat. What part of the puzzle was she missing here?

Oma smiled slowly, surveying the many confused faces before turning to Noor's parents.

"I have her," Oma said.

Hasley? Ember looked wildly around the room, but there were no more people here than there were when she entered. Thoughts began to spiral around her. Did Amic betray them? Was she captive in another room? Her thoughts halted when Noor and his mother stood quickly, both pulling out a knife and pointing it to the dragon matron. His father froze in his seat, tears gathering in his eyes.

They came to radically different conclusions. This was not Hasley. The threat was aimed at Noor and his parents.

"Where is she?" Noor asked and hedged the knife closer in threat.

"Who are you talking about? Noor, where is who?" Ember asked, left in the dark.

"Don't you know, dragonia?" Cindrea said and leaned back in her chair. She crossed her arms and smirked.

"Noor's sister is alive. We have her."

THIRTY-ONE

ACCEPTING A CROWN

The world seemed to circle around Ember like a tidal wave, echoing again and again in her mind with blood rushing to her ears.

Noor's sister is alive. We have her.

Her first thought was, *yes, I know that,* before the second sentence jumped out. *We have her. We have her. We have her.*

"Give. Her. Back," Noor said, a growl rumbling in his chest. He edged closer to Oma, his knife coming higher. His mother moved behind her son, face drawn in anger.

Oma laughed in the face of the knives.

"You think you can get the answers you seek, kill your pair's grandmother, get out of the castle, and get your sister? Is there a rescue party outside that door waiting for you?"

She laughed at the notion.

"What do you want from us?" Cane asked, pulling his wife away. Drae let him.

"Good question," Oma purred, picking off a long silver hair from her dress. "What is it we want, Cindrea?" Oma posed the question to Ember's lady in waiting.

Cindrea dropped her hands on the tabletop and pushed herself up.

"What are you doing?" Jedoriah asked. She ignored him.

"We want," she began with a long drawl, bringing herself between Noor and Oma as if she belonged there, "for Embrence and Jedoriah to *behave*."

Cindrea placed a delicate finger on top of Noor's dagger, pushing it down easily in his confusion.

She smiled, her demeanor mimicking the dragon matron with one distinct difference—the hand on her stomach.

Ember stood, leaving Jedoriah the lone occupant at the table. He seemed immovable, a stone statue while Ember now understood the blood in his veins and the wear and tear of his heart.

"You are Jedoriah's pair," Ember said, the pieces fell together in a horror. Actions snapping into place and just as before, conversations with hidden meanings and stolen moments firing through her subconscious.

Jedoriah helping Cindrea into the carriage on that first day.

Cindrea's comfort in calling Jedoriah by name.

Leaving rooms together.

Arriving within moments of each other.

The day she caught her bringing the tea to his office and Jedoriah's exclamation through the closed door.

A dislike and yet camaraderie with Ember's grandmother. The person who gave them their position.

Her leaving the day after Amir's death.

A swell to her stomach.

Jedoriah's confession.

"No," Cindrea said darkly, her eyes twinkling with mischief as she watched Ember put the pieces together, *"he is mine."*

Words from long ago snapped into Ember's mind.

"Your pair helps you reach your full potential," Ahnika had said in that first lesson.

"If I had the chance to be queen, I would not hesitate." Words straight from Cindrea's mouth. It was right in front of her this whole time.

Cindrea's potential brought her here, a hair's breadth from the throne.

Jedoriah dropped his hand into his hands.

"She got to you," he whispered.

"No, Jed," Cindrea replied flatly. "I chose the side of the person who took care of our family. Not the little girl that doesn't even want to be here."

Ember felt the offense like a splash of cold water. No, she had not wanted to be here. Had that lead to all of this? Amir's death, Cindrea's betrayal of Jedoriah, and the kidnapping of Noor's sister?

"You know the truth of our installed knight as well?" Oma laughed manically. "You are more far gone than even I knew, dear Fireheart."

"Why my sister?" Noor asked, his voice cracking. Drae and Cane observed, taking in what they could. The royal family was riddled in deceit.

"Because you hid her and because your family is a problem," Oma responded honestly.

"I'll do what you say, just let her go," Ember said and gripped Noor's sweaty palm. His posture fell and he leaned into her side.

"I know you will," Oma said. "Let's begin with having breakfast. All this planning has left me famished. We'll talk later on how to rid ourselves of the rebel vermin you decided to play with."

Oma sat back down, with Cindrea on her opposite chair. They each prepared a heaping plate of food before them. The rest of the occupants sat in silence, a heavy weight teetering between them.

"NAIVE LITTLE GIRL, I certainly hope you have a more aggressive plan in mind," Noor's mother sneered as she paced her and Cane's room.

A knock sounded and Wally popped his head in, his expression was drained of color. "They say you only have one minute before we are escorted back to the tower."

Ember nodded to him, and he closed the door.

"That is enough, don't you think?" Noor said once they were alone again.

"Excuse me?" Drae asked with an arched brow.

"I said. That. Is. Enough," he said slowly, exhaustion punctuating his words. "Naomi is captured, and we have nothing to bargain with."

"We are resistance leaders. We can get her back."

"Are you sure about that?" Ember asked.

The three occupants turned to her.

"We don't know how long they've known we were in the resistance. They could have been watching all of our movements to time it perfectly. When was the last time you saw your daughter?"

Cane's face reddened in shame as he said, "two weeks."

Noor sobbed into his hands, giving in to the breaking of his heart. The sight broke her heart too. She hadn't known Naomi, hadn't been able to come up with a plan yet to help her, but she was her family now. She'd find a way to help this part of Noor's heart and history.

"How could you have not seen your daughter in two weeks and not know she was gone?" Ember asked incredulously, she rubbed her hand in circles on Noor's back as she tried to process that fact.

"We move her frequently throughout other rebel homes. We couldn't inconvenience anyone for too long."

"She is your daughter!" Noor yelled, tears rolling into his mouth and nose running. He pushed both his parents against the dresser near the door. It banged back and his mother yelped. He pointed his finger at the both of them. "You were supposed to take care of her! She was yours."

"And who was going to watch her when you left, Nori? Huh? Who did you think would take care of Naomi while we were out working to take on the royal family and you went to *join them*," Drae accused, pointing her own finger at Ember.

"I am not responsible for the world," Noor whispered. A thought he had repeated to himself, undoubtedly, when he decided to leave and make a mark for himself.

"You are a knight," Cane said back as if that proved that Noor was, indeed, responsible for Naomi and much much more. Cane rubbed his arm where a knob had indented with a wince, Ember did not feel sorry for him or his pair.

The guilt that was bred into Noor his whole life was apparent. His need to add humor to every situation, to make light when he was responsible for the care of his sick sister and the pain he felt when he left to the one profession his parents would disapprove of the most. Ember thought again of the Fateless man that ran for her in the woods near the palace and hoped that the madness that took Naomi was calmer, a subtler descent into pain and forgetting.

The door opened and Zhieve entered with Wally and other men she did not recognize.

"Time to go back to the tower, Embrence Dragon Daughter," a stranger said. She nodded to the woman and filled out. Noor held her hand like a lifeline. Neither of them looked back on the couple.

"I'M SORRY," Ember spoke into the silence between them. They stood in the center of the small tower room. Clothes were strewn everywhere from her morning indecisiveness. Had that morning only been a few hours ago? It felt like ages as her body was alight with tension and the figurative crown heavier on her brow.

Ember had never felt this helpless. Years of pain and loneliness did not compare to this embedding dread. Ember pulled him into her until they fell together into bed. She was not as strong as him, not by a long shot, but he let her pull him away.

"It's going to be okay," she said, stroking his curly hair.

"No, it's not," he responded, pushing back her hands and wiping his face. They laid staring at each other, matching each other's breathing.

"I wish our world was just this. Just our arms around each other," Ember said, "but it isn't. I'll solve this, Noor. I may not have wanted this crown, and I may not have been trained for it, but that training doesn't mean anything. My mother was raised to be queen and now she is queen in name only, imposters taking her birthright and leading our people to ruin."

Our people reverberated in Ember. While she had begun to think of them that way after getting to know the resistance, she hadn't said it aloud. She hadn't admitted to herself that she was preparing, actually trying, to take part in this life thrown on her.

"There is more than the wall. More to our oppression than we know. I will find out what it is, and I will get your sister back."

And unbidden, without warning, Ember's mind added, *"and I will be the true queen."*

THIRTY-TWO

SCALED BEASTS

The two weeks that followed were stagnation and whirlwind. The two oppositions threw Ember into a state of confusion. She couldn't help but compare herself to her birth mom. The mad Queen of Ashkadance was seen when necessary and hidden when not. Though Karwyn was more puppet than Ember hoped to be, she still played her part. Oma had successfully kept two of her family members in towers and one faux knight at her beck and call. She was the ringleader here, and Ember knew of only two ways to escape. She would attempt one the night of the ball. And if that failed, she'd figure out if she was capable of the second.

Guests came in and out of the castle as they prepared for the Mutrien ball, taking up the majority of Ember's faux puppet time. She was paraded around and prompted to say and do as Oma asked. Ember saw Jedoriah in passing, but wasn't able to speak with him alone again. How long did he do her bidding willingly? When did he join the cage she was now in?

"I am grateful to Aaleia and Mutrien for bringing me back to my family," Ember would say with a smile.

"Omanox Dragon Matron has been my biggest supporter. I

hope to be as loving to my people as she is." Ember would lie with a smile.

"I aim to understand our history and use that to guide my policies," Ember replied during a scribemaster visitation. Ember was able to add in, "the wisdom of the scribes are welcome in my reign," before Oma pulled her away with a tight grip on her arm.

"This is your only warning, granddaughter. Use that phrase again and there will be consequences," Oma hissed. Ember didn't want to know what those consequences would be. She behaved after that, saving her rebellion for their plan. Well, *behaved* may be a strong word. She did not speak out of turn, which would be more accurate.

Another tower, another balcony, yet so far away from where she wanted to be. Ember thought of the bed she never expected she'd miss, the small hard mattress of her home in Firetop. She wished she could have seen the province one more time. But she had to choose. She chose the side of the kingdom that would lead her to Amic Scribemaster. It brought her back to Hasley. Ember wondered what Karwyn thought of Firetop. Did she have enough awareness to know when they passed through the province that she was riding through where her daughter was found? Did they visit the site of the First Fating?

A knock sounded at the tower door. Noor did not move from his spot on the bed. He had gone deeper into himself. Ember stood from her writing desk, holding a few small bound pieces of parchment in her hand.

"Dinner," Zhieve said as he opened the door. He handed a tray of goods to Ember. She accepted it and dropped the curled papers into his hand. He nodded and left without commentary, pocketing the notes.

Ember closed the door and carefully placed the steaming cups of soup on the writing desk.

"Get up, Noor. Food is here," Ember said firmly.

"I'm not hungry," he said, voice muffled in the pillow. It had been like this for days: food would come in, messages would go out, and he was too stubborn to even notice. But she was always able to get him to eat, eventually.

"Yes, you are. You can't hide your grumbling stomach from me," Ember said with an attempt at humor.

She sat on the bed beside him and brushed a curl from his face. His eyes trailed up to her, the emptiness in them scared her.

"I need you," Ember whispered, hating herself for saying it. She knew that was what pairs were for, to work together to find and accomplish potential. She finally understood it. Seeing how it broke Cindrea and Jedoriah, when they both ascended to powers but never agreed on the reasons for it. They hadn't planned on an out. Ember wasn't going to let that mutual destruction happen to her and her knight.

"Is everything okay?" he asked out of habit. They both knew it was not. She didn't answer the question.

"Tomorrow is the ball," Ember said instead, "and I need you to do something for me."

She outlined the parts of the plan he would agree with, the parts she had designed to keep him out of the way and help aid in his purpose. He would save his sister, and she would help him save the Fateless—her own mother included.

"THANK YOU," Ember whispered in the dim light of the hall. She rubbed her hands down her dress, regretting when the sweat didn't wipe off and instead her palm scratched against sequins.

"You only have ten minutes, then they'll be back to get her ready for the ball," Zhieve warned as he unlocked the door in front of them. He backed away and pocketed the key, guarding the end of the hall. No one was due to check on her until that ten-minute mark. That didn't leave her much time, but she knew it would be enough.

Ember tapped hesitantly on the door before turning its long gold handle. It stood out in the glimmering dark, as bright as her fear.

"Is it time?" Karwyn whispered, turning from a chair in the corner of the room and standing in a flourish. Her long black nightgown reflecting back purple and blue light with the movement.

Taken aback, Ember asked, "time for what?"

"To leave, of course," Karwyn answered as if Ember should be the one who knew this. Karwyn walked to the bed, putting on her robe and pocketing a small notebook from the desk as if that was all she needed to leave.

"And go where?" Ember asked. She fidgeted with her dress, walking further into the room. Was this where her mom slept while visiting her grandmother as a child? Or did they change her to the smaller and more isolated room after she was commanded under guard?

"To the sea," she replied back matter of factly.

"Oh...no, not yet time to go to the sea," Ember said, unsure what to answer.

Ember sat down on the edge of the queen's bed, gazing around her. She didn't even know what she wanted to ask or say. She just felt she had to see her, alone, before she did what she had to do that night. She had never been alone with the queen. It hadn't been allowed. Guards and maids followed her everywhere, and like today, the queen's room was always locked.

The space suited her. Dark grey walls with sprinkles of gold and shadows on the paper. The queen had drawn on the walls, silhouettes of what she presumed were waves based on her reading. Some were swirls of black waves, dark and tremulous in the corner of the room. Others were beautiful simplistic lines, waves with tumbling white fluffs on top. Ember saw a painting once of a wave in a school book, an example of the dangers of water and drowning taught to children. but these were different. This was drawn by someone that had seen many waves up close and understood what they represented. It must be difficult to have seen such beauty, to only have it ripped from you. From the top of Ember's balcony, she could only see the far away still-sea. Nothing like what was depicted here. This must have been her old room, Ember decided, she couldn't have done all this in the few nights they were here.

The queen's balcony was locked shut. Every piece of furniture was black. The bed held soul-thread sheets and furs like Ember's, but there was also tall winding banisters to hold up gossamer curtains around it. If they were privacy curtains, they would do little to hide anything. They were see-through and breezy, loosely tied at the end of each post. In the dark, with little lamplight, the furniture must look like tall shadowed creatures.

"I wanted to talk to you," Ember began, remembering her limited time. She pulled on the ends of her short hair, unsure where to start.

"Then are you here for the truth?" Karwyn asked hopefully. She sat in front of Ember on the floor, eagerness shown through her eyes and smile.

"The truth?" Ember repeated nervously. She tried to calm herself, remembering what Jedoriah had said to her. Karwyn was indeed Fateless. While Ember certainly wanted to know what the queen knew, she was anticipating having to deal with riddles.

"You feel it, right? That things aren't right?"

Numbly, Ember nodded, scared of what her mother would say next.

"You must feel his loss too," Karwyn said absentmindedly. She looked down at floor as if an answer lay there.

"What loss?" Ember asked.

"The loss of your father," Karwyn replied.

"Do you mean Jedoriah?" Ember asked, wondering if her mother was confused by the lie told to their people. After so many years in this state, maybe Karwyn grew to believe it as well.

Karwyn titled her head. "Your father, not Jedoriah," she laughed softly as if the idea were preposterous.

"I don't have a father," Ember said. The nervousness leaked from her as other feelings started to settle in. She was not going to get the answers she had hoped for after all. Her mom was too far gone. Ember stood, disappointed to not have this chance to discuss her moms before it was too late.

Karwyn laughed outright at the movement, a melodious irony in her tone.

"Meerandus is your father, not *Jedoriah*." She scoffed at the last word, as if it were indeed Ember that was Fateless for thinking such a thing.

Ember looked back at her, her breath halted and body frozen. A rushing sound echoed in her, starting from her ears and moving through her body. She turned and stared at the wall of waves, connecting what she saw with the pull and tug in her heart.

"Who is Meerandus?" she asked, a small voice that felt not like her own.

"My fated pair, of course. He's down there!" She pointed to the locked balcony.

Ember felt near fainting, her breath pulling in and out of her in uncontrollable gasps.

"In the city?" Ember asked, hoping for an easier answer, something to stop the fear and panic. This wasn't her mother's madness. This was a clue.

"No, silly Embrence. He is where merfolk live. The sea. Can we go there now?"

Merfolk. Merfolk? Why would she say that? Ember couldn't hold the rushing in her any longer, she fell to the floor, curling herself inward. The sea...the sea? Conversations from the past few months cycling through her brain.

"Always listen to your father!" Karwyn had said after her fight with Jedoriah about the wall. That was before Ember knew, before Ember questioned Jedoriah as her father. She didn't think about that moment again, not after she knew the truth. What other moments were hiding information? That was also the day of their first fight, the day she decided never to listen to his guidance over that of her own heart and mind.

"You look like him," Karwyn told her the day of her debut and the Aaleia ball.

"Dear starlight, don't be upset," Karwyn said, kneeling above her and petting Ember's short hair.

"How?" Ember managed to croak out.

"Oh, there is always a how isn't there. Don't worry. The why is more important."

Ember didn't want to play games. She needed straight answers. She blurted, "why?" and rubbed her arms, hoping to stop the spreading numbness of her panic.

"Because my mother hates merfolk, of course."

And little moments began to click together as they did before.

"How did you become fated to a merman?" Ember whispered.

Karwyn bent closer, helping Ember uncurl herself from the ball she was so tightly wound into.

"I've always been one with the sea. Then I met the sea and he was there too." Karwyn ran a delicate hand on Ember's scales.

Karwyn continued to pet her, from her hair to her scales, in a rhythmic motion, and it oddly calmed her. The rushing began to calm into a crashing wave instead of a waterfall, echoing her heart beat as it slowed down.

"Am I a mermaid?" Ember asked, already knowing the answer. Scales she believed were from dragons, but Ember knew the truth just as clearly as the words that came from Karwyn's mouth.

Karwyn sighed as if talking to a child. "My dear, here you go. Other me will explain."

Karwyn reached into her robe pocket and pulled out a small book. Ember moved up from her sprawled position. Curious and hopeful, she accepted the small book. It fit into her palm, green velvet brushed against her skin. She pulled her knees under her and opened the first page.

Dearest Embrence,

I write this to you with tears strolling down my face and shaking hands. I can't do this. I know I must.

On a diplomatic mission to Grydagia, our ship was turned over by a storm. Myself and the crew were sinking, drowning. I could feel that it was over, that I was losing my light. But that wasn't my end. Aaleia wouldn't let it be. I heard a rushing through my body and bubbles surrounded me. And then, silence. The water quieted, and he was there. My pair. My heart.

Thinking back on it now, it was a little funny. Where did I meet my knight but as I'm falling into the sea? Gold glowed around us, sparks not apparent in the salt water. He smiled at me, his long green hair a halo around his face. I tried to smile back. The happiness I felt was bigger than I had ever experienced, but there was no breath left in my body. He saw this and saved me, kissing me and pushing air into my lungs. He wrapped his arms around me, breathing for me as he swam upward. My legs dimly felt his scales rubbing against them, the kick of his tail, but it didn't totally register to me what he was until we broke the top of the water, and I saw my shipmates.

Every single person was carried up by another one of the merfolk. We were saved. Aaleia had warned them we needed help, and they came for us. Meerandus came for me.

Mother was not happy. Her guards attacked us, separating me from him, and she convinced a Gryffin of Grydagia to fly me home. I was locked away from the sea, confined to my tower. It was the worst moment of my life, tortured, kept from my other half by force. If Pa had been alive, this wouldn't have happened.

Mother would not accept another beast co-ruling the kingdom. She refused, feeling as if Aaleia herself were taking away her crown and giving it to a monster. She was always that way, worried someone would take her power. It was why she hated me for so long, she knew I would take it from her one day. But she didn't anticipate my partner would be a threat too. A merman ruling a dragon kingdom was unacceptable.

Meerandus came for me, like I knew he would. I felt a pull, an unexplainable tug that grew tighter the longer we were apart, and one morning I knew he was here. It was as if I snapped back into place. I looked out from my balcony window, and there he was. I could see him, standing with legs on the walkway of the palace. I wanted to go to him, but I had already been confined to my tower for weeks. The doors were locked and guards stood at my door, but it didn't matter. We glowed purple, sparks erupting around me and from my middle. Aaleia blessed us on our second sighting, from hundreds of feet away.

The guards tackled him, all twenty of the men and

women guarding the palace were ordered to capture him as a threat from a foreign land. They tried to kill him with my mother leading the cry.

But he would not die. Our purple sparks surrounded him, a shield of Aaleia's creation. He ran on shaking human legs. The servants passed on the message to me that he would be back. That he said he would bring help. The merfolk were coming to Ashkadance; they were coming for me.

They were coming for you, my sweet Embrence.

But mother would not take that. She ordered a halt to all travel, brought in all the construction crews Ashkadance had, and killed those that knew the truth. She claimed they were inflicted with a disease from the merfolk. Little did she know, she named her punishment from the gods. Soon, she would be ruler of the unwell.

My mother renamed the sailors, tradesmen, and everyone involved in leaving our kingdom to a new purpose. She told them lies, that the merfolk brought upon the Fateless and they were going to attack again. If anyone resisted the wall, they were killed, thrown and burned in a ditch. She scrubbed their homes and businesses for anything that would help the cause. She spread the lie. I was the biggest lie and the harshest truth.

"This is what they do!" She would cry. "This is how it kills you!" She would tell our people. Her murders explained away by the yet to be named illness.

War and plague. Death on our horizon. An eclipsing loveless death. Build, build, build, build little men and women. Build your cage. Build your ruin.

Build, build, build...

I'm sorry, it's taking me, and I don't know what to do.

I wasn't the same. I am not the same. Being isolated, away from him, it's changing me. And the wall? It's *changing others. She predicted our demise. She built our death with beautiful white stone. A stone no flame could take down, only a dragon could get through this brick. Sickness did come. It started with me.*

Aaleia had given us all pairs. And we trapped people without the means to find them. We are called Fateless but our fates are waiting for us. They are out there. They are waiting. They are suffering. They can't get better, not while the wall stands.

She built our curse. Claimed a sickness had come when there wasn't one. Then it was real, so real. It started with me. May the gods forgive us.

And Jedoriah became my knight, a fool's knight, a facade. Mother controls everything, controls him, controls the guards and the servants. If you don't bend, she breaks you. I couldn't let them break you too. Forgive me.

Forgive me. Forgive me. Forgive. Forgive...

They are taking you now. Safe. Safety with them. I promise. She won't have you. Safety. Forgiveness.

My remembrance. My fire. You'll be what is left of me. I won't forget you. I promise I won't forget you. Remembrance, my Embrence. Please forgive me.

Tears streamed down Ember's face as she took in the rest of the small book. It was just scrawls of words. *Forgive* was a common one, as was *build*. But in the mess, there were snippets of other content, names, her parent's names, Meerandus, flames and waves.

She looked up to see a smiling Karwyn blinking at her. "You see?" she asked, tilting her head like a child waiting to get an answer, hopeful of what was coming next.

"I see," Ember responded, standing up and pulling her mother with her. Hugging her as she did on that first day they met.

"You don't belong here," Karwyn whispered, tears crazing Ember's shoulders. The words didn't hurt now. Ember took them for what they actually were.

Karwyn Dragon Queen, her mother, was telling her that she saved her. That she wasn't safe here and because of that, she had let her go. Her mother was saying, "I love you."

A DESTINY HER OWN

Ember knew that speaking with her mother would be a difficult conversation, but she was not anticipating to learn that another facet of her existence was a lie.

"I am not just dragon-born, I am part of the sea…" Ember whispered to herself, staring into the mirror. Part of a sea she had never touched, only glimpsed. Candles were lit all around the space, illuminating the features she felt she didn't know anymore. Her black hair was her mother's, but was the rainbow appearance in certain light a merfolk trait? With much of her history now brought to light, would that understanding lead her to a better life? She was unsure. But one thing was certain, the moms that raised her, Echoris and Julimore, had been good people. She felt more free than she had since their deaths.

Her scales, of course, were more to do with her father. He was the closer beast to her bloodline. Drakul had died hundreds of years prior, whereas a merman was only one generation behind.

She was more beast than human. What did that mean?

Her moms death, her kidnapping, and her scales were now

revealed to her. All that was left were the Fateless, a hope she would solve once the wall was destroyed.

The celebration of Mutrien was more joyous than Ember's debut ball. The Aaleian festival in Ashkadance had always been a more formal affair. If the First Fating had stopped their war, it needed to be with a calming kindness that it was celebrated with their people. But this was something built for fun, anarchy, enjoyment. Life. Mutrien brought them shelter and continued life and it was celebrated as a party. Mutrien's celebration fell on the longest night of the year. Though oddly, this ball didn't call for her to stay up all the way through it.

Just like on the night she met Noor, the whole of the kingdom was invited to the ball. Keyholders and their invited guests filled the halls of the Cruelindime castle. Ember felt herself comparing the different halls and decorations as she left the bathroom and rejoined Noor.

She gripped his hand and felt her confusion and acceptance of her knowledge bleed into a nervous dread.

She'd have to tell him what she now knew, but not tonight. He had a mission. As did she. Ember was selfish. She wanted to save her kingdom, but not at the potential cost of her pair.

Walking through the palace, Ember noted the staff working on the decor. When the kingdom had dragons, the longest night had been a time of free-flying. Hours of time in the sky, mingling in the night and blotting out the stars with their large bodies. While the wraiths still enjoyed the pleasure, their flying was not nearly as impressive. Still, the influence was there. We could not see dragons, but we could honor them. Ember wondered how the other kingdoms celebrated Mutrien. Did their beasts hold an influence in their celebrations of the gods, even when not directly related to the original cause for celebration?

The ball was held on the roof, open to the stars and night

air. Climbing up the stairs, the wind kissed Ember's skin and she smiled up at the sky.

Every table held sparkling gems, a reflective light. Blues, pinks, greens, shimmered in each table setting. It was not on the table cloths this time, instead opting for a gold-lined fabric. There were some cut neon flowers on each table, basking in the light of the stars before they wilted.

A night filled with charade. Karwyn entered the roof as guests began to settle down. Jedoriah was beside her, her arm looped in his. They were both prisoners, she could see that now. While Ember could never forgive Jedoriah for the murder of her moms and Amir, that brand on his soul would never leave him, she saw they were together in this now. His loyalty to Oma was no more. He would prove that tonight.

"I trust you will be on your best behavior?" Oma had asked her over breakfast that morning, as if speaking to a petulant child. Noor had stared down at his breakfast, pushing around a bowl of porridge. *It's almost over*, Ember thought to herself. One way or another.

The bodice of her dress was a leather and steel marvel, tough, unyielding, and welded to mimic further scales. There was quite a struggle getting it on, the laces in the back helping to torture her. The skirt was heavier than her debut ball dress. Instead of airy and billowing, it was a dark shimmering silhouette. Crystalline jewels and sequins moving in a gradient, combining with the steel of the bodice. Hidden from sight, she had the knife that murdered her friend buckled to the back of her calf, easy enough to get in its low position. She wished she could keep it more secure at her thigh, but with the heaviness of her skirt that would make it impossible for her to reach.

Ember watched as Jedoriah and Karwyn took their place at the head of the space, sitting upon two chairs on an altar. Other chairs sat beside them, one for Oma and two others for Noor and herself. Now that the queen and the person that was supposed to be her knight sat beside her, it was their turn to enter. United. Ember felt like running from their lies, but it was not time yet. She begged her mind to calm down, be patient. This was not like that first ball. They were not here explicitly for her.

She sat at her designated chair, Noor holding her hand beside her. Music began to rise and Ember surveyed the crowd assembled. Several citizens stood out to her: Jade, Jardano, Amic, other keyholders, and resistors. But not all. For her plan to work, all of their supporters could not be here in Cruelindime. They had positions to hold.

Citizens took their seats. Those who did not have space stood in the back, in the halls, and spilled in many other crevices throughout the palace and its walls. On the walkway outside the palace and in the streets, those who could not make it inside also celebrated. If all was as it should be, there was a particular path laid clear for them. The guards that were not present in this room saw to that.

"I present to you, Embrence Dragon Daughter and her pair, Noorworth Knight," a priestess called. The evening would begin with a speech. Ember wondered briefly how many formal evenings would involve speeches from her. They were not her favorite thing to do. She and Noor stood now in front of their junior thrones. It took several moments before the crowd was quiet enough for her to speak.

"I've been asked to speak to you today about unity, about duty, and about the role that the royal family places in your life with the guidance of Aaleia and Mutrien behind them," Ember began, a hush spreading through each person in the room. Noor pumped her hand, knowing these were things that Oma had pushed onto her to say. But he did not know was that this speech would mean different things on reflection, different after what she was going to do.

"It is not an easy role," she continued, "as I've learned in these few months as part of the royal family."

"For I was not raised a future queen. I was raised as one of you, with one distinction. I was told to hide. To lie with each breath. To be invisible.

"We don't always take what Aaleia has given us with grace and trust. We ask the universe for help, like Mutrien did. Sometimes we don't like the answer."

Ember looked around to the people that had gathered to partake in the ball with them, her eyes landing on Jedoriah.

"We fight the destiny bestowed on us and choose another one. There is strength in that resilience, there is strength in hard choices and doing what is right. There is strength in forging your own path, there is power and might in not taking your life for what was handed to you. And I applaud those that go their own way."

Tears gathered in Jedoriah's eyes, seeing between her lies. He tried to do his best with the grace given to him, a purpose he should not have been given but yet was.

"But there is also duty," Ember added.

"Duty to your family, to your neighbors, and friends, to Ashkadance and our gods. Duty requires you to be the best person that you can be and to take pride in your purpose. The most challenging part of duty is accepting that who you want to be and who *you have to be* isn't always the same person. That's a battle I struggle with every day."

Ember swallowed, her throat going dry.

"But we are together in that bond. We come together in that fear that we aren't enough, that we could be more. United in that fear that life may not be what we expected but it could, in the long term, be what we needed. When the dawn comes tomorrow and the world looks different, find that unity together. Find the unity that Aaleia is working to give to all of us. We work with her every day to give you that which will help you feel whole."

She bowed her head, signaling that she finished speaking. Claps began to cascade across the room. The music flowed up with the sound, and Noor spun Ember around into his arms for a waltz. The speech seemed to invigorate him, pushing his old self briefly up to the surface.

"Those speeches of yours keep getting better and better," he commented. "Probably not what Oma was expecting." She could see Oma and Jedoriah talking at the side of the swirling room. "But it will have to do," Ember said.

"I loved it," Noor added and she smiled back at him. They danced and tried to stay as far away from the royal family as they could until the signal went out.

THIRTY-FOUR

THE LONGEST NIGHT

Adrenaline coursed through Ember, her heart maintaining dancing beats as she ran through the passageway. She held up her sparkling skirts, hoping to add a few precious seconds to her speed. Her shoes clicked on the floor with each step. If she weren't so panicked, the sounds would irritate her senses. Noor, Wally, and Zhieve kept pace beside her in their dress uniforms.

"Good luck," Ember said to Noor. He kissed her fiercely and promised, "I'll be back."

He ran off with Wally, going to join other resistors at the closest community home. While on their tour they had completed construction and began to fill their doors. The scribes were able to report back the vital information they needed to know.

Naomi was found. She was with them in the homes, hidden in plain sight. His parents should already be there. Zhieve lead them earlier down into their tunnels.

Tunnels they wouldn't have known about, if not for Jedoriah. His youth at the castle revealing that yes, this place also had secret exits.

Ember and Zhieve grabbed the shovels they hid the night prior and began digging. Right above where they dug was a hairline fracture in the crisp white wall. One that would not have been noticed if it weren't for the meticulous work of the scribes and their network of members. People like Ember's moms. She hoped they would be proud of her.

"Faster," Zhieve demanded as they pushed to create a deeper hole. They had to place the canisters of dragon blood at precisely the right depth to shake the foundations.

"Did someone request a special delivery?" Jade called comically as she drove her carriage to them. She jumped down from the horse and turned to open the door. Rather than a guest inside its walls, there were jugs of the dark fluid Ember had felt remarkably close to. Jade didn't dare drive it over the path to be easier for them to distribute, for she feared what would happen if the carriage tipped over or jostled its contents.

"Is Amic with Hasley already?" Ember asked between puffed breaths. Dirt fell into her shoes. She tried not to glance at what this digging must be doing to her gown. It wouldn't matter anyway. Her involvement in this would be undeniable in moments.

"Yes, they got their supplies yesterday. His people helped me deliver some shipments in the night too. They all looked as dirty as you when I reached them." Jade looked up to the sky, searching for the shadow of a wraith across the stars. Ember doubted they'd get any notices if there was a mishap, the time-line was so tight that sending a wraith wouldn't make sense. The only notice they were going to hear was the sounds of explosions across the city.

"We still have three feet to go," Ember said, out of breath. Jade grabbed their third shovel and joined them.

Looking back to the castle, Ember could see the silhouettes of movement on the roof where she knew her birth family were now with their guests. The moon was climbing quickly, once it reached the center of Ashkadance it would be time.

They had only an hour.

"Pass me the buckets!" Jade called and Zhieve popped up to get them.

Ember and Jade filled buckets of dirt and sand, passing them up to Zhieve. He emptied them in piles a few feet away, dropping them back down again to their shoveling. They worked tirelessly, secluded beyond the trees. No one but resistance members would be looking to the wall tonight. There was too much excitement for the ball, eyes all on the castle.

"That should do it," Ember grunted. Jade climbed her way out and Zhieve held his hand out for her to grab.

"What is this?" a voice called in the distance. Ember froze, eyes wide as she looked up at the shadowed Zhieve. He motioned a finger to his lips before turning around.

"Omanox Dragon Matron, how can I help you?" He embodied innocence in his voice, but his demeanor said anything but.

"I don't know Zhieve Captain, can you tell me why you are leaning over a hole in the ground with a known rebel?"

"I decided I'm tired of taking orders from false idols." His attitude sparked, a new commitment forming in his heart. He had always been true to his kingdom, in his own way, following orders without question. Amir's death changed that.

Ember's chest heated as the anger grappled her heart. They didn't have time for this. They needed to get the dragon blood in the pit before they lost their window of time.

"I can answer that!" she called from below, ignoring Zhieve's call for silence. Jade hauled Ember out of the hole with a gripped hand.

She brushed dirt from her outfit and she knew it didn't matter now. The hole was deep enough. All that was left was the blood.

"I was hoping you were smarter than this," Oma said, sucking her teeth with raised eyebrows. "Unfortunately, I misplaced my judgement of you," she added.

A horse was beside her, and off in the distance there were two other figures riding towards them in the dark. An audience it would be then. She should have known that it would be this way, with her family a part of it. There was no other way it could end.

"We have to talk," Ember said to Oma. She opened her mouth but before she could speak a syllable, she held up a hand. "Privately," she said as she walked past her grandmother. As she hoped, she followed indignantly. She did not like being showed up. Omanox needed the last laugh, always.

"I trust you know what to do," Ember said pointedly over her shoulder to Zhieve. Jade was already inching back to the carriage.

Twenty-feet away, Ember positioned herself so that she was facing the wall. Oma looked at her, away from the action.

"You dare to make commands of me," Oma said with malice. Her hair was not braided today. Instead, it lay straight down her back, her peach dress brightening the yellow in her skin.

"I am the queen," Ember said, hands on her hips. The sentence had the effect she hoped.

"You are not queen," her voice boomed with immediate anger. Ember saw Jade startle in her peripherals, but Ember didn't stray her eyes from her grandmother. They had to work faster and she could not draw attention to them. The blood of her heritage sloshed into the dirt, creating a pool of history. They continued to pour the jugs, careful not to get too close to the opening, using gloves to protect themselves.

"My mother is Fateless, due to the loss of her merman pair. Her knight is a fraud. You are a murderess, defying the will of the gods, and locking up your daughter," Ember listed. "I am in charge here."

Ember inched closer to her, speaking the words she knew would burn.

"If you get in my way," she threatened, "your deception will no longer be maintained. When the kingdom knows what you've done to your daughter, I will be the least of your concerns."

"You would not reveal her madness so easily," Oma hedged, reaching into the folds of her peach dress. She pulled out a gold knife, a delicate weapon made for close combat.

"Oh really? I have a feeling Karwyn would want me to share it. To stop you, I know she'd forgive me." Ember laughed bitterly, remembering the scrawling words of her Fateless mother.

You'll be what is left of me.

"As sure as the sun will rise, your time will run out. In fact, it has already begun."

The moon reached its height. In response, the party on the roof soared in celebration. The night was halfway through, but their plan was coming to a close.

Booms sounded first at a distance then closer. Explosions. A rumbling. It climbed like a tsunami.

"NOW!" Ember screamed across Oma's shoulder. She turned as the match was struck. Zhieve let go of the flame, and it fell into the material as he threw himself to the ground. Jade was already clear, hidden behind the carriage.

Ember and Oma fell, the blast of the impact pushing them to the ground.

The cascading sound rushed towards them and the stone wall shook with it. The kingdom tremored. It had begun. Ember coughed, heat and smoke curling around them as flames licked blue.

Peiradonne stone fell from the sky, crashing with the simultaneous hits on its weak points. The wall was opening, the sea calling and crashing into the slivers of stone falling to the ground. It called to her.

Omanox screamed a curdling sound unlike any that Ember had ever heard.

"We need the wall!" she cried, dust and dirt across her face and bright red murder reflected in her eyes. Zhieve lay unconscious in front of the broken wall, a slab of stone lay on his feet. Jade advanced from her hiding spot, hoping to help him.

All around them, the world continued to shake and screams collided their senses. The party on the palace landing strip stopped their revelry, running down the steps to see what was happening to their kingdom.

"No, *you* needed the wall. You couldn't let go of the crown!" Ember screamed back at her. Oma stood above her, face twisted and eyes wide.

"This is my kingdom!" she cried, her hands grabbed Ember's hair and pulled her up. Ember screamed, pain shooting her temple. Oma slapped her with one hand and held her knife to Ember's neck with the other.

"You don't know what you've done," Oma hissed.

"I've set us free. You'll have to answer to the people now," Ember whispered, happy for it to be her last act.

"I answer to no one," Oma declared, pressing the knife harder into her skin. It drew blood and Ember's eyes prickled with tears.

"I love you," Ember whispered, knowing it to be true. She didn't want to die saying hateful words. She did love her Oma, despite it all. She loved everyone in her family. She didn't like them, hated much of what they did, their actions irrefutable.

But love would always win out. Even in this.

Oma hesitated, her eyes pooling and mouth tense.

"I wish you hadn't said that," the dragon matron whispered. A decision passed through her, resolve becoming stronger. Oma moved the knife from her neck and Ember breathed a sigh of relief, but one that came too soon.

Oma repositioned the knife over Ember's heart, pressing it into visible scales.

"The dragon part of you, that is honorable. What you have from me, my daughter before she turned from me, and our heritage. This arrogance, this rebellion, the sniveling bits of you that belong to *that man*," Oma spat the word *man* like an insult, for her father was more than that. "That part damns you. It cannot survive."

She drew the knife back, arm out to strike a hard blow into her chest. Ember closed her eyes, not willing to see her grandmother's killing blow. Instead, she listened. Listened to the water lapping into their kingdom. She had done her duty. Ember would be free now.

But the blow didn't come.

"Get away from her," a voice cried in the distance.

Ember opened her eyes to see two figures running toward her. Three others were farther away, two men and a woman. She couldn't see their faces yet, but she recognized that voice.

"Karwyn," Oma said in surprise.

Her mother stepped forward, Jedoriah standing behind her with a sword extended.

Ember reached down while Oma was surprised and took out her hidden blade. She inched back away from them, loosely holding the weapon. She stood in a wide circle with the Fateless queen, dragon matron, and acting knight. Three of the four held a weapon, all but Karwyn. She didn't seem to notice that she was unarmed and pushed forward. She advanced fearlessly to her mother.

"I will not be shackled. I will not be burned. I do not drown. I am unheard. You hold me no more, mother, for my home is here. *My time to rule is now.*"

Oma backed up as her daughter kept moving forward.

Shocked, disturbed, seeing her daughter act on a clear conscious. As if the breaking of the wall freed her, Karwyn Dragon Queen stood tall and unafraid.

Ember stumbled to the floor, and Jedoriah stood in front of her. He reached for Ember's hand, taking the jeweled dagger he used to kill Amir. He called to his pretend pair, "Karwyn!"

She glanced back and extended her hand. He tossed the dagger and the queen caught it effortlessly. She kept moving forward, the dragon matron backing away without looking behind her.

Karwyn kept speaking, using her voice as the weapon, the dagger held without malice in her hand. As if a baton. A beacon of truth. Ember recognized the dagger now. As if the surrounding trees pulled her back in memory.

Outside of Azororion on the day of the Fateless man's death, two people stood before her. Cindrea and Wally. Wally held a sword not that different from Jedoriahs. But Cindrea, she held a dagger with a green gem.

"It's him or her," Oma had said on the night Amir was murdered. She handed Jedoriah's Cindrea's knife. Cindrea had been who was threatened. Now that same knife would be used against Oma. Or would it be needed?

"My destiny no longer twines with yours. Thank you for all you taught me," Karwyn said. Another tremor jolted through the world as more pieces of the wall crumbled. It shook her foundation, and Oma fell back, not realizing she had brought herself perilously close to the still-burning flames.

With a broken cry, the dragon matron fell into the pit of blood fire, and her scream was snuffed out. In an instant, the sea salt air was filled with the smell of burning skin and silver hair. There was no time to feel pain. She felt the fire and was consumed by it. Alone. Karwyn stood staring at the flames that consumed her mother. Tears did not fall. Instead, she stood resigned.

"Em," a voice called behind her. Ember turned her watery eyes to see Noor running for her. He held a woman's hand, his sister. She was laughing, finding joy in the run. Her wild orange hair held tighter curls than Noor. She was a flame. Wally ran past them, calling to Zhieve. He was free of the stone but still lay on the floor with bones broken.

"Are you okay?" Noor whimpered, falling down to her level. He let go of his sister's hand, and she immediately began to wander. Jedoriah placed a hand on Naomi's shoulder and tried to soothe her whirling mind, used to working with the Fateless queen. The queen that now stood at the edge of the world, hands touching the gaping open wall and looking beyond. Her shoes were off and in the water. She was searching. Ember now knew for what, but still gestured to Jedoriah to try and watch her too. It was dark, Karwyn would not find her pair tonight – but Hasley must have already.

"I will be," Ember finally answered. "We will be okay."

THIRTY-FIVE

A NEW TOMORROW

It was only two days, yet it felt like weeks.

Ember stood hand in hand with her mother as they watched the waves tumble over debris. Salt air circled towards them, carried on the wind. Ember couldn't help but take in a deep breath, holding it as part of her.

"How do you know he'll be here?" Ember asked. The sea rushed up towards the rubble, water leaking into Ashkadance after nearly two decades. She wanted to touch it, but her soul told her to wait. He was coming. She had to be ready to greet him. The kingdom needed her more than her desire to touch what had, until now, been forbidden. This was her first time near the water since the night she brought the wall to the ground.

"Aaleia told me," the queen answered with a smile. Ember had never seen her this happy. Karwyn bounced back and forth on her heels, dress swishing with her like a bell. Wraiths flew past them, letters in their claws. The letters hadn't stopped, the activity hadn't either. Revealing the knight of the realm was an imposter and that the queen matron had died trying to murder the heir? Well, it was enough. And the people didn't know what Ember now knew, the true knight was on the way. And he was a merman.

Ember squeezed her mother's hand tighter, happy that the fresh air was doing her good. If her true father came back, maybe she'd recover entirely. Ember hoped for that, but almost seventeen years away from her pair may have created irreversible damage. Did Aaleia actually speak to her? Hallucinations and voices were a symptom of the Fateless. She hadn't had a lucid moment since that night.

Noor watched them from a respectable distance away, not wanting to get in the way of their reunion but also not willing to leave Ember alone. Noor had been pulled between many duties these past couple of days: helping the kingdom clear the wall's debris, to help keep the peace in the fear of what was to come, the helping of the Fateless (his sister included) and that of his princess. While their love was irrefutable, that didn't mean it didn't take work. They would both be overworked for quite a while. They had opened a door to the unknown, now they had to step through it. Her new heritage a big question mark in the dark.

"I hope we get along well," Ember admitted out loud, rearranging her thoughts back to her father.

"That's a silly thing to think," her mother commented before a gasp escaped her lips.

"What is it?" Ember asked, she turned to follow Karwyn's pointed finger.

Out in the sea was movement. There was a shape in the waves coming closer. It moved just below the water, pushing it up in a curl as it raced faster.

Before she could stop her, the queen ran toward the waves. Her shoes slipped off, her skirts flew back, hair wild and smile beaming. The queen pushed through the rising water until she was within feet of the shape. It slowed down, knowing it was almost at its destination. Ember stood frozen, shocked but unafraid, she watched the shape and her mother flinging herself towards it.

Jumping up from the water was a man. Scales covering his body from head to toe, patchier on his face and more dense the farther down his form. As he emerged from beneath the water, the scales receded in uneven lines. Half his body stood covered in the mirror reflection of Ember's own scales, the rest of him now appeared human. He ran forward to meet the queen, using powerful legs in a way that Ember wasn't sure he should be able to do. His green hair was long, almost as long as the queen's. Their bodies finally reached each other, and Karwyn crashed into his chest with bursts of laughter and happiness. He met them in kind, a deep chuckle escaping his mouth as he pressed his head onto hers. He inhaled the scent of her hair and smiled.

"I found you," the man said.

"I waited," she answered.

When they pulled back to look into each other's eyes, purple erupted all around them. Sparks covered his partially scaled body and jumped onto Karwyn's. They gasped, the glow surrounding both of them. The smile that filled their faces could not be denied. After years apart, they would now get to experience the blessing together.

A tear fell down Ember's cheek. That should have been how she was brought into this world, not with the turmoil of a queen locked in a tower, away from all that made her whole.

As if sensing her tremulous thoughts, the merman looked up. His eyes met Ember's for the first time.

All her pain and doubt leaked from her chest with a sigh. The peace of meeting her mother for the first time came back to her, and Ember too began to glow. Not in the same way as the blessing, but a more a subtle glow with no sparks. The blessing bound, what she had felt when she met her mother and what Jedoriah claimed to have felt but lied.

Noor walked up behind her and stroked the back of her hair.

"Go meet him," he whispered, hugging his pair.

"I'm scared," she whispered back.

"All good things in the world come with fear," he reasoned.

Ember kissed him briefly and turned back to the water. She took one step forward and then another. She made it to the edge of the crumbled wall and took a deep clearing breath.

"I found you," the merman said again. His strong arms still held her mother, who looked between both of her favorite treasures with glee.

"I didn't know I was missing," Ember replied, in more ways than one. She stepped over the wall and into the water. Her parents began to walk towards her.

The sea—she was finally in the water. She looked down, its cool liquid washing over her linen pants. It filled her with joy. A spark of happiness soaring through her body.

Something was wrong. No, *something is right.* The happy spark turned into a tingling.

Cold and heat moved up her body, swirling fingertips pushing up from her feet.

"What's happening?" she called out, fear and exhilaration mixing in her blood.

"Ember!" Noor screamed. He ran towards the water just as Ember's vision began to blur. The color of the world changed, everything was bright and sharp. Her father pushed forward just as Ember began to fall. Her skin transformed, pain erupting from her chest as her scales grew up her arms and down her stomach. She dropped into the shallow water. Ember looked down, the water held pieces of her clothing, and where her legs should be, there was now a tail. Her legs knitted together into one and her grey and purple scales spread.

Noor and her father reached her at the same time, kneeling before her as she stared horrified at her body.

"It's going to be okay," Noor responded firmly. He held Ember's scaled hand. Meerandus held Karwyn's.

"I—I'm a mermaid," she whispered. Her eyes were wide, unable to look away from her bobbing tail and the skin turned scales. All that remained of her human self was her face, the scales stopped in a gradient around her neck. She had known she was part merfolk, but this? Ember had not expected to have a tail. To be a beast, truly.

"I'm a merman," her father said in answer to her statement. He shifted back into his merman form, his scales mimicking the same pattern with a tail that spanned longer than hers.

Ember looked into her father's gold eyes and said, "Hi. I'm Ember."

"I'm Meerandus," he said with a smile. He took her free hand and Karwyn took Noor's. They formed a circle around each other: human, dragon, mermaid, merman, all kneeling together in the foam.

"It's nice to meet you," Ember said with a tear.

"We're all together now," Karwyn said, her dress and hair wet.

A horn blew in the distance. Boats were silhouetted on the horizon as the neighboring kingdoms came to investigate the explosions, the tremor in the world as Ashkadance set itself free. Closer than that, heads began to pop out of the water one by one. Ashkadance was no longer the siloed kingdom. It was part of a whole new world.

"We're together now," Ember echoed.

EPILOGUE

The Betrayal, as the citizens called it, of Jedoriah Pretender was wide-spread news. Ember knew now what his sacrifices had been and the burden he had to wear each day that he assumed the duty of the knight. And some of it, she actually understood. But it didn't excuse the murder of Amir Captain or that of the Fateless that came before the community homes. It did not excuse the death of her adoptive moms in his search for her.

For the kingdom, it was seen as an unforgivable crime. They did not deem someone that would fake the will of Aaleia worthy of survival and called for his death.

What Ember did not understand was why he decided to try and reverse the killings of the Fateless. Whether it was guilt or some other reason, she was glad that he had convinced Oma of that change. Could it have been a changing opinion on her mother the queen? Or was the blood on his hands already too much to bear, and with the heir now found, less necessary?

Regardless, Jedoriah could not be seen in public again. Not if he wanted to live. Sequestered to a small room near the dungeons, Cindrea and their child were with him. It was a willing solitude, one he had to convince Cindrea of regularly. When the time came, they had agreed that his child would be allowed to go to school with the children of the other staff and come and go. Their child would be free. Ember would not punish someone for the sins of their parents.

With Oma gone and Karwyn sick for years, Jedoriah was the only one who held the information Meerandus would need in his role as the true knight. Part of his repayment to society was his cooperation. Seeing Jedoriah and Meerandus together was confusing to Ember's mind. Her family dynamic had shifted wildly this year.

It was about to change again.

Ember smiled at her mother across the dinner table. Karwyn smiled back, her hand idly running along her swelling stomach. For the first time in Ashkadance history, there were two heirs to the throne. They didn't know yet what that would mean.

"Are you ready to go?" Meerandus asked. He turned his head to her. His long green hair was shorter and more maintained than when they first met in the ocean those weeks ago. He had grown emotionally too, now more used to being in his human form. The way Karwyn smiled at him was different than the way she smiled at everyone else. She was the clearest when they were together, like Hasley and Arsenio. The time apart had impacted her, and the damage had yet to completely reverse. Meerandus did answer their suspicions about beasts and the Fateless, his status as a beast kept his mind safe. As part beast, Karwyn was more lucid than the others affected for as many years. For that, Ember was grateful.

"Of course she is," Noor said with pride. Ember squeezed his hand under the table. Noor had flourished, brighter and more focused on his task as knight now that his sister and parents were safe. The resistance was no more, just concerned citizens that were heard and taken care of. The secret spaces beneath the kingdom were being addressed and a council was coming together to see how to best use them. Jade was head of the committee, reporting ideas and requests to Noor on a weekly basis. While they were gone, she would report to Meerandus. The prejudice of merfolk was a new challenge for them to explore, one that was not apparent in those that came off those first boats to visit Ashkadance in diplomacy.

But just as dragons became part of who they were, so would the merfolk.

"I'm happy to represent our kingdom," Ember answered instead. Ready wasn't the word she would use. Scared was a lot more like it. Her palm began to sweat in Noor's, and she let go, rubbing her hands down her dress.

They were free now. The wall was gone, all debris cleared. To re-open trade, Ember was going to leave with Noor to visit Grydagia and Faeinto tomorrow. A new start, new purposes, and an exchange of the Fateless. Their hope was that more people would be paired and the Fateless would dwindle, but they knew not everyone would be. The earlier deaths in the kingdom saw to that. Naomi and other Fateless would come with them. They hoped her pair would be found at the other end of the sea.

Despite the opening of their kingdom and how much Ember had wanted it, actually taking the leap to leave was more challenging than she had anticipated.

At Meerandus' inquisitive expression, Ember added: "I will be ready."

She had to be.

As the curtains billowed from her open balcony that night, Ember curled into Noor's embrace. From her view in bed, she could see beyond her kingdom, a wall no longer blocking any part of her eyesight.

She watched as the ships in the distance slowly grew larger.

Where they sailed, there were holes in the darkness. A silhouette within the stars.

Did you enjoy *Ember Dragon Daughter*?

Leave a review of *Ember Dragon Daughter* and then continue reading in *Hasley Fateless*.

A SPECIAL PREVIEW OF

HASLEY FATELESS, CHAPTER ONE

Hasley Jeweler and Arsenio Trader were meant to meet, but their fating was derailed by the building of the impenetrable wall around theirkingdom. Little do they know that love finds a way, and Hasley's journey as a Fateless will teach her that order isn't always the answer and rules are meant to be broken.

CHAPTER ONE
CARRIAGES

An anger that was unlike Hasley's usual disposition boiled in her veins. How could Ember do this to her? They were best friends. In fact, Hasley was Ember's only friend. Didn't that mean they should tell each other everything? Hasley's heart hammered in her chest as she walked into the back of the jewelry shop Ember and her apprenticed at.

Her fingers gripped the paper in her hands, crumbling the edges as she stared at her friend's empty workbench. When Hasley had come into purpose apprenticeship that morning, her only care had been to ask Amlin Jeweler, her mentor, if he had heard from Ember. After Ember didn't come back from her delivery the day before, Hasley had begun to fear the worst. She walked back to Ember's home and found that Ember hadn't returned there either. If Amlin hadn't heard anything, Hasley's next stop would be to report her absence to the province guards. What if one of the Fateless had hurt her?

It happened sometimes. Those crippled by the madness were prone to acting out in violence. This was one of the reasons why the Fateless were often...silenced...by the province guards. The Fateless were too dangerous to be allowed to live, and while Hasley found that difficult to stomach, she understood it.

That is, she did until recently. But she pushed that thought aside. This morning she was angry, not sad and confused. She was not going to focus on her own concerns when her best friend was revealed to be the missing princess.

The Dragon Daughter had been missing for sixteen years, stolen from the newly minted dragon queen's birthing bed. Despite the many years that have passed, Karwyn Dragon Queen and her consort, Jedoriah Knight, were not blessed with another heir to Ashkadance's throne.

Hasley hadn't thought too much about it, unlike other citizens. She instead focused on her future, rather than that of the crown. Their god Mutrien and goddess Aaleia would not leave the throne without a ruler, she had reasoned, so she didn't need to worry.

And apparently, she was right. Ember was the heir. Her best friend was a princess in hiding and Hasley didn't know.

Hasley wanted to kick herself. She had been worried all night, thinking something terrible must have befallen her friend. Instead, notices were passed out at dawn and pasted on every building to spread the happy news. The princess was found, alive, and had been in Firetop under the name Ember Julimore.

How could she not have told her?

The crumbled notice fell to the floor.

Amlin Jeweler walked into the back room, the door slamming behind him. Wherever he went, he made plenty of noise. His default was a shuffling walk that spoke of disinterest. Today he walked faster, his intent leaving loud and purposeful steps.

"Did you know this?" he asked Hasley in an accusational tone, as if she were tainted by a secret she didn't know. His yellow eyes squinted and his skin appeared burnt from recent sun exposure.

"I-I..." Hasley struggled to find the words.

Her anger simmered and she instead felt drowned in dread. How did Ember's true identity impact her purpose apprenticeship here? Amlin controlled whether or not she would receive her purpose name as a jeweler. She had been working towards this for a year and it could all tumble down.

Nothing was going according to plan. She would get an apprenticeship, get her purpose name, move out, get fated, and open her own shop with Ember. Ember would do all the actual jewelry-making, as Hasley always knew. But with this big mysterious moment before her, Hasley realized without Ember's talent, was she anything at all?

Why did Ember keep this from her? Her hurt bubbled to the surface. She wasn't truly angry, Hasley knew. She was heartbroken and mourning a future she thought they had together as friends.

Hasley ran from the confrontation, making her way passed the market and to the inns. Bounding down the street, she felt her feet hit stone as if it were her heart. She hastily pulled up her blue hair as it whipped around her. If Ember was still here, as the other workers on the street had been gossiping this morning, maybe she could fix this, somehow.

"I don't know. I don't understand," Hasley muttered to herself as she ran, answering unvoiced questions.

When she reached the inns, she saw there were dozens of people already gathered at the end of the street. She could only get five people deep, pushing between them to see guards in purple holding everyone back. The street was blocked off and she pleaded with them to let her through. Grumbles came from behind her over her rude interruption of their own gawking.

Were they ever friends? Why was she hiding for so long? Did Ember not trust Hasley?

She wasn't who she thought. She was the royal heir. And Hasley had no idea. Hasley wasn't trusted. Hasley was alone. How could she compare to the future queen?

*To the wall...*a voice whispered in her mind.

"Not now!" Hasley screamed and the guard she had been pleading with a moment prior looked to her annoyed.

Over the guard's shoulder, the street was clear save for two anchoris pulled carriages. Figures far away walked towards them. Hasley lost her breath as she recognized one of the figures as Ember, unmistakable with her black hair reflecting the sheen of a rainbow in the sunlight.

"Ember!" Hasley screamed, desperate to break from the crowd.

Her best friend did not turn around. Instead, she entered the carriage without a second glance. As the carriages rolled away, Hasley fell to the floor in a heap. She wanted to cry and admit she was alone, letting her self-pity take over. But on the floor, she saw an opening and crawled around the guard's feet. Hasley pumped her legs as hard as she could down the street, two guards hot on her heels, but she was too late.

The carriages were already further than she could reach. Hasley stopped running and took one long sobbing breath. The future she thought she had with her best friend rolled away in an elegantly drawn carriage.

Continue reading in *Hasley Fateless*

ALSO BY R. K. SAMPSON

The Fated Tales Series:

Ember Dragon Daughter

Hasley Fateless

Kariana Dragon Daughter

See art like this, character profiles, and more in the special edition hardback!

Order the special edition hardback:

Leave a review of the book:

ACKNOWLEDGMENTS

Written on March 5, 2023

Here we go again! I am so grateful to republish and rebrand the Fated Tales series this year and bring this story to life for new and returning readers. I only have one additional thing to say that isn't covered in my original acknowledgments...

Life throws curve balls. You can curve with it.

Written on April 7, 2018

It is with these words that I take a deep breath. It is with these words that I shout and cry. It is with this soul that I breathe the fire that will become *Ember Dragon Daughter*.

While there are so many people that I'm sure my future self will want to thank, there is only one person on my mind as I write Ember's story.

Chris, I wrote this book during the worst period of our lives. Cancer. The C-word that is whispered and screamed. The scariest monster we've ever faced. If we can do that together, nothing can stop us.

Thank you for believing in me and for believing in this book. It would never have come to be without you.

Written on June 19, 2019

I wrote the above and told myself I would not open that file until I was ready to publish. I'm so glad I was able to record those emotions for me to explore now.

This novel was written over the next year in waiting rooms, on the floor of the ER, in uncomfortable hospital chairs that double as twin beds, and on the floor of our spare bedroom because getting in and out of bed was difficult for my husband. For a year, we slept on the floor.

Ember Dragon Daughter helped me escape and feel empowered at the same time. Now, my husband is safe and clear. We are cancer-free! But neither of our journeys are over.

I hope as you read this book you enjoyed learning about Ember and her world, there are a lot of influences from my personal life. Like my need to protect. The amount of pressure I put on myself to solve everyone's problems. My inability to hide even when I want and need too. My hope that things can get better. My husband's heart, beating in Noor's and mirrored in his laughter. The importance of friendship and community.

Tragedy helped me put this into words, but it doesn't have to be that way for you.

So, dear reader, whether you are a writer or not - I hope you know that you CAN make your dreams come true. Just take it one decision at a time.

Thank you to my toddler son for saying, "Mommy book," because that made my heart melt. Thank you to the other authors that helped me bring this to life. As an indie author, choosing who I get to invest in means a lot to me. Thank you to Mandi Lynn for creating the cover for *Ember Dragon Daughter*, to Kim Chance for your help, and to PS Malcolm for your guidance and support. Thank you to my critique partner and fellow indie author, Emilia S. Morrow, for talking to me about plot and revisions at all hours. Thank you Kate Weiler for helping me learn how to give and take feedback, I hope we can work together again soon.

Thank you to everyone that supported my business and projects on RebeccaKSampson.com. It helps me cover publishing costs!

I cannot wait to share with you more in the Fated Tales series.

As younger me expected, there are too many people to thank. I'm sure I'll forget somebody and be very embarrassed, but as of this first printing here is a list of wonderful people that have helped support me and have grown with me during this process of writing and publishing my first novel. I am forever grateful.

Thank you to my middle school crush for inspiring my first attempts at poetry, thank you to my mother for continuing to encourage my creativity all throughout my childhood. Thank you to my husband for inspiring only romantic poetry and for being the first keeper of my secrets, novels, and heart.

Thank you to my sisters, brother, dad, my in-laws, and extended family for encouraging my big ideas all these years. A response of "why not?" instead of "why?" makes a big difference in a dreamer. Thank you!

Thank you to my beta readers, and the expansive writing community on Instagram, YouTube, and through NaNoWriMo for giving me a home away from home. It was you and this book that distracted me while I was in chemo-center waiting rooms. I know it took me a little while to share that part of my life with you, so thank you for the warm welcome when I was finally ready for more support.

In particular, thank you to writing friends and inspirations Brittany Wang, Bethany Atazadeh, E.C. Woodham, Peggy Spencer, Jessi Elliot, Bruna Reis, and J.M. Buckler. I have learned so much and connected with all of you. There is so many more people I can mention! If you've thought of me, I guarantee I have also thought of you.

Thank you to my coworkers Erin, Danae, Matthews, Molly, and Melissa for the encouragement these past two years as Ember came together. This big dream of mine kept me away from lunches, happy hours, and events and you still invited me anyway. Thank you!

Now for some famous people. Thank you to my author influences and "Mac & Cheese" comfort books! Thank you Lynne Ewing for creating the first YA series I devoured, *The Daughters of the Moon*, and to Stephenie Meyer for my young obsession with *Twilight*. An extra special thank you to Marissa Meyer for *The Lunar Chronicles* and Keira Cass for *The Selection Series*. Those two are my most re-read series!

I am a very grateful indie author. Thank you for reading through this and thank you for leaving a review!

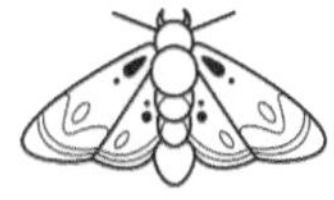

ABOUT THE AUTHOR

R. K. Sampson is a YA and NA fantasy author. Her favorite scenes to write are plot twists, betrayals, and unique takes on love in fantasy settings.

She writes novels that help readers take on scenarios that can seem insurmountable like swift change, massive responsibility, and being different through the backdrop of magic, creatures, and flawed characters.

Rebecca is a mom and married to her high school sweetheart, living in Miami, Fl. You can read her blog chronicling her life and interests on rebeccaksampson.com

instagram.com/fictionbyrks

tiktok.com/@rksampson